His Lordship

Leslie Thomas was born in South Wales in 1931 and when his parents died, he and his younger brother were brought up in an orphanage. His first book, *This Time Next Week*, is the autobiography of a happy orphan. Aged sixteen, he became a reporter on a weekly newspaper in Essex and then did his National Service in Malaya during the Communist bandit war. *The Virgin Soldiers* tells of these days ; it was an immediate bestseller and has been made into a film with Lynn Redgrave and Hywel Bennett. *Onward Virgin Soldiers*, the follow-up to this, is also published by Pan Books.

Returning to civilian life, Leslie Thomas joined the staff of the *Evening News*, becoming a top feature writer and travelling a great deal. His second novel, *Orange Wednesday*, was published in 1967. For nine months during 1967 he travelled around ten islands off the coast of Britain, the result of which was a lyrical travelogue, *Some Lovely Islands*, from which the BBC did a television series. He has continued to travel a great deal and has also written several television plays. He is a director of a London publishing house. His hobbies include golf, antiques and Queen's Park Rangers Football Club.

**Also by Leslie Thomas
in Pan Books**

Orange Wednesday
The Virgin Soldiers
Come to the War
The Love Beach
Onward Virgin Soldiers
Stand Up Virgin Soldiers
Tropic of Ruislip
Arthur McCann and All His Women
The Man With the Power
Dangerous Davies, The Last Detective
Bare Nell
Ormerod's Landing
That Old Gang of Mine

Some Lovely Islands
This Time Next Week

Leslie Thomas

His Lordship

Pan Books London and Sydney

First published 1970 by Michael Joseph Ltd
This edition published 1972 by Pan Books Ltd.
Cavaye Place, London SW10 9PG
9th printing 1981
© Leslie Thomas 1970
ISBN 0 330 02943 6
Printed in Great Britain by
Richard Clay (The Chaucer Press) Ltd, Bungay, Suffolk

Dedicated to my friend
Desmond Elliott

'... And with the girls be handy.'
                Edward Bangs
'Yankee-Doodle or Father's Return to Camp' (1775)

Until that evening I had truly tried to fight it. I was surprised and shocked, at first, to find that they affected me at all. But once I realized they did, I honestly tried to prevent it getting a hold on me.

Then one of them came in to me, a fifteen-year-old called Susan Belling, and stood in front of my study desk. It was about eight o'clock, and just getting dark. I switched on my green-shaded lamp. She was just over five feet tall and, although she was one of the senior girls, she should have been in bed in the dormitory by then.

At first she looked as though she were going to laugh. But then she shut up and I asked her what she wanted. She said: 'Mr Herbert, I have come to tell you that it was I – or is it me? – who pushed Vivian down the steps of the tennis court last Monday.'

I knew it had been her. 'You know she had a compound fracture of the left arm?' I said.

'Two places,' she nodded.

'You seem pleased with yourself.'

I walked to the window and watched the gardener watering the evening lawn. At that point I made a strong attempt to steady myself. Then I said: 'In a boys' school you would get six of the best across your little backside, believe me.'

I turned to face her.

'Why don't you try me?' she suggested.

Signed : William Herbert,
HM Prison,
Wandsworth,
London, SW18.

1

HE WONDERED if by some quick fortune he might be able to trap a spider in the exercise yard that day. A good sporting spider, or even perhaps a beetle with some nice jockey stripes down its back. He had been inside for three days and there was nothing to do. The others, he was told, captured insects in the yard and played with them for hours, making them run or jump over outstretched fingers. One of the elder men had described a beautiful curly caterpillar which he had found the previous April and would never, ever, forget. It used to sit, exotic but tame, along the top rim of his ear, either the right or the left.

It was the authorities' pathetic idea of a joke, William thought, to toss a book called *Little Women* into him. Seven days remanded in custody, followed, so he was assured, by a further seven days, and then probably yet another seven, and so on until they had the charges all arranged and they were ready to attack him. And he had to wait for them.

There was nothing to do. He hunched on his bunk and pretended it was a raft and he was shipwrecked, as he had done so many years before, but the game needed childhood to make it convincing. The easy magic had gone. He had read *Little Women* twice, the second time very carefully, and although he liked Jo well enough he thought the other girls were a trifle old-fashioned.

His fingers went craftily to his hidden brace of ten-shilling pieces, slotted with cunning into the bunk, and touched also the folded paper upon which Jackie MacAllister had written the poem. *The forward youth appearing; the remote Bermuda's riding; not overlooking the lady breast-high among the corn and good old Angel King of Smiling Morn.*

William grimaced at the schoolgirl arrogance of it. The effrontery. The ingenuity too. Jackie MacAllister of the terrible dipping eye and the caked lipstick, trying to get her strong fifteen-year-old arms about him on top of the lighthouse. Perhaps Connie had helped with the verse. His beloved Connie, now carrying a full tummy before her down the main street of Gary, Indiana, USA. And Susan the sweet giggler, little Yum Yum, Tina of the twins. He was lonely in his cell, all he had were the remembrances and his collection of knickers – if ever the detectives had the decency to return them to him. The girls were gone, all gone, scattered through the country, through the world, growing to womanhood, losing their girlish ways, making statements to the police.

They had given Mr Decent to him as defence counsel, and Mr Decent had suggested that he ought to try and write some of it down, so that they could see if there was *anything* good, no matter how small, which could be told to the court in mitigation. The magistrates would not deal with him, of course. It would have to be a judge and a jury. At the moment, they had him on a charge of being drunk and incapable at the buffet at Victoria Station, sitting in some elderly person's dinner, they alleged, plus larceny of the Clifton Tennis Cup from Southwelling School, found with the five pairs of knickers in his suitcase. They told the magistrate that other charges would be preferred following investigations and William did not at all like the sound of that.

He had tried writing something down, as Mr Decent had suggested, beginning with the evening when Susan Belling had blatantly provoked him in his room. But he hardly knew how to continue. So he merely signed it and left it at that. Mr Decent had sniffed through the meagre document and then shrugged and put it in his briefcase with what William could plainly see was a collection of children's comics. Mr Decent saw him looking and volunteered that he read the comics for relaxation but refused to lend one to William because he required them for his train journey home to Effingham Junction.

It was July, nearly August, with summer going berserk outside the bars. William was thirty-five, a handsome man in an outdated fashion, straight-featured, short-sided hair Brylcreemed straight back. It was the sort of face they illustrated on bottles of hair restorer in Edwardian times. Connie had once described him as beautiful like an old-time prize-fighter and just as stupid. He did not believe this to be true, even though they had deceived him so easily. Even now he was not, after all, without his memories.

Mr Decent had asked him all about his parents, his jobs and his Service career, and had evoked William's earliest memory, that of his father, a county tennis player, striking him powerfully in the ear with a prodigious service as he, a three-year-old, had toddled negligently across the court.

His jobs, with the final spectacular exception, had been dim and unprogressive, his achievements being confined to the tennis courts where he managed more ably than in any other aspect of his sorry life. His Service days were marred, indeed ended, by what he insisted was a flying accident, although it did not actually involve an aircraft but a bed.

All these things were relevant to the case, of course, but only in minor ways. It was the girls that were causing Mr Decent to mumble dismally and reach for the *Beano* when William launched explanations. William felt slightly silly trying to formulate a defence with a counsel who became engrossed in a comic paper at the very moment when his client was seeking to expound the deceits which had tripped and trapped him. The girls were the subject, Mr Decent confirmed to him, of the unspecified further charges. Undoubtedly it was the night of the bathroom business that those terrible events began, minutes after he had overheard two of the juniors arguing in a prep room as to whether shit was a legitimate word for use in the game of Scrabble.

Not that he was normally in that part of the building at all. His room was at the tail of the school, on the ground floor, and they must have spotted him walking across the lawn before they perpetrated the rotten trick on him. Hearing the Scrabble-players reaching violence over whether their foul word could be found in the Gospels was shocking enough, but then he heard the screams that Mary Bosham was drowning.

He was in the long corridor of the school. The girls called it Death Row because of the series of doors fixed into its frowning green paint with the regularity of large pictures in a dull gallery. All the screams began at once and the bathroom door at the end was banged open. Steam elbowed its way out and through its fog emerged a frail and frightened girl wrapped in a blue towel. Streaming bathwater and tears, she stood, wide-mouthed and weeping, in the corridor, spectacularly out of control, crying out about somebody drowning. Then she spotted the gaping William,

13

screamed louder, and perversely ran through the door and slammed it.

Doors fell open along the long run of the corridor as though forced by a huge abrupt wind. William had not moved. The steam from the brief opening of the bathroom door was moving sedately as a ghost about him and continuing on up the corridor. He feebly flapped his hands like fans to push it away. The Scrabble squabblers had come from their room like two small ferrets in gymslips and were at his side staring with pale fascination at the mute green bathroom door. It was explosively reopened. Another girl, this time, a red towel sticking to her, hair hanging like liquorice in the fleeing steam. She screamed: 'Mary Bosham's drowned! She's drowned!'

William moved now and got there before they could slam the door again. There was a clutch of senior girls in the writhing vapour of the bathroom and they screeched outrageously when the master charged in.

'Shut up!' he shouted at them. 'Be quiet all of you!' His own firm voice surprised him.

He could only half see them, trembling like slim animals in the steam. 'Where?' he demanded. The wet, towelled girls seemed to close about him. 'Who's drowned?'

Then Tina Ferber, cascading wet hair on her face and shoulders, towel run tight under her armpits, her breasts like flannel cushions, walked directly in front of him. 'She's over there,' she said dramatically. 'I'm afraid it's too late.'

'For God's sake!' he cried. He started forward, banged his knee on the second of the four baths, and then saw the girl draped like a mermaid over the end of the last one. He felt he should not be there. 'Get a mistress,' he ordered. 'And quick.'

Trembling in the steam he went towards her. She was slim and white and hanging head first over the end of the bath. He forced himself to move decisively and put his hands under her, lifting her clear of the grubby water, and lying her tenderly on her back on the tiled floor. He began to give her mouth-to-mouth resuscitation.

Mary Bosham was fourteen. She had fine dark hair in short curls, a beautifully round face, and small pink breasts, like the snouts of little pigs. The steam was in William's hair, down his collar, inside his shirt and sticking all over his face and hands. Her mouth was conveniently open and each time he lifted his lips from hers he tried to decently close his eyes so that he would not have to see her, but he could not do it. She was lying quiet as a white fish on the floor, but she was still breathing shallowly. As he bent to her he could sense the youth of her body, the wetness of her skin. After three minutes, Mary Bosham began to stir quietly. The girls who had stood around under the steam, now risen to the ceiling and loitering like an indoor storm, stirred too. Those who had been in the bathroom stood in static, ecstatic, excitement at the front of the audience and behind were the others in gymslips and dressing-gowns who had piled down the corridor. When the lips and the face directly below William's lips and face began to twitch, a long beautiful sigh went through the towelled spectators. Then Mary opened her eyes and looked wonderingly at William. As though realizing what he had done, fourteen-year-old fingers moved up and touched the side of his face. The girls jumped and laughed and wept and put their arms about each other. A towel slipped exposing a pink steamed bottom and again William was forced to close his eyes.

2

'THE WHOLE thing was staged, Officer. Yes, really! A bloody put-up job. I tremble when I think about it. They'd watched me, waited for me like an ambush, and I walked right into it. Even then it was weeks before I realized.'

'Now don't let's start by you calling me "Officer", William. My name's Rufus, and I'll be glad if you'd call me that – Rufus. I'm a detective-sergeant, but I definitely want you to call me Rufus. Is that reasonable? Right, that's reasonable. We'll get on a lot better like that, Bill.'

'Are you Irish, Rufus? You sound quite Irish.'

'My grandfather was. Came from Coleraine.'

'I'm glad you've got some Irish in you because you people

have got a nice sense of the ridiculous, and I think you're going to need it.'

'I expect we'll have a few laughs along the way, Bill. Now, do I understand that you want to make a statement?'

'Oh, yes, I'd certainly like to make a statement, Rufus. For God's sake! Right at the very beginning it was a put-up job . . .'

'You are not obliged to say anything, but anything you may say will be taken down in writing and may be given in evidence against you.'

'Why do you have to say "taken down in writing"? It's a funny way of putting it, isn't it? Taken down in writing. What do they expect you to do, take it down in pictures?'

'A good point, Bill. You're familiar with the caution then?'

'Riding a cycle without lights. That's all up to now. It's a bit more serious this time, I suppose.'

'You *could* say that, Bill. Let's see. Larceny of a silver cup, the property of the governors of Southwelling School . . .'

'I've told them. I told the magistrate I don't remember stealing that cup at all.'

'Also, drunk and incapable at the buffet on Victoria Station. That's probably why you don't remember the cup.'

'That could be true.'

'But what you really ought to appreciate, Bill, is that these are what we would call holding charges. There were the knickers we found, for instance, and things you were saying at the police station while you were pissed. You've been remanded for seven days for what is known as further inquiries, old friend. After that we'll probably be asking for a further remand. Of course, it's for you as well. It gives you time to get your defence together. Have they sent anyone to see you?'

'Mr Decent. Is he any good?'

'Good for us, but not so good for you.'

'I see. He's not very well regarded, then?'

'He's laughed at, Bill. But you've got him so that's that. It's no use crying now.'

'No, well I won't.'

'Good chap. He *may* be all right on the day.'

'I hope so, Rufus.'

'Anyway, these inquiries will be going on and I'll be popping

16

in to see you quite often. I'll try and assist you in piecing the story together. I hope you'll cooperate and you can think of me as a friend. Even after it's all over and you're doing your sentence.'

'I certainly will, Rufus.'

'Now what were you saying ... about the phrasing of the official caution?'

'Well, I've seen it on the television, of course, and on films and I've always thought it was a very quaint way of putting it, that's all. I'm not making a complaint or anything.'

'I'll tell the high-ups. Nevertheless, we've got to start in the usual old dull way. It doesn't make exciting reading, I'm the first to admit, but it's the way they've always done it. Now, let's see, Bill, your full name is what?'

'William Bridgemont Herbert.'

'Nice ... nice. William Bridgemont Herbert. Let's get that down. Is there an "e" in Bridgemont? There is. Good. I really *like* that for a name, Bill. We've got a youngster on the way and I'd like to have a name like that for him. I know it's going to be a boy.'

'Just don't let him be a tennis coach at a girls' school, that's all.'

'I'll try to keep him away. Age, what is it? Thirty? Thirty-five! Well, you're in fine shape, that's for certain. That's the tennis, eh?'

'It certainly wasn't the girls.'

'No? Well no, I suppose not. Thirty-five, then. What do you call yourself, Bill? Tennis coach? Professional tennis player? Ah, Tennis professional, that's better. You know, we *don't* get many tennis professionals in here. Not on this sort of charge anyway.'

'I'm surprised. They're in all the rackets.'

'They are?'

'That was a joke, Rufus.'

'Oh, *rackets*! Yes, sure, Bill. Rackets. Now, I suppose your address would be Southwelling Girls' School. No? Southwelling School for Girls. Right, I see. Might as well get it right. At Southwelling in the County of Sussex.'

'That's a picturesque way of putting it, Rufus.'

'What?'

'Saying: "In the County of Sussex." Makes it sound extraordinarily grand. Historic, if you see what I mean.'

'Oh, sure, it is Bill. It goes back years and years. Long before there were any tennis coaches and girls' schools, I suppose. Now, let me jump right in here a minute, Bill. Back to where we were having our little general discussion earlier, before tea. Would you like some more tea, by the way? You've had two? So you have. Well, I hope you enjoyed it because it's not a general privilege. It's just for today, as it's our first day. Now, the two little girls you heard saying that word when you were in the corridor. Yes, shit. I lost you a bit there, Bill. What were they playing? Some sort of lexicon?'

'Scrabble. Sarah Curran, one of the two, was the sort of Scrabble Queen of Southwelling. Miss Bonner, the English mistress, says that the child knows every last word in the English dictionary.'

'And some that are missing, eh?'

'Most certainly. My God, I'll say she does. Plays for cash, so I've heard, or getting other girls to do her schoolwork.'

'Now there's a thing. You wouldn't think that of a twelve-year-old kid, would you?'

'Thirteen. Sarah's thirteen. Thirteen and four months, actually. No, you wouldn't. But then you wouldn't believe a lot of things about them, Rufus.'

'Bill, how do you *know* that the kid nearly drowning in the bathroom was a put-up job? Did anybody actually tell you?'

'I began to suspect it after a while, and especially when all the other involved business started . . .'

'Involved business?'

'Oh, you know. All this bother with the girls. That's when I began to think back and put matters into perspective. Connie more or less spilled the beans and then Yum Yum told me about it in the changing-room. They'd spotted me coming across the lawn and decided to do it then. I hardly went over to that part of the school at all. But the courts had been flooded, and they'd drained that afternoon and I wanted to tell Connie and Tina Ferber about an early tennis practice.'

'This was not very long after you'd started at the school?'

'That's right, Rufus. They started on me right away, the little bitches.'

'Connie. Now she's the American girl, isn't she? You talked a lot about her when you were drunk in the police station. Something about a baby.'

'Oh, well. Yes, I suppose I might have done.'

'It doesn't matter now, Bill. There's plenty of time for you to tell me. Now – Yum Yum. We haven't met Yum Yum to date.'

'Stupid of me. Pamela Watts. She was the smallest and prettiest child in the school, Rufus. Lovely kid. Everybody called her Yum Yum because that's the part she had in *The Mikado*.'

'This Scrabble interests me, Bill. I'd like to play that.'

'It's very interesting, Rufus. Not that I played a lot myself. I'm not all that good with spellings and you have to be very quick with words.'

'And you heard them arguing about shit.'

'Well, arguing about the word of that name. The girl with Sarah was Penny Scott-Wallace, I remember, and it was the first word on the board – and that gives double points.'

'You were a bit shocked to hear them say that?'

'Naturally. I was right outside the door, just before all the commotion started in the bathroom.'

'And it shocked you, you say?'

'It's not a word I've ever been fond of, quite truthfully. I had a nasty experience with it when I was a child.'

'What was that?'

'I was about seven or eight, I suppose, and I met a railway-man at a bus stop and he taught me to say it. And I went home and said it to my mother.'

'You remember that pretty well.'

'Very well. So would you if you could have seen my mother's face. Somebody was having tea with her, some elderly lady, and I remember the old girl simply dropped her cup, tea and all. It was a nasty shock for everybody.'

'The railwayman only talked to you. I mean, as far as you recollect, he didn't try to mess about with you or anything while you were standing at the bus stop.'

'Good God, no, Rufus, it was nothing like that. I suppose I was partly to blame because he had just missed a bus and he stood there puffing and blowing, with his greasy railwayman's bag across his shoulder, and then he said "shit" and looked down at me and said it again. So I said it back to him and we carried on saying it to each other until his next bus turned up. As a matter of fact, I was so pleased with the word that when he was on the platform and the bus was drawing away I called it after him and the conductor nearly fell off the platform.'

'I can imagine. You were seven or eight?'

'About that. My mother got rid of her guest and she simply went berserk. Weeping and pounding about. Quite berserk. She was so upset and it upset me so much that I never used that word again.'

'At the station you were gabbling on about Miss Tilling.'

'The music mistress, Rufus. It was she who came into the bathroom when I'd brought Mary Bosham back to consciousness – well, I *thought* I had. She'd been conscious all the time, of course. But Miss Tilling was a wicked woman, you know, thoroughly wicked.

'She arrived in the bathroom just as I was getting up off my knees after giving mouth-to-mouth treatment. She sort of rushed through the girls, and pushed me aside and started giving Mary the kiss of life all over again. Well, it was quite ridiculous. The child didn't require it. But Miss Tilling was hanging over her and blowing into her like mad. Mary was almost choking, but every time she made to get up Miss Tilling pushed her flat again. Quite violently too. It was most extraordinary. Then she started pressing young Mary's stomach and massaging her heart. I could hardly believe my eyes. Afterwards, a long time afterwards, of course, I woke up to it all.'

'She sounds a villain, Bill. Now let's go back, way back to the time before you went to Southwelling School for Girls. Tell me about your marriage. What was that like?'

'It was a good marriage, Rufus. I was very, very happy.'

3

HAPPY HE may have been, but Louise was not. They had lived at Midford-Pallant, an obstreperous new town of boxed houses and hideous fountains, which had stretched over quiet fields and was callously throttling an old and innocent English borough which had been minding its own harmless business since the Middle Ages.

Pallant was the old name, a crouched and ancient place, streets hiding behind houses. Midford, the newcomer, spread itself with neither taste nor tact across unsuspecting meadows and woodlands. William and Louise Herbert were among the new people ushered in. He had a job in Barclays Bank where they were understanding about allowing him to attend courses at the Lawn Tennis Association coaching centre. They also gave him occasional time to play tennis for the county in the summer and he coached at the local club and the Midford-Pallant Evening Institute.

They lived in a maisonette, the top of three, with outside steps descending like a chute. It was not very well built, and Louise was annoyed that the toilet had a high flush and not a low modern one. After they had been there six months, William was on the lavatory and absentmindedly pulled the chain as he sat. The cistern came away from its poor fixing and struck him on the head. There was a cascade of water and blood and neighbours had to help Louise to break down the door. They said it looked quite funny when they got in to him. Louise said it was about the only genuinely amusing thing he had ever done.

She *wanted* him to be amusing, *required* it, you could say, and told him that he ought to develop his personality and do amusing things. Being good at tennis was not enough. William spent two weeks in hospital after his joke with the cistern and during that time Louise met and committed adultery with George Sherman, the deputy town clerk of Midford-Pallant, a man with a lot of personality. George had gone to the house to apologize personally for the faulty cistern and the injury to William. Louise said that they had tried to discuss it seriously, but their sense of humour over-came them and they wound up laughing in each other's arms.

It was not as though he had not made an honest attempt to amuse, to *be* a personality. But, as Louise and Mr Sherman had both told him, he was not *positive* enough. They had sat down together on his settee, in his maisonette, informed him that they had decided to set up house together, and had given him good, sound advice on how he could and should better himself in life. How, as Mr Sherman put it, he could make *more* of the world belong to him.

William had sat, his head a miserable egg of bandages. It was the day they had discharged him from hospital and he knew every damned nurse in that place was laughing hysterically as he tottered down the steps with his little suitcase and his bald dressings. It was because of the way the accident had happened, of course, not because his bandages looked so odd. Very few people pulled the chain and tugged the cistern down on their heads. When the story had gone around the hospital, nurses and doctors, patients who could leave their beds, and even casual visitors who had gone to see other sick people, used to troop along to his ward to ask him questions about it, or simply stare at the phenomenon of a man injured in such a strange way.

On his return to the maisonette that day, Louise made him a salad lunch which included two graphically bald, boiled eggs. Then Mr Sherman came up from the town hall and the two of them sat and tried to help him straighten out his life by making himself more positive and more of a personality. At first, he could not comprehend what on earth it had to do with the borough council because he had never before met Mr Sherman and knew nothing about him. He imagined that the deputy town clerk had come in some kind of official capacity, or even for charitable reasons, perhaps working at a spare-time occupation for some after-care organization.

But when Louise sat so close to Mr Sherman on the settee he began to worry; then they slipped their hands together and he knew he had misconstrued the entire situation. He mentioned the hand-holding to them and they told him what had happened between them when Mr Sherman had come to look at the fallen cistern. They said they were in love and were going to live together. They knew he would understand and they hoped that he would take this break as an opportunity to start life afresh and to make something of himself.

Sometimes, with all his uncertainties and outrageous misjudgements, he felt like a man destined to stagger through life weighed down by half a dozen heavy, free-swinging, slop buckets.

Only on the tennis court was he sure of what he was doing. That first blow in his baby ear when he walked, as a child, in the line of his father's fierce service, had been his first drama on the court. At twelve he had won the Southern Junior Championship. At eighteen he had beaten a Wimbledon seed and had won his county's championship. Out there, in the sun, with a racket he had power and decisiveness. But only there.

In the winter before Louise went off with Mr Sherman, however, even his sporting career was blighted by his misfortunes off the court. It was the annual dinner dance of the County Tennis Association and he had promised Louise that he would develop his personality and make the evening something for her to remember.

William confessed when it was done and over that he had drunk a lot. He was, as he tried to explain to the committee, strictly a two-glasses-of-sherry-man, but on this evening he had been under pressure to develop his personality and had therefore drunk more sherries and, indeed, more of everything. Louise had looked exquisite in a black lace dress. She had pale, marvellous shoulders. Months later, Mr Sherman had chatted to him in the street and told him about some official dinner they had attended. And said: 'Our wife's got such marvellous shoulders.' On the night of the tennis dance she was getting into her lace dress and he was enjoying the husband's pleasure of simply watching her. She told him to stop gaping and asked him to try, that night, to promote some interest in himself. Not to crawl off to a corner where no one would see him and expect her to hide with him. He had promised.

All through dinner he told random stories and jokes to his neighbours, forgetting the endings or other important factors. He made up a deliberate lie in attempting to engage one lady, saying

23

that he had seen her husband the previous week and commenting on how well he looked. She began to weep into her prawn cocktail and then went howling from the room because this was her first evening out since the death of her husband three months earlier.

The cold hand of failure was held against William's heart. He dared not glance at Louise. He began drinking brandies as though his personality was a dormant Christmas pudding within him. Then some champagne-type sparkling wine, which he found he liked, and then more sherries, sweet, medium and dry. They were drawing the raffle tickets and through the rebounding festive noise from the tables he heard his name being called. Louise's hand came across the tablecloth and pulled at him roughly like a sergeant catching a sleeping sentry.

Faces like plates were turned to him and the mouths were saying: 'It's you. It's you.'

Louise impatiently motioned him to go out and get his prize. Suddenly he was terrified he would not be able to remain on his feet. He rose experimentally and then went towards the dance-floor, at the backs of the chairs, with a baboon crawl which everyone thought was hilarious.

Then, without the friendly chairs, out on to the maple floor. He stood and waited to see if he would be all right. He remained marginally upright and began fumbling for his raffle tickets in his dinner jacket. Where were they, the little salmon devils? Ah, yes. Here. Number which? Forty-two pink. Yes, he had forty-two pink. Well, he did have the damned thing before he dropped them on the floor. He bent and sorted them out among the french-chalk. Forty-two pink. There. He stood and held it high and the guests laughed and applauded and made remarks. He was being noticed. Their eyes were with him. His personality was bursting through, coursing up his body, oozing out of the top of him. This was it at last. *Personality*. He thudded confidently down the floor towards the table set like an altar with baskets of fruit and biscuits and bottles of whisky.

Any prize was his, they said. *Anything* he liked. His was the first ticket out and he could take his pick. Mrs Elbert-Keir, the wispy wife of the president of the County Tennis Association, squeakily instructed him to choose. She was a sad-eyed little woman, pinioned in a drab shawl. William stood, the prizes before him, while the voices from the tables shouted advice. 'Leave the Scotch for me!' 'The fruit's only wax!' 'All the biscuits are broken!' All sorts of amusing things.

William sensed his chance. His personality *had* to erupt right there, *that* moment. Afterwards they had to say: 'God, wasn't he marvellous!' There he stood, there were the prizes, and there was nice, shawled Mrs Elbert-Keir. The excitement almost choked him. He shouted: '*Anything?* I can take *anything*?'

'Anything!' They all cried. Heavens, he thought, I bet Louise is enjoying this.

'*Anything?*' he called again like a pantomime clown getting children to repeat his lines.

'Anything!' everyone replied.

'Right,' shouted William. 'I'll take Mrs Elbert-Keir!'

She was much lighter than he imagined and when he picked her up and threw her across his shoulder he did it with such force and enthusiasm that she did a nose-dive, sliding down his back towards the floor. He caught her by the skinny tops of her legs as she, and everybody else, began to scream and shout. William was elated. After this who could say he had no person-ality? He began to do a high trot down the dance-floor and he could hear Mrs Elbert-Keir's jewellery falling off her as he pranced along. He was calling out and laughing and there was a tremendous row going on all about the hall. He had sensations of men moving towards him, but he dodged them deftly and carried his prize onwards. He was almost back to his seat and Louise when he skated on some spilt beer, lost his balance and dropped Mrs Elbert-Keir on her head.

4

'JESUS, BILL. On her head?'

'Actually, Rufus, she fell on her elbows. Yes, I'm afraid so. Slid down my back like a kid in the park going down a chute head first, and I suppose she stuck her elbows out to break her fall. Anyway it was the elbows that got most of it, Rufus. Both broken. Her head was only bruised, although they did think there might be a fracture. Believe me there is nothing more embarrassing than having broken elbows, especially for a thin, elderly lady like that, because, when they put the plaster-of-Paris on, the person has to keep her arms hanging out before her. Stuck out like this. She looked like a praying mantis.'

'Louise didn't go on it very much I suppose?'

'No. You're absolutely spot on. She didn't. Far from helping with my personality development it seemed to have just the opposite effect. She said it was like being married to a performing seal. She actually got up and left before they'd even picked Mrs Elbert-Keir off the floor. She simply cleared off without me. Things began to get much worse after that, between us, I mean, and I felt terrible because I loved her tremendously and I thought we'd had some marvellous nights together. But apparently she didn't think so. After she met Mr Sherman she told me that she'd never enjoyed a single moment in our bed at home, and I had to accept that, Rufus, even though it hurt. I accepted it.'

'Tell me, Bill, did you ever have any bad feelings about girls – young girls, I mean, schoolgirls – in that time? At the tennis club or anywhere?'

'No, honestly. I didn't feel like that. Even at the club where some of them were very pretty and nice and used to wear little white pants under their tennis dresses . . .'

'But you didn't feel like . . . well, like you felt later. It was just the girls at Southwelling.'

'Oh yes, truthfully, it was *their* doing. Before that I thought fourteen-year-olds were children. I was very wrong of course. Mind you, Rufus, I was aware that *some* men felt like that. We used to get the *News of The World* and there are always items like that in there, of course, AFTER HE HAD GIVEN FIFTH FORMER A LIFT, and that type of headline. Oh God, yes, I was aware that such things went on. Men used to stop their cars on the road outside the school sports ground at Midford-Pallant, and gape at the girls doing the high jump or throwing the discus. I suppose it was because they wore gym knickers and white blouses. On one school sports day there were three collisions because drivers were looking at those little schoolgirls instead of watching the road. A commercial traveller drove smack into the back of a baker's van there one afternoon.'

'This was when you worked in the bank? When you were still with Louise?'

'Yes, Rufus, that's correct.'

'Bill, how did you know the man was a commercial traveller? The man who hit the baker's van.'

'I heard him saying so. They had the usual bit of an argument about it and I overheard.'

'You were on the spot, then? Right there by the sports field?'

'Well, yes, actually I was, Rufus. It was my lunch hour from the bank and I used to take a breath of air, go for a walk, you see, and if you know Midford-Pallant you will appreciate that you can only more or less walk up the main road or down it.'

'And you, more or less, walked down the road and along by the school sports field where the girls were doing the high jump and throwing the . . . what was it they were throwing?'

'Discus, Rufus. No, I walked *up* the road, more or less, not *down* it. *Up* the road. That goes by the sports field. But there are only two ways to go if you take a walk from the bank. The *what*? Oh, the discus. You don't know about athletics? Nor about Ancient Greece? Well, it's like a heavy flat plate and the girl . . . or whoever is throwing it . . . brings it back with her . . . their arm and throws it.'

'That's all there is to it?'

'That's about all.'

'Doesn't sound very thrilling.'

'Well it isn't, I suppose. Not particularly. I'll tell you something though, Rufus, some of those men got into a terrible state in their cars outside the sports field. I was going by there once . . . on one of my walks, as I said you could only go up the road or down the road . . . and I actually saw this middle-aged chap almost doubled up in the seat of his car, beetroot-red . . .'

'What?'

'How do you mean, what, Rufus?'

'Beetroot-red what?'

'Face. He had a red face. You understand? And he was all crouched up and staring at the schoolgirls like a madman and

27

muttering and groaning to himself. I heard him say "beautiful", "exquisite", and words like that. He didn't even notice me.'

'Maybe he was a discus-throwing fanatic, Bill.'

'Now you're joking, Rufus. I *know* when you are because your face gives you away. It's the Irish in you, I suppose. No, you know as well as I know what he was up to, groaning and staring at the girls in their blue knickers. Now come on, Rufus, you know don't you?'

'I can take a good guess, I suppose. How are they treating you here, Bill? Of course, being on remand is not like the real thing, you know. They say it's the boredom that gets you with the real thing. Nothing to do.'

'I always thought the dim ones sewed mail bags and the bright ones worked in the library.'

'Bags is a sought-after job, Bill, because it gives you something to occupy yourself. Now, tell me, why did you leave the bank, Bill? I mean, you had another job before clearing out of Midford-Pallant, didn't you? Delivery service or something.'

'You've been making inquiries about me, haven't you Officer. I thought you had.'

'Well we have to, you know. It's part of the job. It's no good being a detective unless you like asking questions.'

'And very true, I suppose. Well, I left the bank after Louise went off with Mr Sherman. I thought it would be better to get a job where I got out into the fresh air a bit more. I got to feeling very morose; claustrophobic they call it, don't they? Hemmed in. So I took this job delivering lemonade and lime juice and all that sort of thing. I had it for a few months in the summer and then I left the town altogether.'

'Any particular reason for leaving, Bill? I mean, did you just clear off quite suddenly or did you plan it all?'

'Well, I suppose a bit of each, really. I wanted to get out, to go somewhere where nobody knew me where I could start again. I kept seeing that bastard Mr Sherman around, and sometimes I saw Louise when I was on my delivery round. They even had the cheek to order their lime juice and soda and suchlike from us, so I had to deliver it to the door. Mostly I just used to leave it on the step, but sometimes I knew she was watching by the curtains in the front room so I used to annoy her by leaving the van right outside her house and going around the corner to the pub for my lunch.'

'So you'd started having lunch in the pub? No more walkies.'

'No. Well I was outside all day anyway, so I didn't need the air. So I went and had a shandy and a sandwich or something. But, as I say, I seemed to keep seeing that bastard Mr Sherman in the town, and he was so jolly and oozing with personality. He was terrible. He'd have stolen the limelight at a bloody funeral, Rufus, really he would.'

'Now you're starting to curse and swear.'

'I know. I keep control as a rule but, God, he really did upset me. Do you know he was the president of some club or other, and Louise went to a dinner with him and he had the nerve to parade my wife around while all the other buggers clapped in rhythm. You know, The President and His Lady stuff, and He's a Jolly Good Fellow. My wife! They even had their picture in the local paper. Nobody cared a damn about how *I* felt. So I decided to get out of Midford-Pallant for good and I did.'

'Anything else, Bill? Anything else make you leave?'

'Well, there was. I had a bit of an accident with the van. Nothing very much. I knocked down a woman and they said it was my fault, although it wasn't. She just ran out into the road. She wasn't hurt much. Just bruises and that sort of thing. They didn't even keep her in hospital. But the boss said I had to go. So that helped me make up my mind. I just packed up, locked the maisonette and threw the key in the pond where those ribby old fountains are in the middle of the town, and I got on the first train going anywhere. I just got out.'

5

THERE WAS the awkward accident with the van. He had been spying that afternoon through the crafty little hole he had made, lying along the shelf in the back of the van and looking and looking until he was sick with the heat inside the vehicle and the excitement of the things he had seen. He felt like a man in a midget submarine. He must have been still thinking about it all because he went carelessly through the summer traffic in the hazy afternoon town and the accident happened as he turned the corner by the library and Sainsbury's. She came out between some parked cars and somehow the side of his van hit her.

It was strange because there did not seem to be people around. It was about two o'clock and the shops were quiet and because of the parked cars no one saw what had happened. William went around and picked her up. She was lying in a strange, frightened crouch, almost against the front wheel. Her eyes swivelled up to him as though he were a hunter and she his victim. She was silent and he picked her up (oh, that picking her up!) and carried her to the pavement where some people came to see what had happened and someone went to get the ambulance and the police. It was not his fault, and she said that herself.

But, God, that picking her up and carrying her. His left hand and forearm under the widening part of her legs, his right arm beneath her armpits and around to her front. The extraordinary feeling of those steps to the pavement. The triumph! The great protectiveness!

He had got out because of that really. Left the town; taken the first train he could that came in to the Midford-Pallant station. It should have been mysterious and romantic, as he planned for himself, a journey into the unknown, and he purposely covered his ears when they announced where the train was going. He had bought a ticket to Doncaster, the first town that had come to his mind, and it cost him two pounds. But he could go anywhere. He was free. There were no limits, no horizon but the next one.

In the end it was disappointing because the train had stopped at Pallant Minor, the next station, and that was the end of its journey. Foolishly, he stood on the platform, observed by a puzzled porter of whom he had asked directions to Doncaster. He tried not to look at the house on the hill estate where Louise now slept with Mr Sherman. It stood up among its squared fellows like a deliberate taunt.

He had taken the next train back to Midford-Pallant and then another one to Derby which he thought was as near to Doncaster in spirit as made no difference.

He had found his town which did not know him. It knew nothing of him and he nothing of it. It was a mute Midlands evening when he came out of the station and walked among the quiet shops and the dumb fronts of the offices. There were a few entwined couples around, all arms and aimlessness, looking at the engagement rings in the windows of Bravingtons or the enticing three-piece suites displayed in the Times Furnishing Company. It was too early for the cinemas to empty and the pubs were subdued. William walked on his search for lodgings and on his journey passed the post office, which he liked. It looked solid and decent, the sort of place to make a new start behind a metal grille. He got a room and the following day went to the post office and got a job as a counter clerk. He was beginning again.

At four o'clock on his first afternoon a strawberry-haired schoolgirl came to the grille, smiled at William and asked for a fourpenny stamp.

He managed to tear the first one almost in half on the sheet. He gave it to her and saw her expression fall as she saw how it was ripped. So he gave her another and told her to keep the first. Then another girl came in for two penny stamps and had lost her money. Her face was about to squash into tears. William smiled at her uncertainly, and then decisively pushed the stamps to her and straightened his finger against his lips with a shushing sign. She had a blue school hat slung around her neck like a sombrero and bright green eyes. She smiled at him with instant gratefulness. Within ten minutes William's grille was besieged by clamouring schoolchildren shouting, 'Free stamps! Free stamps!'

The other counter clerks stared bitterly at William as though he alone had discovered the secret of being loved. Then the postmaster arrived and the children were pushed into the street and the doors closed. William bashfully explained the occurrence to the official. The postmaster said there was no place for humanity in a post office. William had better look for another job by the end of the week.

He did not need to. On the following day they gave him the

harmless occupation of weighing the parcels and he stood there watching the slim, unerring arm of the scale as it waved to him. There was one parcel like a shoebox with separate small bouncing sounds and movements within it and he knew it was tennis balls. A voice said: 'Surely, you're William Herbert.'

He raised his lids like a criminal. The woman was forty and fluffy, with a tennis-club tan and tight greying hair. 'Why are you here weighing parcels?'

'They won't trust me with the stamps,' William shrugged.

They had a tennis court in the back garden, two gardeners and two Pomeranians. Their twin daughters were at Southwelling School in Sussex.

'Starting a new existence,' explained William casually after dinner. 'Life gets too rich,' he continued bravely. 'Too many things come one's way. In the end you're in the gravest danger of losing the most important thing of all – yourself.'

'How true,' sighed Mrs Ferber. 'Isn't it very true, Daddy?'

'How true,' echoed Mr Ferber, a former Warwickshire umpire.

'But why work in the post office in a strange town?' his wife asked. 'The last time I saw you was at Sutton Coldfield in the mixed-doubles final with Hazel Milling.'

'Fine backhand,' nodded William. 'I thought that the post office would be a humble sort of place to start a new life. There are few things so levelling as licking other people's stamps.'

Mr Ferber said: 'I thought they licked their own these days.'

'Some of them' agreed William. 'But others watch you and give sharp nods showing that you ought to lick the stamps for them. Fortunately most people are decent about it.'

'From licking champions to licking stamps, eh?' Mr Ferber gurgled at his joke. 'Why didn't anyone recognize you? Before Mary, that is?'

'Well I wasn't there long enough, and it's not as though I'm Wimbledon Champion or anything. Nobody really knows my face.'

'Well *we* do,' said Mrs Ferber dramatically. 'And you are not to go back to that terrible place.'

'Terrible place?'

'The post office.'

'Oh, no. Well, it wasn't really for me, I suppose. I was thinking of chucking it at the end of the week in any case.'

'How long since you played for the county?'

'At the beginning of May,' said William. 'I told them I wasn't available for the rest of the season. Too busy.'

'Tragic, isn't it, Daddy?' said Mrs Ferber.

'Tragic, certainly,' said her husband. 'Southwelling ought to be right for him, don't you believe, Mary? That's what you're thinking, aren't you?'

'*Clever* of you,' said Mrs Ferber. 'That was exactly what I was thinking. Mr Herbert – William – our twin girls are at Southwelling and I know the tennis coach has just gone. Died too. Died across the net poor man.'

'That's the good way to go,' mumbled Mr Ferber. 'Across the net.'

'They're looking for someone else. Tennis is terribly important there you know.'

Mr Ferber said: 'Best tennis school in the country. That and St Margaret's.'

'I'm sure they would find you of great use,' said Mrs Ferber. 'Do you think you would like it?'

6

'BILL.'

'Yes, Rufus.'

'Bill, can we go back to the bathroom. The scene in the school bathroom. Are you with me?'

'Yes, of course. We're in the bathroom.'

'Now *why* was the girl supposed to be drowned? I *know* they were fooling you. But what was the *reason* she gave – was it that she was just drowned or overcome by the steam, or something? What did they say?'

'Oh that. Mary Bosham. Yes, well they said, Rufus, and I believed them of course . . .'

'Of course, Bill. You don't have to look at me like that when you say "of course", you know. I *believe* you, Bill. Everything you say, I *believe* you. But later I want to ask you about a few of the things you told me yesterday. Like the accident with the van.'

'The day before. Yesterday was Sunday. You didn't come.'

'No. You're right. It was. We don't ask people things on Sundays. But let's get back to Mary Bosham in the bath. I'll ask you about the van in a minute.'

'About the accident. What did you want to know about that, Rufus? Oh, Mary Bosham first. Yes, of course. Well the girls said that they usually had a competition to see who could stay under water for the longest time. And Mary was the champion, you see, and she was trying to beat her own record and stay under while the others counted up to a hundred or something. And that's how it happened. She had a remarkable talent for staying under water. So they said, anyway.'

'It's a gift, I suppose, Bill. Some of us have got one gift and some of us have others. The wife went in yesterday, by the way. Right in the middle of Sunday dinner she started having the pains you know. Off we had to go to hospital. Now I'm just waiting.'

'That's wonderful, Rufus. Just keep him away from being a tennis coach, remember.'

'Oh, I'll remember that, Bill. When you were in the bathroom, Bill, how were the girls standing? I find this interesting.'

'They *are* interesting. No doubt about that. How were they standing? Well, all around. Just all around. In towels and all steamed up. Some of them were still standing in their baths, because girls nearly always dry themselves standing up in their baths, you know. They don't get out and dry themselves like men. Probably something to do with not leaving the security of the water. Or getting the floor wet. Yes, they were standing there just like those birds – herons – standing in the water. With their towels around their bodies of course.'

'They dry themselves standing up in the bath, do they? We learn something every day. I didn't know that before.'

'It's not something you think about, Rufus.'

'Oh, I don't know.'

'What was it about the van accident?'

34

'Yes, now Bill, you were fibbing to me, weren't you. You told me a fib about the accident. *That's* for fibbing!'

'*Don't* do that, Rufus! You mustn't slap me like that.'

'Only playful, Bill. But you mustn't fib about things. We want to get everything right for the court, don't we? Otherwise they're going to get the wrong story. Understand?'

'Yes, Rufus. But don't slap me, please *don't*! You did it again! You're hurting me, Rufus. My nothe! Snnnnoppitt! Snnnoppitt, Rufuth! You're bloody hurting . . . I'll tell you . . . damn, that hurt my nose, holding it like that. No . . . No, don't do it again, please.'

'It was a *girl*, wasn't it, Bill? It wasn't a woman, like you told me. It was a fourteen-year-old girl you knocked over in the van.'

'Yes . . . yes, it was. I lied because it looked so bad. It sounded bad, didn't it? But it was a girl all right. Mind she was a *big* girl and at first I thought it was a woman.'

'She was in a blue school summer dress, Bill, and she had a satchel.'

'Yes, I suppose that's true.'

'And you picked her up and carried her to the side of the road.'

'Yes, of course. I did just that.'

'How did it feel carrying that helpless little girl like that, Bill?'

'Heavy. I told you she was a *big* girl. Don't move your hand towards my nose, Rufus. Not again, Rufus. It makes my eyes water.'

'Did you *like* carrying her? Did you like picking her up and feeling her in your arms, Bill? What was it like?'

'Stop it, Rufus. You're getting all worked up.'

'Sorry, Bill. Yes of course. Let's keep calm. Well let's forget the fib you told about the accident. But we've established that it was a schoolgirl and not a woman, haven't we? That's the main thing. Was she wearing a school hat, at all? Can you remember?'

'No, I can't remember.'

'Let's get on to that van of yours. The one with the spyhole in the side.'

'You've been checking up on me!'

'We have to. I told you that. It's part of the job. Why did you make the spyhole there?'

35

'Not for what you think.'

'Why?'

'It was there when I got the van. It was right in the middle of the letter "O" in the name Thompson. The first letter "O". Thompson was the man who owned the drinks business. The one I worked for.'

'Why the hole?'

'I told you. Oh no! *No* Rufus. You mustn't hit me. Christ, that hurt! Not my nose. No, not my nothe, again. Pleeth. No. Thath my bloodith nothe. Let go!'

'There, I've let you go!'

'Thank you. You make my eyes water doing that. I told you. No, I'm not crying, but you hurt me, Rufus.'

'The hole in the side of the van. Why did you make it?'

'You think it was for spying on the schoolgirls in the playing field, don't you? Watching them doing high jumps in their gym knickers and all that. That's what you think, don't you? WELL, YOU'RE BLOODY WRONG, RUFUS, COPPER!'

'Don't call me "Rufus, copper", Bill. I thought we had this on a friendly basis. Don't let's spoil the relationship.'

'Well don't pull my nose again. That's what spoils the relationship.'

'Not to mention spoiling your nose, eh, Bill. Hah! *That's a joke, Bill.* Come on. Right, that's the style. Now let's shake hands and try again. There. Okay now? Tell me, then. About the hole.'

'You think I had it made to watch the schoolgirls in the afternoons, don't you? Well I didn't. I had it made to watch my wife. Oh, God Almighty. I used to park the van outside the house where she lived with Mr Sherman and pretend I'd gone off to the pub. But I didn't. I'd crawl into the back and lie there on one of the shelves with the bottles of lemonade and raspberry soda and all the rest of it. And I'd lie and watch her cleaning her windows or sweeping the front path or weeding the garden, so happy and carefree, and not even looking at my van. I'd watch her for an hour at a time, until I was nearly suffocating in there.'

'What did you do while you were watching her?'

'I just used to watch. Sometimes I used to cry for her.'

'I'm sorry, Bill.'

'That's all right. You weren't to know, Rufus. But don't pull my nose any more.'

'I won't. I promise.'

'That was all there was to it. I just wanted to be somewhere near her and to see what she was doing. She seemed so happy with him too. That's what was terrible.'

'How long did this go on for, Bill? Did you stop and watch her through your hole every day, or every other day?'

'Most days. But it got me down, you know, Rufus. It simply got me down. Seeing her and not being able to kiss her or touch her or even speak to her.'

'So what did you do?'

'I couldn't stand it any more. So I stopped looking at her and I took the van up to the road by the school and looked at the schoolgirls, instead. But I didn't have the hole made especially for that. Honestly. Oh, don't! That's my nothe again, Rufuth. You promithed! You promithed!'

7

CURLED LEAVES were lying in worried groups about the paths and lawns, waiting pessimistically for the wind or the broom. A lemon sunlight was on the Sussex Downs, trees fidgeted along the distant road line, and the school looked more settled, more permanent than anything in the landscape.

Some girls on the opposite side of the tennis courts heard Miss Smallwood's owl-hoot voice as she walked with William. They loitered and spied at him through the diamond wire, chatter and giggles drifting in the autumn afternoon.

'You've arrived in fine time, Mr Herbert,' enthused Miss Smallwood, making bad imaginary forehand volleys with her screwed-up fist. 'Our splendid new indoor court will be completed when you begin your coaching. So we can ignore the elements, at last, thank heavens.

'I'm sure the girls are going to enjoy having you. They adore someone with a perky sense of humour. Poor Mr Fielding, our last tennis coach. A sadly lacking man, in some ways, I fear. Especially as he got older and slower on the court. Most of the senior year could beat him easily and I'm afraid he would have had to go anyway.

'When I saw him hanging across the net that afternoon, quite dead ... yes, quite dead ... with his racket still held rather pathetically in his hand ... somehow I felt that it had saved me an unpleasant job. God moves, indeed, in a mysterious way.'

'He does,' agreed William.

Miss Smallwood said: 'He was soaked through, you know. Soaked right through. The little girl he was coaching went off when she saw him collapse across the net and was too upset and frightened to tell anyone. Apparently she had struck him with a forehand drive shortly before and she was under the impression – mistakenly of course – that she was somehow responsible for his collapse. So she crept away, as little girls will, Mr Herbert, and said nothing to anyone. Then it rained heavily, quite a storm, and poor, dead Mr Fielding was out there through it all, hanging across the net and no one there to see him. Most sad. The rumour went around the lower school that he had actually been drowned on the tennis court. You know how children exaggerate.'

They continued their walk through the grounds. October sun was calm and rosy on the walls, and the windows reflected the mild agitation of the trees in the park.

'I'm afraid you will be organized here, Mr Herbert. In a female society a man is invariably organized. It's in the nature of things, I suppose. Mothered is perhaps a better word than organized, but they both mean the same thing in the end. Have you been in one of the Armed Services?'

'Oh yes,' William assured her. 'I was in the Royal Air Force, but a flying accident finished me.'

'How frightening. It was a crash?'

'Yes,' admitted William. 'It was a crash, all right.'

'I don't suppose you want to recall it. Men who have been through such experiences rarely do.'

'I'd rather forget it, Miss Smallwood,' he replied.

She nodded seriously and four little girls who walked by sang: 'Good afternoon, Miss Smallwood. Good afternoon, Mr Herbert.'

William felt warm and flattered.

'They know me,' he smiled.

'I imagine they will have been talking of little else since the term began, Mr Herbert. A new tennis coach! You know how excitable girls can be.'

The school was in a spectacular half-bowl of the Downs so that you could see it from the upper ridge, its grounds spread out like skirts, concentrated trees hemming it and only three or four peaked roofs of other buildings showing like red islands above the trees. William walked with Miss Smallwood away from the school.

'Three hundred and thirty girls, Mr Herbert and twenty-five staff.'

She paused, strode a few wooden steps and then began to recite: 'Armitage, Arnold, A'moore, Bonner, Bennett, de Berenger, Chevalier, Donovan, Elliott, Everett, Frewin, Freemantle, Hartley, Hecht, King, Ling, Miles, Paget, Quinlan, Robertson, Scott, Tilling, Unwin, Vernon, Whitefriar.' She twinkled triumphantly through her spectacles. 'That's the staff,' she affirmed.

'I thought you were listing the girls,' said William.

'A funster!' Miss Smallwood hooted. 'A veritable funster! We could do with some humour, Mr Herbert.'

She ambled on towards a house set like a small cake at the edge of the encircling trees. 'We keep the girls until they are sixteen, Mr Herbert, and then off they go to Kelly's, our associate establishment in Kent, a finishing school, you understand, or occasionally to finishing schools abroad or in London.

'My cottage,' continued the thin, pink lady pointing to the house ahead. 'I like to get a little removed from all the school bustle, you understand, at the end of the day. I am a Gilbert and Sullivan fanatic, Mr Herbert. I keep up a correspondence with past and present members of the D'Oyly Carte wherever they may be. I have all their photographs and all the gramophone records. Marvellous, marvellous.'

'Marvellous,' agreed William.

'You like Gilbert and Sullivan! How appropriate. I shall play you all my records.'

They went to the cottage and the twin daughters of Mr and Mrs Ferber of Derby arrived while he was having tea among all the hanging opera singers, captured open-mouthed along the picture rail.

'Tina and Claire,' announced Miss Smallwood. 'We have to thank their mummy for your being here, Mr Herbert.'

William heard his teacup rattle as they came in. They were tall, just fifteen then. Their hands felt identically shy in his as they were introduced. They were alike but not indistinguishable. Tina smiled, Claire was soft-eyed and solemn. They had tea, balancing the awkward cups on their thick black stockings, sitting on a flowered couch opposite him, their clear faces turned and listening as he talked about tennis.

They were closely attentive and they nodded politely as they ate their fairy cakes, their four long legs each slightly apart from the other. Four slim black legs in a line, like piano notes, a space between each. Then, at Miss Smallwood's tentative suggestion, they brightly sang and danced *Three Little Maids From School Are We* as an asthmatic record played, the headmistress herself suddenly jerking up and joining in, taking the middle maid's part.

They kicked and chorused lustily to the running, rousing music, plunging across the formal cottage room in front of the stiff William. Miss Smallwood had a wooden voice and straight hard legs and the two young girls, their jolly arms around her shoulders and hers about theirs, seemed as though they were supporting her rather than dancing with her. The twins sang with fullness and enthusiasm, without shyness, throwing back their long fine hair and laughing at William's fixed face. Their legs flew within inches of his hands. Beneath their school blouses their young bodies boiled to the music. They ended laughing and breathless with their final 'Three little mai—ds from schooooooooooooool' and fell deliciously backwards on to the couch with Miss Smallwood her limbs mixed with theirs like two lightning-struck old trees between four supple saplings.

William applauded violently and choked over his fairy cake, throwing out a shower of crumbs. Tina Ferber poured him a hurried third cup of tea and smiled at him inquiringly while he used it to clear the cake blockage in his throat. Miss Smallwood was still panting, her pink now deep maroon, her eyes alive with achievement. 'Lovely! Lovely!' she cried. 'Wasn't that fun, Mr Herbert?'

'Great fun,' agreed William honestly.

Before he went they did the routine again, but more subdued, in deference to Miss Smallwood's age and condition, and also sang *The Lord High Executioner*. William took the train from Lewes station where he bought a paper and never looked at it. He stared into the window all the way to sunset London, seeing half a ghost of his face. It watched him suspiciously.

8

'You had a crash in a plane, did you, Bill?'

'No, Rufus. I've never said that. I've only said I had an aerial accident or a flying accident. But I've never mentioned a plane.'

'What was it then, a tightrope?'

'You're not far out. I'd only been in the Air Force about five weeks when they did it to me. It was a rotten lousy trick. And, to think, I was quite keen to be called up.'

'This was national service, wasn't it? That's right, you're thirty-five. They just caught you.'

'I'll say they did. But, as I explained, I was quite keen to get in. My father said it would separate the man from the boy. He kept on saying it, too. He never gave me a lot of credit, my old man.'

'Hard on you, was he?'

'Very hard. He fell about laughing when he heard what they'd done. It didn't matter that I'd got three broken ribs.'

'What did they do to you, Bill?'

'Actually, I fell out of bed, which doesn't sound all that dangerous, I know. But some silly bastards had tied some ropes on the bedstead and hauled it up to some iron girders in the roof of a hangar, and I was fast a-bloody-sleep in it. I was on guard duty in this hangar and once they'd pulled me up there the flight-sergeant – he was in it too – bawled: "Call out the guard!" Of course, being keen, I rolled straight out of bed and I fell eighteen feet to the floor. Apparently they were supposed to catch me, but they were all laughing too much. Christ, I looked up from the floor and you ought to see them holding on to each other, wetting their bloody selves. And I was lying there with a greenstick fracture of the left arm, three broken ribs, and multiple bruises. You're grinning, Rufus.'

'No, I'm not grinning, Bill. I've got something caught in my teeth from breakfast. A bit of kipper, I think.'

'Kipper! You make me drool, Rufus.'

'Very tasty too. A little pat of butter on each one.'

'We don't get much like that in here.'

'Well, you wouldn't expect to, would you? It's a prison, for Christ's sake. Anyway, you were invalided out of the Air Force.'

'I was in hospital for a long time. Even that was disastrous. There was a chap in the next bed called Buller who was having fun with one of the nurses. He used to say she had more things to play with than the average toyshop. When he went from the hospital she had a go at me and broke two of my ribs again the first time she gave me a damned hug.'

'You made up for all that, though, didn't you, Bill. I'll bet you were pampered at Southwelling. Were there any other men there at all?'

'Only the gardeners and the porter – that sort. And Major Prescod who lived a mile away and took a sort of interest in the girls.'

'What sort of interest?'

'Oh, he liked their shoes. Really. Wasn't that odd? I thought it was very odd. He used to let them hide in his house when they were on the cross-country run. The old rascal! When they went to his house – sometimes he got them over to tea on a Sunday as well – he was always looking at their shoes and saying that they needed a clean. He used to like to clean them. He would go and get a special little box where he kept all his shoe brushes, polishers and Cherry Blossom and he would kneel down and take the girl's foot in his hands and clean her shoes for her.'

'While she was wearing them?'

'Oh, yes. They always wore them when he did it. He used to buff them up beautifully. You always knew the girls who had been to Sunday tea at Major Prescod's because they always had such nice shiny shoes on Monday morning. It used to be quite a joke. And when they used to dodge into his house on the cross-country runs he always cleaned the mud from their spiked shoes.'

'Sounds like a very clean man, Major Prescod. Imagine going to all that bother.'

'Nothing was too much for him, Rufus. Sometimes if the cross-country run had been very muddy he would wash their legs down for them as well. My goodness, apparently the girls used to have a huge giggle about that in the dormitory! You see, they always had to put mud on their legs afterwards anyway, to dirty them. Otherwise it would not look as though they had been on the cross-country run at all. Talking about shoes, Rufus, has your wife had the baby yet? No. Still waiting are we? Never mind. Yes, my nose is a bit sore, still, Rufus. You did pull it rather a lot yesterday, didn't you. It's very tender. Yes, when you touch it like that. Oh Rufuth, you didth ith again! Yeth, you're hurthing . . .

'Thanks. I wish you wouldn't do that. It *does* bloody hurt. I only asked about your wife and the baby because the shoes reminded me, that's all. If you knew how much my nose ached this morning you wouldn't keep doing that. Look I've got to wipe my eyes again now. It's as tender as anything, Rufus. Please don't do it any more. I'm cooperating, aren't I? I thought we were friends.'

'Sorry, Bill. Thoughtless of me. I was just looking at it and I thought it was looking a bit red. All I was doing was seeing if it is as tender as it looks. You've got an interesting hooter, Bill, if you don't mind me saying so. I think it's swelling up a bit, too. It's bigger than it was.'

'I don't wonder, the way you keep squeezing it.'

'Christ, I *am* sorry, Bill. I won't do it again. Not unless it's necessary. Look – tell you what.'

'What?'

'If I do it again, without any cause or justification, *you* can have a pull of my nose. How does that sound?'

43

'Scout's honour, Rufus?'

'Scout's honour, Bill. Now where were we? Ah, yes. These shoes that the Major kept so clean? Did all the girls wear the same sort of shoes?'

'In the week they had neat little black shoes with small buckles, but at the weekends they could wear other sorts of shoes if they liked. Brown or black or whatever they preferred as long as they were not common-looking.

'But Major Prescod used to like the proper school shoes. He used to make a point of asking the girls who came to tea if they would wear those shoes because they were the ones he wanted to clean.'

'They had little buckles?'

'Yes, he had a special little tin of Brasso in his shoebox just for the buckles and he made a special thing of cleaning those. The girl would have to lift her leg up really high when he did that because he used to pretend that he wanted see his face in the buckle when he had polished it. He *was* an old scallywag, Rufus. Everybody used to laugh a lot about that. The girls, especially the younger ones, always thought it was a great game and the old Major used to pantomime about making a big show of it. The girls told me all about it. Mind you, Rufus, I couldn't help thinking that underneath all the laughter he had some ulterior motives. I don't want to prejudge the man, but you can't help thinking like that, can you?'

'You *don't* mean? . . .'

'*Exactly*, Rufus. Perhaps you ought to keep a quiet eye on Major Prescod. He may be perfectly all right, of course, and I'm the last one to make accusations. I realize that. But he might just be worth watching.'

'Just a moment, Bill. I'll write that down. M-A-J-O-R P-R-E-S-C-O-T . . . Not T? Oh, a D. Right, PRESCOD. Well, that's got *him*. Thanks a lot, Bill.'

'Anything to help, Rufus. Now where were we? We seem to wander off at the slightest thing this morning, don't we? By the way, could you ask them if I could have the fishcakes today? I like fishcakes, but I always get the second choice. Like that diabolical soup yesterday. It was awful, terrible! It's enough to give prison a bad name. Ask them will you, because I'm only on

44

remand, remember. I should be getting the better choice of food because I haven't even been on trial yet, and I could be proved innocent. There'll be plenty of time for horrible, mucky old soup when I'm doing my ten years or whatever it is.'

'I'll tell them, Bill. Fishcakes. As soon as I go, I'll tell them. I think that the trouble is that the fishcakes are all gone by the time they get to you. This cell is 304 and that's a high number. The low numbers get all the fishcakes.'

'Ask them to start from the high numbers, for once, will you? Sometimes I'm near to tears in this dump, you know, Rufus. What with my nose and no fishcakes and being in here anyway and Connie expecting our baby. Sometimes I feel so sick about it. I have to admit to you that there are moments when the future looks very, very unpromising. The prospect of ten years! That's a long time out of anyone's life, Rufus.'

'Sure, sure. But cheer up. Just think, some of those South-welling girls will be all of twenty-one when you get out.'

9

HE HAD never ceased to think that Connie Rowan, the American girl, was at least partly responsible for the unpleasantness concerning his motorized bicycle and the French letter. She would laugh about it when she was with him in the extraordinary days that followed; hoot hysterically in her young animal way, which used to offend and annoy him.

'You did it,' he had pointed at her. 'You were in the gang which put that revolting appliance on the end of my exhaust pipe. My God, Connie, you made me a clown that day! A damned laughing stock. All the town – women, children, bus-drivers, everybody – saw it. Who knows, some of the teachers might have been in town. Miss Elliott or Miss Hartley, or – God forbid – even Miss Smallwood.'

It had gone to hideous lengths and had, in many ways, been the beginning of his unsettled period at Southwelling. That and, of course, the dwarf. Until then he had followed a circumspect life, keeping carefully to himself at the school when he was not tennis coaching in the new indoor court, or preparing, as an additional duty, for *The Mikado* which the girls were presenting at Christmas. Occasionally one or two of the younger teachers, the stocky, blonde, Miss Elliott, or Miss Hecht, the games mistress, would play on the indoor court but he had comparatively little contact with the other staff outside the dining-room and his rare visits to the common room.

It was late November and he had just bought the motorized bicycle, a little weakling on wheels, to cover the occasional journeys he made into Lewes for replacement tennis equipment, or for bits of shopping, or to go to the cinema. He was feeling a kind of peace about life then, away from the towns and the people, not having to see Louise or her Mr Sherman, having his own enclosed room and his television for the windy evenings.

The terrifying confusion of his life was losing its pace. Now the outdoor tennis courts were unused he coached the girls in the fine, echoing indoor court, doing something in which he was confident and competent, eating sedately with the rest of the staff, between Miss Smallwood and the elderly Miss King, at the table at the top of the girls' dining-room, and beginning to lose the fragile sensation of being a solitary male in a female menagerie. He began to know life again. One afternoon he had seen three cruising swans, necks elongated like regal airliners, navigating a few feet above the Lewes telephone lines. Stopping his motorized bicycle he had watched them neck their way south, while he stood awkwardly among motorists at the traffic lights. He had seen them go away into the curry-coloured sky of the dying afternoon.

Even the young girls did not upset him as he feared they might. He watched them at their tennis and kept his mind on the game. They were children, after all, with runny noses, pink knees, hairs on their arms, voices calling childish things, and pathetic backhands. Most of them anyway. Once, involuntarily, almost involuntarily – he *thought* about it a second before committing himself but he followed through anyway – he patted one of the podgy juniors on her small rump as she was leaving the indoor court. He remembered how genuinely hard she had tried on the court and she was sweating heavily when she went off. He was honestly pleased with her, truly, and he had given her an encouraging little tap on her damp white knickers as she went out. She had turned, savage and flushed, and he had hidden his hand guiltily behind his back and smiled his confident, playful, grown-up smile at her.

But the matter of the French letter had upset him. He had parked his motorized bicycle outside Smith's in Lewes and had bought a tennis magazine and some notepaper there before going out into the street again. It was a half-day and some of the girls had been in a group near the school gates as he had left that afternoon and he remembered seeing their round innocent faces in a bus that had overtaken him a couple of miles short of the town. Connie Rowan had been one of them and Susan Belling another.

This Connie had marmalade eyes and long drifting hair. She was tall, sixteen, with none of the half-promises of a schoolgirl's body. She was firm and lean with refined legs and an American laugh.

He had come out of Smith's and put his tennis magazine and stationery in the saddlebag. The motorized bicycle was second-hand, but the saddlebag was new and its straps stiff and he had some difficulty in opening it. Had he glanced down then, at the mouth of the exhaust pipe, none of it would have happened. But he did not.

He clambered on to the ugly vehicle and started it up. Looking back, he remembered thinking that, at that instant, a woman with two children in one pushchair was staring down at something behind the bicycle. Then the piebald man who sat by Boots the Chemists, selling newspapers, began to laugh. He had a strange laugh, more like a long cough. William, looking unsurely about him, realized that there was some excitement in the immediate area. People were colliding into other people and a lot of them were smirking or beginning to splutter with laughter. A child cried: 'A circus! It's a circus!' William looked across the road to see what was causing the diversion. More people had gathered there in small clusters, looking across at his side. Some of them were pointing. Three girls had come out of Boots and were blatantly screeching, bending down, and holding each

47

other's pea-green nylon overalls. More children had become excited and were tugging at their mothers' arms. William swivelled desperately on his saddle. It was *him*, he knew it was *him*. They were getting at him again.

'A balloon,' a boy cried. 'Mum, a big-big balloon.'

The stupid old fool selling newspapers was braying now and throwing himself around on his stool. One of the Boots' girls was in hopeless tears and another had slumped against the window of the shop and had her face in her hands. The newspaper man howled across to the girls: 'Is that one of yours?'

'We don't sell 'em!' one screeched back hysterically. And the people on the pavement all fell against each other again. One ruby-faced woman waved an umbrella at him.

William looked down angrily. The contraceptive sheath which had been fixed over the exhaust pipe of his motorized bicycle was blown out, long, white and obscene, for five feet to his rear. The exhaust gases were swelling it every second. He could hear the tight, pallid rubber squeaking as it expanded.

William whispered: 'Oh, dear God.'

Traffic had stopped in the channel of the street and a coarse lorry-driver on his high perch was foully advising other motorists to leave their cars and have a look. Some jumping boys were trying to touch the huge, fat, dragon condom with extended fingers. William, filling with tears of embarrassment, put the bicycle into gear and charged chugging away. The increase in gasflow blew the balloon out even longer behind him until it was waving and screeching twenty feet behind his bicycle like a pursuing ghost. He felt his face tight, white, and contorted. The whole street, the entire idiot world, was screeching with laughter. Then the French letter abruptly escaped from the exhaust and went rasping rudely up the shopping centre like a rubber banshee, wriggling, writhing through the traffic and the hollow-mouthed shoppers. William looked behind and saw it fizzing in the opposite direction.

He saw an innocent, elderly woman knocked over in the ridiculously hilarious panic to get out of its way. Sick and horrified he bumped speedily out of the town on the bucking vehicle. There were acid tears in his eyes. Somehow he was never safe.

When he drove into the school he realized that they all knew. He might have guessed they would. A lower school hockey match became petrified in the mud of the riverside playing field as he phutted along. They forgot the game and twenty-two quagmired infants stood still and watched him journey by. He heard Miss Hecht's whistle piping in vain, and, as he went under the yellowing chestnuts towards the main school, he could hear the miniature hockey teams cackling across the damp air.

There were dozens of dappled faces at the school windows when he arrived along the drive. He tried not to look at them. There were so many. He almost made his misery twofold by braking too heavily and allowing the back wheel of his wretched machine to skid through the wet leaves. But, almost breaking his forearms, he kept it upright. He knew they were howling behind their windows, the horrible bitches. He ran into the school, through the empty corridors, out across the tennis courts and into his own safe room. Without taking his heavy trench mackintosh off, he grabbed a pillow from the bed and, trembling with choking rage, put it across his knee and spanked it unmercifully. First he lifted the pillowslip up like a skirt. 'Take that, you little swine. And that! And that! It hurts, doesn't it! Yes, it hurts!'

10

'Jesus, you should be glad you're in here, Bill. In the dry. It's pouring out there this morning.'

'I didn't get any fishcakes again, Rufus. For God's sake – you *must* talk to them about it. I had that filthy, disgusting soup, but I know for sure that they brought the fishcakes right up to the cell next door. Next door! I could smell them. I was so sure I was going to get some, and I was looking forward to them like hell, and in they came with the rotten soup. They tried to make out that there were no more fishcakes left.'

'Well, Bill, maybe they did run out.'

49

'Oh, *come on*, Rufus. You know they did it on purpose. I'll tell you something, the man next door had some. I knew he did, I bloody knew it.'

'How *did* you know?'

'Because I'm clever, that's why. Not only could I smell them but I know when he's got soup because I can hear him slurping it. He leans up against his bars and slurps it, and he always bangs his mug on the wall to get the soup that's stuck to the sides to drop into the bottom of the mug. But today there was no slurping and no banging, so I reckon he had fishcakes without any doubt. And if he had them, why couldn't I have them? Damn it, I'm right next door. Don't tell me they *happened* to run out of fishcakes just as they got to me! I'll damn well write to the Home Secretary.'

'Now come oh, Bill, don't you go writing to the Home Secretary. You'll be getting somebody into terrible trouble. I tell you what . . .'

'What?'

'It's dead against the rules, and I'm risking my job by doing it, but I'll bring you in some fishcakes tomorrow.'

'You wouldn't!'

'Cub's honour. I'll bring them in. Do you want them hot or cold?'

'Now you're taking the piss again, Rufus. You mustn't be so cruel.'

'Bill. I'll bring some hot fishcakes in for you tomorrow . . .'

'No fooling?'

'I'll get my wife to cook them herself and . . .'

'There! You're lying, Rufus. You're bloody having me on again. Your wife's in hospital; how can she cook them?'

'Christ, I'm going daft, Bill! You're dead right. I meant my mother-in-law. Myra had the baby last night, by the way.'

'The baby! Oh, Rufus, why didn't you say?'

'You were threatening to write to the Home Secretary, that's why.'

'What is it, then?'

'Little boy. Well, a big boy really.'

'Marvellous, Rufus. Congratulations.'

'Thanks, Bill. He's all there by the look of him. Hair and everything.'

'And your wife?'

'Fine. Took it in her stride.'

'What will you call him?'

'I don't really know yet. Quite honestly, if you weren't on a criminal charge, I wouldn't mind calling him your middle name.'

'Bridgemont?'

'That's right, Bridgemont. That's a really impressive-sounding name, Bill. People would respect someone with a name like that.'

'It didn't help me, Rufus.'

'That's true. Anyway, I can't do it. Not with you on this sort of indictment. Maybe I could call him after one of the train robbers.'

'Oh, Rufus!'

'Only a joke, Bill. I think he'll probably end up with one of the names you hear on television. Cheyenne or something.'

'Yes, well that sounds nice and ordinary. What have you got in that bag, by the way?'

'Scrabble. I've been learning how to play. I thought we might have a game.'

'I'd like that, Rufus. But you won't forget about the fishcakes, will you?'

'I'll tell my mother-in-law.'

'I won't believe you until you've actually brought them. In fact, I won't believe you until I've *eaten* them.'

'All right. You'll see.'

'No questions today?'

'Well, I thought I'd ask you some while we're playing Scrabble.'

'I thought there was a catch in it.'

'No catch. It's just a change from the same old routine, and I know you like this game. You played it with the girls, didn't you?'

'Yes. On the island. When we went there.'

'The island. You're going to tell me about the island a bit later, aren't you? My mother-in-law plays this very well, Bill. We play it all the time now that my wife's in hospital.'

'Ha! Don't let it stop your mum-in-law making the fishcakes, will you?'

'Now, Bill, I've promised, haven't I? I won't go back on the fishcakes. Now let's have a game. Take seven letters . . .'

'Now, now, Rufus. You can't have "Durex". One of the rules is no proper nouns. You should know that.'

'Yes, you're right, Bill. Pity. It was double bonus points.'

'It's a good word, Rufus. Anything with an "x" is a good word for scoring. But it's trade name.'

'When you come to think about it, that trick they played on you with the French letter must have been a huge laugh.'

'Truthfully, Rufus, it wasn't. I can smile about it now, well almost. I suppose girls will be girls. But it was difficult to see the funny side of it that day. I don't think you would have found it very laughable if you'd been in my place.'

'I like the bit – I have to confess I really *do* like this bit – where the thing took off and went down the street rasping and wriggling. Christ, Bill that strikes me as being very funny. I can see it now . . . thrrrrrreeeeeeep . . . thrrrrraaaarp . . . thrrrurp . . . and all the people scattering and falling over. Dear Jesus, when I told that to the solicitor and his clerk they just about split themselves laughing. We were having a bit of lunch in a pub in Lewes, just along the street from Smith's, now I come to think about it. They knew something about it, of course, but when I really filled them in on it, well, I thought they would never stop. You'd have enjoyed that, Bill. It was a pity you weren't there.'

'I was in here, Rufus.'

'Yes. A shame, Bill. We had quite a laugh.'

'Well, I'm glad you enjoyed it. It's nice to give a little pleasure, I suppose. Funny how Louise always wanted me to be a joker, an extrovert, you know. She wanted me to to have *personality*. Now, when I'm apparently making people laugh, I'm stuck in here. And, from what I hear, I'm likely to be here for a long time yet.'

'There, look, I've made it "exude". Just took the "r" away and put another "e" in its place. Double score. Right?'

'Right. Now *this* is mine, Rufus. I've been waiting for you. Look – watch this, copper . . . z-i-p-p-e-r-s. Ha! You fell right into that by putting your "e" in there. Triple points there for me!'

'Don't call me "copper".'

'What was that? What did you say, Rufus?'

'Don't call me "copper", Bill.'

'Sorry. It slipped out, I suppose.'

'Well don't let it slip out. Call me "Officer" if you like, that's if you want to be formal. But that puts an end to our relationship.'

'Sthowy, Rufuth!'

'I've got your nose again.'

'Oi know you hath, Rufuth. I'm noth sthupid.'

'Does it hurt?'

'Courth it hurths! Like blooith hell, it hurths.'

'Ith tenderth from lasth time.'

'Right, well I'll let go. Now no more calling me, "copper". It's understood?'

'You're sthill holding it, Rufuth.'

'Well, I'm letting go . . . now. There, it's your nose again. Now remember.'

'Oh God, yes, I'll remember. I'm sorry.'

'All right, I am, too. Don't let's damage our friendship. I didn't hurt it much today, did I?'

'Well, not as much as usual. But it's so damned tender. Can't you see how red and tender it is?'

'Yes, it looks a bit touchy. Tender as a little girl's bottom.'

'Was that said lightly, Rufus? I mean, it was just a joke, wasn't it?'

'Sure, sure. Just a figure of speech.'

'I'll write down my points. Twenty-three, three times. That's sixty-nine. Your turn.'

'Let's give it a rest for today, eh, Bill. Let's put it over here on your potty.'

'You want to finish now? You're not upset because I got all those points, are you?'

'Christ, no, Bill. We'll just adjourn it. Leave it until tomorrow or the next day. We can carry on then. We'll play it like they play those grand-master games of chess. Sometimes they take weeks.'

'As long as I don't upset the letters when I use the potty, Rufus. I'll have to be careful. I'll hold the board carefully in my hands when I'm having a wee.'

'It will be all right, Bill. But hold it a bit to one side or it will get in your view. You won't be able to see where you're weeing, will you? You'll be missing the pot – doing it all over your socks, or something!'

'Rufus! I can't help feeling we get a bit coarse, sometimes, don't you? If Miss Smallwood could hear me now. She would be upset. She always thought I was a bit of a goody-goody, you know. Don't grin, Rufus. She saw the *best* in people, that's all. It's a pity there aren't a few more like her around. The world would be a damned sight better place, believe me.'

'I do believe you, Bill. Right, let's put the Scrabble over here on the potty. Just be careful not to upset the letters, that's all.'

'I'll remember.'

'Good lad. Now, Bill . . .'

'Yes, Rufus.'

'Some of the girls . . . well, we've had a policewoman going around to them for statements . . .'

'A police*woman*?'

'That's right, Bill. Really I haven't had the time to talk to them. And Connie Rowan is in America, of course . . . But wait a minute. You reminded me of a joke just now. When we were talking about what happened with the French letter in Lewes. Oh, yes. Let me tell it to you before we start on the serious business.'

'Connie . . .'

'Wait a minute. Yes, I've got it. Do you know why the doctor always ties a little knot in your belly button when you're born?'

'No, I don't, Rufus. Well I *do* know, the true reason, of course. But I don't know the answer to the joke.'

'Because if he didn't tie a knot there and he let you go – you'd go threeeeeeeeeep . . . thraaaaaaarp . . . thruuuuuuup. Like a balloon, whizzing all over the place! Like your thing at Lewes.'

'Humour is a very personal thing, isn't it, Rufus? I don't see that's very amusing. Now what about Connie? . . .'

'Connie. Yes. Jesus, how you can't think that's funny, Bill, beats me! Thrrreeeep . . . thrrrrraaarp . . . thrrrruuuuup. Just like a balloon! Imagine a baby doing that!'

'What about our baby? Connie's and mine.'

'It's a long wait for that little bastard yet.'

'Yes, it's only a few months, not much more than weeks really. It seems like years and years. She was beautiful, Rufus. Really beautiful, in a grown-up sort of way. The others . . .'

'What about the others?'

'Well, they were just kids.'

11

ALL MEN, he was sure, felt these complicated feelings about young girls. He appreciated that. Books had been written about it. It was an attraction to innocence, a natural desire to get in on the ground floor, an irritation, an awkward tickle beneath the flesh. The important thing was to keep it there, to imprison and confine it, let it lie. One morning, when perhaps he was an elderly man, he might awake to find that he wanted someone over sixteen.

He admitted to himself that this would bring a considerable sense of relief. Even so, he considered, at first anyway, that he was doing very well; keeping cool and clean. He kept them more or less at a distance even during tennis coaching, not looking at them more than he could help and, even when he did look at them, concentrating on the ugly ones.

But there were fateful things for which, he felt, he should not be brought to account. The trouble in the bathroom with Mary Bosham for one, and having to do those emergency things to her, the mortifying scene with the contraceptive and his motorized bicycle, Susan coming to his room so late in the evening, and the unfortunate accident over *The Mikado*. But he *had* tried.

The curly blonde, Susan Belling, had stood in his private lamplight that evening, sweet and assured. He had tried to converse with her without looking too fully into her face. She knew it and kept waiting for his eyes to turn up. Once, he fancied, she had the damned nerve to crouch so that she could look under his eyelids.

He had tried to concentrate on his comfortable green desk lamp with the light oozing out from beneath its smooth round skirt. When he did allow himself to look at her, her face was warm as an apricot. Her blouse was crumpled and saggy at the collar and her hair squashed around the nape of her neck. The sash about the middle of her gymslip was lolling like a gunbelt. She looked as though she had been lying on her bed in the dormitory before she had decided to see him about Vivian Puller's broken arm. She wore a smirk as carelessly as she wore her clothes. Her eyes were on him, fondly he thought, as though she knew he would understand.

She should have been in bed in the dormitory by then, anyway. He knew that. Something strange, panic-stricken, was running around within him like a family of disorganized mice.

She said: 'Mr Herbert, I have come to tell you that it was I – or is it me? – who pushed Vivian down the steps of the tennis court last Monday.'

Stop it, he told himself. Keep your hands on the desk, press them down so they obey and keep still. He knew damned well it was she – or was it her? – who gave poor dimpled, pimpled, Vivian a shove. Now, standing there in his quiet room, she was pushing her girl's breasts out. He could see she was.

'You know she had a compound fracture of the left arm?' he said.

'Two places,' she nodded.

'You seem pleased with yourself.' He attempted to make it sound grating, but his voice turned traitor and he merely squeaked. She closed her eyes and extended her small, heavenly, smirk. He turned quickly to the window. Now why couldn't he be like the gardener out there on the indistinct lawn, conducting the evening water, going home afterwards to his chummy wife and his satisfying dinner? He had to be steady. Strong and steady. He could not afford to squeak again. He turned his voice down a couple of pressures as though it were a gas cooker. It came out thick and low. 'In a boys' school,' he said, 'You would get six of the best across your little backside, believe me.'

He turned to her.

'Why don't you try me?' she said.

No! Why had he said that? He had *wanted* to say it, God knows, as she stood there, the blatant little devil, but he had thought he was capable of keeping it back. When he heard the words escaping he could hardly believe they were directed, dispatched, by him. But he *had* said it. And *she* had said what she had said. The trembling was awful. His hairy tweed suit felt like a tunnel, a burrow, with his agitated body shivering inside it.

He decided to be formal, but understanding. 'Susan, Miss Belling,' he began carefully. He said the rest of the sentence cautiously, deliberately, like a novice on a tightrope. 'You and your friends will have your jokes, at my expense. I appreciated when I took this post that, as the only man – apart from a gardener or two – at Southwelling, there would be particular difficulties.'

'Yes, Mr Herbert.'

He continued with more confidence, his voice straighter. 'There are bound to be, these difficulties. But I am here to coach the pupils at the game of tennis, and I don't intend to let *you*, or any of the others, get away with too much acting up. I'm telling you, and you can tell Miss Connie Rowan, our gift from America, and the rest of your friends, that I have been very patient, but I cannot be patient for much longer. Try to think of me as you do about every other member of the staff of Southwelling. Try to think of me just as you would a woman.'

Jesus, why did he have to ruin it like that! His thought collided with hers. He could see she could hardly wait to get away and tell them in the dormitory. The smirk streaked across her face even though she tried to pull it in. And he had been doing so well. It had sounded so adult, so firm. She had some little fair hairs on her forearms, and on the slope of her neck. The lamplight made them into fine gold streaks.

Eventually, she answered: 'Yes, Mr Herbert.'

'Good,' said William. 'Now let's have no more of this messing about. I'm not unaware of what has been going on, you understand that, don't you?'

'I understand, Mr Herbert.' She pulled the smirk entirely in, like someone tightening a string bag. 'What about Vivian's arm?'

'Does Miss Vivian Puller know you have come to me?'

He enjoyed calling them Miss Puller and Miss Rowan, and so on. It gave him a sensation of remoteness, some relief from them.

'No, sir,' said Susan. 'She doesn't even know it was *me* who pushed her.'

'Why did you own up?' he asked logically.

'It was on my conscience. I can't live with something on my conscience. So I came to see you.'

'Yes, I understand.' He thought a while. She stood quietly looking at him. He wanted to touch her somehow. 'Well,' he said quietly. 'Well, let's see.' He moved towards her purposefully, like a real schoolmaster, and gave in to his desire by putting his arm and fingers around her shoulder. He could feel the warm cutlets of flesh at the top of her slight arms. He tried to be uncaring and jovial but he was trembling so much his voice squeaked again. 'Right . . .' He desperately brought the level down. 'Right. Well knowing who did it won't bring poor Vivian back . . .'

Susan looked up abruptly. 'She's not dead, Mr Herbert. She's only got a broken arm.'

He laughed unconvincingly. 'Ha! That's what I meant. I've been watching too many plays on the television. What I meant is it won't mend Vivian's arm. Well, I am not letting it get any further. I should report it but I won't. But listen . . .'

He had led her to his respectable door now. He turned her around firmly so that they were facing. There was a chasm only an inch wide between the front of her gently swollen chest and his flat stomach. Her confidence had drained. He could see that. His miserable hands were on both her ungrown shoulders. 'Listen . . .' he said with sudden frankness. 'Just leave me alone, will you?'

She nodded. 'Yes, Mr Herbert. We'll all leave you alone.'

'Please,' he said.

She went out. He sat down on his bed and looked at his hands that had touched her young shoulders. He undressed and put out his lamp. Then naked he crawled into bed and clutched his pillow to his body. He talked a while to her in the private dark. Come and try me, she had said. But she had such a warm apricot face and the face of the pillow was white.

Before the curtain staggered up on *The Mikado* during the final week of the Christmas term, Miss Smallwood stumped in her warm wooden way to the footlights and held out her arms to the audience like a tweed crucifix.

The Southwelling school orchestra was cut off in mid-agony by one spearing glance shooting down under her rimless spectacles. Then she brought her hands across her chest and thrust her pink face towards the main hall.

'Dear parents, friends, old girls and young girls of Southwelling,' she began. 'We are pleased to present for your delight our Christmas production of *The Mikado* – *not* the Mick-a-doo as I heard one member of the lower school pronounce it today . . .'

She painfully constructed the same joke every time. Ruddigoreee for *Rudigore* and Princess Adder for *Princess Ida*. But they always assisted her by laughing.

'This term, we believe that we shall be better than ever since our music mistress Miss Tilling has had a male hand in the pudding . . .'

There was an uncertain giggle from the dim back rows and some fatherly coughing from the front. Miss Smallwood waited. '. . . and I believe that you will agree that Mr Herbert, our splendid and popular tennis coach, who took on the task of co-producer in his spare moments and out of the goodness of his heart . . .' There was a shower of young applause from the dim back rows. '. . . has added a man's touch to the production . . .'

Connie was playing The Emperor. To William, at the dress rehearsal, she had looked tall and ravishing in her costume and she had an uninhibited American voice that gave a touch of *Annie Get Your Gun* to the Gilbert and Sullivan score.

William had been entranced by her. She was so stately, so nearly grown to a woman. He wandered restlessly backstage while Miss Smallwood was out in front of the audience.

'I'll quit,' he told himself firmly. 'I'll turn it in. It won't be *that* difficult. After the holidays I just won't come back.

59

'Where is there to go? Well, that's not so hard. The world's a hell of a big place. I'll go somewhere. Why couldn't I get a job at a boys' school? That would solve it all. It's these ... little buggers I can't ... withstand.'

Connie should have left the dressing-room by now. He stood uneasily and watched the door. Miss Smallwood's creaky voice still came through the wings. He could see Miss Tilling holding herself ready to scrape the school orchestra together.

Connie really ought to be out and dressed before this. That was her trouble, her damned independence. There were two young girls and Miss de Berenger, the French mistress, standing in the wings at the opposite flank of the stage. He knew he should have called one of them around the back to go for Connie. But he went himself.

He intended to knock on the door and call to her from outside. He moved irresolutely towards it, then stood an inch outside, not moving. Then it bounced open and two small Oriental courtiers came out, heads bowed under heavy head-dresses, almost colliding with William. They saw him in time and scurried around him, holding their hats.

William was pitifully transfixed. There were several senior girls in the room. Pamela Watts, who was Yum Yum, was facing him, reading her script, wearing only her school vest. Its hem was short of the white half-moon of her lower belly; the pale sweet seams between her trunk and her legs were set deep, running down to a powder puff of pubic hair. Another girl, a sturdy, unappetizing child called Jackie MacAllister, stood naked apart from her school blazer hung about her heavy shoulders. Two others were adjusting their Gilbert and Sullivan costumes before the mirror. Connie was standing with her back to him. She was clad in the top half of her Emperor's costume, brilliant greens and purples, with a splendid Eastern coronet on her full hair. But her backside was uncovered. Two full, turnip mounds, white and pink, running up smoothly to the hollow of her back. Her legs were still fawn from the summer, set apart on the wooden floor. Her feet were bare.

Jackie MacAllister saw him first. Her heavy jaw dropped and a soundless shout came from her throat. She clutched her school blazer about her sprawling breasts with both hands, then let go with one to point at William and emit a horrified bellow. Pamela looked up and screamed, trying to pull the end of her vest down between her legs, then frantically turning away, giving the hapless William a full and exquisite view of her tiny buttocks. All the girls began to screech and William stood still and closed his eyes. Connie alone made no sound. She picked up a robe and hung it around her naked middle, then she advanced upon William at the door. He opened his eyes and looked into her angry iron face. The orchestra had begun its overture.

'You're on, Connie,' he muttered miserably. 'You're on.'

12

'WHAT WAS this business about a dwarf, then?'

'Ah yes, the dwarf, Rufus. Well it upset me, that's all. It was just before Christmas and there were all these hundreds of people in the street – in London – and it was sleeting. Everyone was hunching along with their heads down because of the sleet, including poor old William here, but poor old William had to be the one it happened to.'

'Well, what?'

'I bet you brought the fishcakes.'

'Yes, they're in the bag. Now what about the dwarf?'

'Wouldn't you just bloody well know. I *had* fishcakes today! I was the last one. Apparently they move up one cell every day. That's why the horror next door got his yesterday and I didn't. But I'll be getting them every day now until they've moved right up the cells and I'm stuck on the end of the line again. But that won't be for a while yet. It might even be when the case is on, with any luck. Fancy you bringing me some fishcakes on the very day I got them from the prison. Getting your wife – no, it's your mother-in-law isn't it – to cook them specially juth for meeeeth. Thath my nothe again, Rufuth. For Godth thake!'

'Hell, Bill, I've got to stop you somehow. You blather on like some old biddy. Pulling your hooter is the only way to shut you up.'

'Well I've stopped now.'

'And I've let go now.'

'It was getting a bit better, too. It didn't keep me awake last night.'

'Now don't let's start on about your hooter, Bill. That's as bad as gabbling on about the fishcakes. I want to know about this dwarf.'

'You're a bit irritable this morning, Rufus. A bit "off". Something worrying you? You can tell me. I mean, I'm not likely to tell anybody, am I? I'm not likely to be going anywhere.'

'Right. So I'm irritable, Bill. I'm sorry. It's the wife being away and all that. I get a bit pent up, if you understand.'

'Do I understand! My God, Rufus, if I don't, I don't know who does. I've felt pent up enough even when my wife was right there, lying in bed next to me. That's worse than when she's in hospital presenting you with a new baby. At least you've got something to look forward to in the future. Cheer up, old chap.'

'*You* cheer me up, then. Tell me about the dwarf. It might have an important bearing on the case, you see, Bill. It could throw some light on what happened afterwards.'

'Oh, it certainly did, Rufus. It upset me so much and I get so damned confused when something like that happens in public and everybody starts creasing themselves laughing. It was the same as the French letter. And it's always *me*.'

'The dwarf.'

'I'm coming to it. Well, it was just before Christmas, Christmas Eve in fact, in the West End. I'm not all that sure where because I don't know London much. But there were coloured lights banging about in the wind in that street. And I was going along with my head down a bit. Everybody else – hundreds of them – seemed to be going the other way. Then slap.'

'Slap – what?'

'It was this dwarf. I'd knocked him flat on his poor little back and he was lying there on the pavement, madly kicking his legs and all purple in the face. And all his Christmas parcels were all over the place. They were such little *tiny* parcels, too,

Rufus. That was one of the awful bits which sticks in my mind. I suppose he was buying presents for all his minute friends. Anyway, they were strewn all on the wet pavement and he was kicking and struggling to get up. He was very well dressed, very smart miniature overcoat and everything. I suppose he was a theatrical dwarf.'

'Did you pick him up?'

'No, Rufus. It was so horrific, like a short, nasty nightmare. I ran away.'

'You buggered off.'

'Yes, I did. I have to confess that's exactly what happened. The police aren't looking for me for that, are they? I mean, he didn't die or anything?'

'You dwarf-basher, Bill. God, first schoolgirls, now dwarfs.'

'It was an accident! For heaven's sake, stop prodding me like that.'

'So you ran. What next?'

'Well, that's where all my troubles really began . . .'

'Every time I come to see you, Bill, you tell me another situation where your troubles *really* began. It's like what-d'you-call-them . . . you know streams that go into a river?'

'I don't know.'

'Tributaries. That's it; Tributaries of Tribulation. You ought to write a book with that title, Bill.'

'I'll have tons of time, I expect.'

'Well, it will be a nice long book. Anyway, where did you run?'

'In this dance hall. It was the middle of the afternoon but it was all lit up in the foyer and I thought it was a picture place. So I went to the cubby-hole, the paybox, and got a ticket and walked in. I had a hell of a shock when I got inside and saw the people dancing and the pretty silver light that they have spinning in the middle. I mean, I thought it would be all dark and there would be cowboys shooting away on the screen or some film stars having a kiss and cuddle or something. It was quite a surprise.

'But I didn't mind it in there. Not at all. It was a tea-dance, they said; no alcoholic drinks, and there were a few people sitting around having cups of tea and buns and that sort of thing, served by waitresses. It was nice and warm and the music wasn't too bad. I was quite glad I'd gone in. Have you ever been to a tea-dance, Rufus?'

'No, Bill. Tell you the truth, I haven't been to a dance since my last hooley in Coleraine. Last Christmas holiday that would be.'

'It was strange because it was all people you *knew* had no business being there. They'd crept out to meet other men or women. They couldn't get out in the evenings, see. Well not *all* of them. That's an exaggeration. There were some couples who obviously knew each other because they've been dancing together for years and years. Some of them were very good. Just like you see on television with all that hundred feet of blue tool and that . . .'

'Hundred feet of what?'

'Blue tool! Hah! Caught you that time, Rufus. That was a joke! Haven't you ever seen it when they do ballroom dancing on television? They have a lady telling you what the women dancers are wearing, the colours and sequins and that sort of thing. But they always . . . well, not always but quite often, wore this material called tulle. And it's pronounced "tool". The girls at Southwelling used to giggle themselves silly about that. But you don't think it's funny?'

'It's sort of mildly amusing, Bill.'

'Oh . . . well, there it is.'

'Can we get back to the dance hall?'

'Yes, the dance hall. As I said there were these expert dancing partners, sort of whirring about with frozen expressions. And, oh yes, there were these little kids who were done up like ventriloquists' dummies and they were dancing too. I suppose in the afternoons their parents took them there because there were not all that many people around. They couldn't be knocked over.'

'Not like the dwarf, eh?'

'No! Certainly not like the dwarf, Rufus. You won't forget that dwarf, will you!'

'No. I reckon I'll still be laughing at the dwarf when you get out.'

'It's not *that* funny, Rufus. I can't see you laughing at it then. It'll be a bit stale. Like me, I expect.'

'Maybe it will. Maybe it will.'

'Anyway these children looked very strange because they danced with amusing little clockwork steps, just as though somebody had wound them up at the side of the floor and pushed them out. They sort of click-clacked around, and all the little boys had their hair over their eyes and the little girls all had pleated dresses with bows. They looked quite nice, the little girls. The one I danced with . . .'

'You! The one *you* danced with! Dear Jesus.'

'Yes, well I did. Now look here, Rufus, there was nothing like *that* about it. Be reasonable. Don't look at me like that . . .'

'All right. So you danced with one. How old?'

'About twelve, I suppose. She was very pink and light and she danced very nicely.'

'You just went up to her and asked her for the next tango?'

'No, it was a fox-trot. I can't do much else. And it wasn't *quite* like that. She was standing by herself at the side of the dance-floor waiting for . . .'

'Someone to wind her up?'

'No. As a matter of fact she was waiting for her little boy partner who had gone off to the bog and hadn't come back.'

'Maybe he couldn't reach the chain.'

'All right, Rufus, have it your own way. You seem to think my whole story is some gigantic joke. It isn't to me.'

'Sure, it's not to you. That's the difference between us, Bill. Let me put it like this, old pal – I'm not in your shoes.'

'Very true, Rufus, very true. I suppose you can see the entire tragedy from the different angle. One or two of the things might seem quite funny to you.'

'Well, serious, with a funny tinge, shall we say. So you danced with this small, pink girl.'

'It was her dress that was pink. She had a pale face, like a sixpence. I thought she looked very sad.'

'Sad? Maybe that was because she was dancing with you.'

'Christ Almighty, Rufus! Do you want me to go on with . . . thith or noth? Alrigth I willth go on, if you wouldn'th mind getting your fingerth off . . . my nose. That's better. I wish you'd do something else, Ruf, old boy. Couldn't you kick me in the knackers for a change? Yes, I'm *swearing* now. You might

65

well stare. Quite honestly, I don't know that my nose can take any more squeezing. I'll have to show it to the prison doctor . . . No? No, all right then, if you say so, but I *am* trying to help you . . .'

'I'm trying to help you, too, Bill. So let's get on with helping each other. Do you want these fishcakes now? I brought them specially for you.'

'Yes, of course, I'll have them. Wouldn't mind a nibble now, come to think of it. They're not very hot now, I suppose. Still I'm very grateful to you and your mother-in-law for . . . Funny thing, Rufus. Very funny.'

'What is, Bill?'

'These fishcakes. They look just like the ones they give us in the prison here.'

'I suppose once you've seen one fishcake, you've seen the lot.'

'Yes, there is that to it. But your mother-in-law *did* make them for me, didn't she?'

'Just for you.'

'She doesn't make them for the rest of the prison as well?'

'No. Certainly not.'

'And she didn't buy them – and pretend she had made them because she's ashamed that she can't make them like your wife? Perhaps she doesn't likth to tellth youth the facths . . . No . . . no . . . not when I've got my bloody mouth full of *fishcake*, Rufus! If you hold my nose when I've got my mouth full I could choke or suffocate.'

'The tea-dance, Bill.'

'Yes. All right. I finished the fox-trot with Paula-Marie. That's a pretty name, isn't it? I remember saying to her: "A pretty name for a pretty child," and she blushed beautifully. Her chin just about reached my chest and she had a job reaching up to the back of my neck. She was very slim under her dress. I couldn't help noticing them – I mean *that* not *them* – very slim. No puppy fat or anything. She seemed a bit shy and she didn't tell me much except that she came from Croydon. Anyway we had this little fox-trot and that was that.'

'Didn't you ask if you could see her home after the dance?'

66

'That supercilious look is in your eye again, Rufus. Just as though you're having a laugh at me inside.'

'It's my Irish eyes, Bill. You know they're supposed to smile.'

'I'll take your word for it. No, I didn't ask to see her home. But at five o'clock, when the dance was finished, somebody *else* asked me to take them home.'

'Oh?'

'I honestly wish I'd never gone. But there, I'm always wishing I'd done one particular thing when I did something else. I suppose even you've noticed that.'

'I have, Bill.'

'Well, I made another mistake. I took this girl – this woman she was really – home. She just came up to me as we were going out of the dance hall. I was feeling very fed up about going out of there because, truthfully, I had enjoyed it. It was cheerful and warm and there were people. I don't think half of them went to actually dance anyway, Rufus, because there were only about twenty couples on the great big floor at one time – and they kept crashing and banging into each other like ships in a storm. They all danced the old-fashioned way with their arms sticking out like those poles that stick out in the front of sailing ships. That was except two women, who looked . . . common, I suppose you could say. A bit out of it. They were wriggling and twisting in one corner. What I was trying to say was that I think most of the people went there just for the company and to be in a cheerful sort of place on Christmas Eve and that's why I liked it.'

'This girl, woman, who asked you to take her home?'

'Oh, yes. She was one of the two who were twisting or whatever they call it. Just as I was going out, I'd stopped to ask the attendant if the dance hall was open on Christmas Day because I would have liked to have gone there. He said something that was supposed to be funny, like I ought to go to church on Christmas Day. And this woman came up in her fur coat and asked me to take her home. Just like that. To be honest, Rufus, I just didn't realize what it was all about. You might not believe this, but I'm a bit of an innocent in that way. I thought she wanted me to escort her because it was dark and this was in the West End of London. So I gave her my arm. I felt really pleased for a minute because this was the first time I'd ever felt that a woman needed me.

'Then we went out. All the lights were jumping about and it was still sleeting a bit. I felt very happy walking along with her. I looked at men going along by themselves and I felt really sorry for them. I asked her what her name was. She said it was Blanche but she didn't tell me her surname, so I asked her. It was d'Smith. A sort of French version of Smith, I suppose. She spelt it out for me because she was quite proud of it. I told her I was William Bridgemont Herbert and I shook hands with her in the middle of the street. She looked slightly shaken when I did this and some of the people stared when I shook her hand.

'Then she said: "It's business, you know," and I asked her what sort of business and she said: "Fucking business." I was shattered, I can tell you. She was on the game. A prostitute!'

'I'd more or less worked that out, Bill.'

'Well with your training I expect you can spot these things. But I was a bit stunned.'

'Did you go with her?'

'Yes . . . yes, I did. I didn't want to be by myself again after having such a good time at the tea-dance. I asked her how much it would cost and she said five pounds, so I agreed. I thought of it as a sort of Christmas present to myself.'

'Did you like your present?'

'Some horrifying things happened, Rufus. Really terrible things. Do you want to hear about them?'

'Yes.'

'Could I have another fishcake?'

13

HE FOUND himself lagging, self-consciously, a few feet behind her as they turned into Soho. She looked around at him every twenty yards or so like a woman taking a tired dog for a walk. William began to shiver, a mixture of anticipation and apprehension. The custard-coloured lights of the little shops travelled across his face and he felt that every pair of hurrying eyes that went by took a moment to look and carefully note him.

A cherry-faced formation of Salvation Army personnel were bawling carols to a rude sousaphone outside the door where she waited for him to catch up.

William stood, like a boy by his mother, while she screwed the key in the lock and the singers proclaimed that it came upon a midnight clear.

'Sod this key,' said Blanche amiably. 'Never known *any-thing* so difficult to get in. As soon as we *do* get inside, shut it behind you love, because the wind shoots in here like a funny-man's fart.' She managed the door. He obeyed her instructions, glad when it closed on them.

'Jesus,' she said, taking off her fur and nodding towards the sounds of the Salvationists. 'You'd think we could have Christmas to enjoy without all that bleeding row, wouldn't you? Come on down here, love, I'll put the fan heater on. In this game in the winter, you know, you have to spend a fortune on electricity.'

He was looking at her. She had a round, young mother's face under the scars of make-up, and her bust beneath her cream dress was full and fluid. It rolled maternally as she moved about the room. William stood formally, uncomfortably, with his hands behind his back. She carefully took the silk eiderdown from the double divan and folded it with equal concern.

'Sorry about this,' she said, pointing to the patchwork quilt now revealed. 'Not very sexy I know, but it can't be helped.'

'It's all right,' said William unsteadily. 'Perfectly all right.' He tried to look interested in the quilt. He said: 'It looks as though there's a lot of work gone into that patchwork.'

'There is really, I suppose,' she agreed, stopping and staring at the quilt like a housewife. 'Some of the men I get in here you wouldn't credit, believe me. So if one or two of the patches get a bit mucked up I can just whip them out and sew a couple more in. I'm always having to do it. You know, I doubt if there's hardly a patch there that was in the quilt when I first had it. One or two around the edges maybe.' She looked at him. 'Come on,' she smiled busily. 'Get your overcoat off. You don't bang in your overcoat, do you?'

The room was small and like a pleasant cellar, low-ceilinged and with no window. The walls, the ceiling and the floor were all painted slapdash cream. The bed and an apologetic table and bedside lamp took up most of the space. Let into the wall at the side of the bed was a dead gas fire and above it two miniature doors which were open. From the doors, like a strange tongue, projected a solitary greasy gas ring. There was a three-tier bookshelf on one wall, lined on all its levels with shoes. A framed map of Ceylon showing the main tea plantations took up the remainder of that wall, and there were two other posters on the opposite cream space, a BOAC blandishment advising 'Try a Little VC Ten-der-ness', and a hand-scrawled effort, with the initials W.H.A.M.S. drawn out in lipstick red.

Blanche leaned over the bed and pushed the projecting gas ring back into its neat recess, and closed the small doors on it. 'It always falls out,' she grumbled. 'I wouldn't be without it though. Very handy for the quick cup of tea when Babsy isn't here to make it.'

She pulled the zip down at the back of her dress and shook her dark hair like a short mane. It was the most feminine thing she had done. William had taken his overcoat off and pretended to become occupied with the posters as she began to strip.

'Come on,' she said, without heat, 'Gaping at those things. It ain't the Tate Gallery.'

'Sorry,' said William. He turned abruptly around and she was standing white and naked except for her heavy pink bra which she was tugging free of her breasts. William was surprised, and she looked at him, surprised too that he should be taken that way. He stared at the brazenness of the display. 'I wondered what that was?' he muttered, pointing over his shoulder at the hand-made poster. 'What's W.H.A.M.S.?'

She pulled the brassière away. Her breasts lolled like two heads dropping off to sleep.

'Can I have my present?' she asked confidently.

'Present?'

'Oh, Christ. The money, love. The fiver. What d'you think I meant, a box of After Eights?'

'Present. Oh yes, Blanche. You don't mind me calling you

Blanche? Five pounds. There it is. One, two, three, four. Sorry, one pound has to be in silver and copper. There we are. Ten, twelve, fourteen, sixteen, seventeen, and threepence . . . and one, two, three, four, five, six, seven, eight, nine, ten, eleven . . . rather a lot of pennies, I'm afraid. Oh no, wait a minute. There's a sixpence hiding in this lot! No more though. It will just have to be coppers.'

'Has your mummy let you open your piggy bank for Christmas?' she sniffed. 'What am I going to do with all those bleeding pennies?'

'Well, isn't it all right?'

'Blimey, I picked a real lovely one in you. Still, you must be strong to be able to carry that bloody lot. That's something, I suppose. Haven't you got a quid note anywhere?'

'No. It's all silver. And copper, of course. The rest of my money is back at the hotel.'

She brightened. 'I bet you stay at Claridges, don't you?'

'No, I don't,' he said. 'Listen if the small change is no good, why don't we forget it and I'll go . . .'

'Oh no you don't mate. Now I've changed for work? You've got a flaming nerve. No, leave the coppers there, I'll give them to those howling Salvation Army buggers outside.'

Immediately she seemed to soften towards him. As though that moment, now the finance was settled, was the time to start. She smiled a professional smile and told him to take off his things. She helped him with his shirt and tie.

'You know,' she said, looking at his chest and stomach, 'you're not bad really. Not bad at all.'

'Thank you,' said William meekly.

'Mind you, after some of the human wrecks I get in here, it's not surprising I'm keen. Pitiful some of them, I can tell you. Sometimes, honest, I'm scared they're going to fall apart on the bed.'

William smiled gratefully. 'You didn't tell me what W.H.A.M.S. stands for,' he said as her hand dropped to his fly. She unzipped it with the accustomed ease of a factory girl pulling a lever on a machine, and pushed both her soft, fat hands into the dark cave of his trousers.

'Oh, that poster thing,' giggled Blanche. 'Well, it's just a

71

laugh really. Dorsey, the boy who runs us, did it. He used to be an art student before he was a ponce. I reckon he's quite clever, don't you?'

She pushed her hands outwards in a not ungraceful butterfly movement and peeled his trousers and underpants away from his legs.

William was now naked except for his singlet. He was quite pleased to see how he was reacting to her. She playfully pulled his singlet over his head and then hung it like a white flag of surrender over his organ.

'W.H.A.M.S.,' she said reflectively. 'Now, what was it? Dorsey made it up and he drew the poster, too. It's a Christmas party for the maids. You know, *our* maids. Mine, Babsy, is gone. It's on now, actually. It's just a sort of annual piss-up. W.H.A.M.S. means – what was it? – Whores and Harlots Annual Maids' Supper. That's right. He's really very cute our Dorsey. He drew the poster, too, or did I tell you that?

'Come on then, love, let's slip this on. There. That fits quite comfy. Righto. Climb on gently, there's a good chap.'

14

'D'YOU KNOW? . . . Well, I've got to admit it to you, Bill, that for someone who doesn't seem to know his way out of his own front door, you do get in some extraordinary situations. You! Banging on Christmas Eve!'

'Why do you people keep calling it "banging", Rufus? She kept on about that. Bang this and bang that. Do you prefer to bang this way or bang that way? Have you ever been to a gang-bang, which turned out to be some kind of orgy? Bang, bang, bang. You'd think she was flying the Concorde.'

'Sometimes you're really worth talking to, Bill. Honestly, I mean it. But the main thing is, did you enjoy it? Did you get your fiver's worth and get rid of some of that stuffed-up feeling – the old inhibitions?'

'I wish I *could* tell you that was how it turned out. But the whole business was a tragedy. Yet another one. Quite honestly I don't want to talk about it. It doesn't seem to have much bearing on the case to me. Why can't we go on with our game of Scrabble? It's still there on the pot. I have to lift it up and put it down pretty carefully, I can tell you. I don't hold it while I'm having a pee now because, just like we thought, the damn board just obstructs the view and I pee all over my feet, which isn't as funny as you might think. So I always set the Scrabble board on the bottom of the bed and then replace it when I've done.

'Listen, Rufus – I've thought up some marvellous words for Scrabble. How about onyx? That gives you a hell of a lot of points for only four letters.'

'I don't feel in a Scrabble mood today, Bill. Come on, tell me more about Christmas Eve. Be a sport.'

'No, I don't think it matters. I'd rather talk about almost anything else. How is your wife and the infant?'

'*Bill*, how's your nose?'

'You're NOT going to touch it again? No, Rufus! You did promise. Doesn't a policeman's promise count? Don't start flexing your fingers like that. Please. Now, be reasonable. Yes, yes, yes. I understand. All right, you win. Christmas Eve. Yes, it was all fine. Just what I needed, as you pointed out. Then this Babsy came in – the maid — and after that it was too terrible to describe.'

'It's *not* too terrible, Bill. Describe it.'

'Oh, all right. I don't see what bearing it's got, but still. Everything was going fine, in fact, I was enjoying the whole caboodle, and she was lying underneath grunting away quite contentedly. It was very warm in there – in the room I mean – and to be truthful I wasn't at all disappointed. Then Babsy came in.

'My God, Rufus, you should have seen her. She was petrifying. I bet she was fourteen stone, blonde dolly curls sticking out like wood shavings, big fat face all painted up, and smashed out of her senses. She came up the corridor like a bloody tank. And she was wearing one of the Salvation Army bonnets. They started pounding on the front door as soon as she was inside and

73

Blanche made the silly cow take it back to the Salvation Army people. She was afraid they'd call the police.'

'Very wise, Bill.'

'I thought so, too. So Babsy, after Blanche swore at her, took the hat back to the door. Blanche shouting! It nearly strangled me, if you know what I mean. Well, it nearly damned well strangled my thing! If ever you're having intercourse with your wife – or any woman for that matter, Rufus – let me give you some brotherly advice – don't let her shout while you're at it. When they shout it sets a sort of trapdoor going in their vagina and it's as painful as hell for the chap.'

'It's the same when they cough, Bill. Exactly.'

'Is that so. We know now, anyway, don't we. Never have a woman with the flu or who wants to bawl out anyone.'

'That could have been Confucius talking, Bill.'

'Thank you, Rufus. I'm glad, at least, that you take *some* notice of me. Sometimes anyway. Well, back this Babsy came down the passage, without the bonnet, but shouting and carrying on, waving a bottle which turned out to be cherry brandy. And I'm slap-bang in the middle of doing you-know-what. It had put me right off, I can tell you. Blanche was trying to be serious with her, but she herself kept bursting out laughing. That, by the way is almost as bad as shouting or coughing.'

'Confucius, he say: "Never tell a funny story to a shouting woman with influenza."'

'That's *very* good, Rufus. Anyway, this monster is charging about the room, and there wasn't a lot of room as I told you. Careering about and waving her bottle. Then she came out with one of those blower things. You know, the coloured paper things that unroll like a trunk and rasp when you blow them. She was rasping about the room with this thing like a kid gone mad. She kept coming up to us and blowing it in our faces – while we were still lying there! I would have got up and cleared out, without finishing the job, as it were, even though I'd already paid, but this Babsy suddenly smashes her great fat fist against the wall right over where we're lying and the two little toy doors fly open and the gas ring flops out. It was just like a cuckoo clock. Then she staggers into another room and comes back with a kettle. To my horror, Rufus, she then puts a match to the gas and puts the

74

kettle on to boil right over my arse. Go on, have a laugh if you like, but I didn't think it was all that amusing, believe me.

'I was pretty well petrified, I can tell you. I'm not afraid to admit it. There was I, still hanging on to Blanche, who's laughing like a maniac, and there is Babsy belting around the place like another maniac, and the kettle spluttering on the gas ring about six inches over my bum. If you think that's funny, well all I can say is you've got a pretty peculiar sense of humour.'

'Maybe I have, Bill. Sorry, but the kettle . . .'

'All right, have your laugh. Well, that was that.'

'No. Don't stop there, Bill. Tell me the rest.'

'Nothing much to tell. Not really. *Stop* flexing those nasty fingers of yours, Rufus. There was *hardly* anything. They kept pouring this cherry brandy down my throat, afterwards, and the fat monster had a terrible row with the man in the Indian restaurant next door.'

'There *is* more, Bill. Come on, tell me.'

'I can't remember much about it because of all this horrible sweet cherry brandy she'd brought back from the maids' Christmas treat. I suppose the Indian started banging on the wall because of all the row that was going on. I mean, Babsy was making a terrible din, and then the blessed kettle started to boil and I must have made a bit of a fuss trying to get out from underneath it. And then Blanche started having hysterics, sitting on a pot in the corner.'

'On a pot in the corner?'

'For professional emergencies, I suppose. I don't know. I didn't ask her. It was just a pot, like that one over there.

'There must have been a lot of noise because this gentleman from the Indian restaurant began banging on the wall and some of the plasterboards came loose. Babsy went right up to the wall and I really thought she was going to tear the plasterboards down and get through to give him a going-over.

'But Blanche stopped her and so she started screaming through the wall at him, calling him names like "a curry-faced cunt" and all that type of coarse thing. I must have been a bit drunk on the cherry brandy by this time – I reckon everybody was, Rufus, because the kettle boiled all over the bed – but I made some remark about the Indian man wanting to curry

75

favour, you know, something not even very laughable, and the two girls went into fits and made me go right up to the wall and shout it through to him. Today, of course, I wish I hadn't. If I ever get in that neighbourhood again I'll call in and apologize. That's the least I can do.'

'After that?'

'Well, after that, truly, I don't remember very much, Rufus. I'm telling you quite honestly. I must have drunk half that bottle and I don't remember.'

'Nothing? Not *one* little thing, Bill?'

'Oh, all right. You squeeze everything out of me. Well, I was very drunk remember, so I'm not really all that responsible. But it must have got out about the girls – the girls at school, I mean – and the next thing I remember is this great big Babsy, bloody enormous she looked too, Rufus, had got herself all togged up in a gigantic gymslip and a great big pair of blue knickers. They made me put a pair on too – now stop bloody laughing will you, Rufus! I'm being fair with you. I was drunk remember. It wasn't my fault. You wouldn't think it was funny if a big bird like that whacked you across the backside with a sting from a sting-ray.'

'A sting-ray? Oh God, Bill.'

'Only once. Christ, I nearly went through into the Indian restaurant. You know a sting-ray, the fish – it's got a long sting on its nose that's like a whip – and these two mad bitches, that's what they'd got. Dear Jesus, I let out such a yell. And then they both jumped on me and I was like a damned turkey sandwich between them. And the bed was still sopping wet from the kettle. They knocked all the breath out of me. It was a nightmare, believe me. I can only remember pulling my clothes on and staggering out of the door. To tell you the truth I went into the Indian restaurant next door and tried to calm myself down with a Madras curry. Naturally, I didn't let on who I was. I sat there eating the curry and trembling and I could still hear them laughing through the wall. Shrieking their heads off. The bitches.'

15

LONDON WAS very empty on Christmas Day. He did not know his way about so he walked without aim through the streets and across the muted green parks until the buildings opened out to the river. The Thames was like a sloven. No one moved anywhere on its grey banks or among the cold streets. It was as though people had fled from the earth and forgotten to tell him. Two gantry cranes on the far side leaned their heads together over a grubby barge, like a pair of cadaverous surgeons consulting over a fat patient.

William was miserable, not just because it was Christmas Day and he was wandering alone in this void city, but because he thought he had a dose.

He shuffled by shuttered tobacconists' and provision shops with sadly stranded plum puddings, cakes and crackers left in their windows, abandoned, unbought, unwanted. A dose! What did it feel like? What did it look like? Without doubt there was a nasty sore place down there. Where could he go?

He had missed his Christmas dinner at the Abbey Castle Private Hotel, Bayswater Road, because he had meandered so far he had forgotten the way back. Not that it bothered him; in fact he had not very seriously tried to find the road to return.

Immediately after breakfast, while the enormity of what had occurred on Christmas Eve was still as strong with him as the heavy, sour memory of the cherry brandy, the twenty guests that Mrs Lilley of the Abbey Castle Hotel had gathered in were assembled for carols, followed by games. William had lugubriously allowed himself to be bullied into the singing around the piano, his fellows welcoming the Babe of Bethlehem in hideous voices strongly accompanied by blasts of port-laden breath. But when the games had commenced, he had craftily allowed himself to be sent out of the room during hide-and-seek and then had callously run away while the others were still plotting merrily in the parlour. He wondered if they had given up looking for him by now. Or were they still hopefully calling.

Why had he gone to that place? Why anything? Why Blanche? Why the dynamic Babsy? Why Louise? Why Mr Sherman? Why William Herbert? Yes, by God, why William Herbert? Why had he walked in on the girls in the dresssing-room at *The Mikado*? Why had Miss Smallwood been so soothing and understanding about it, steadying him and blaming her girls for their carelessness, and sincerely hoping he was not too embarrassed?

He had left the school with the rest; goodbye until next term, hurrah for Christmas. Goodbye, have a good time. See you in January. In the train to London he had shared the compartment with Miss Elliott, Miss Bonner, the English mistress, and three of the girls. They had prodded him trying to discover where he would be spending Christmas, laughing at his secrecy, wondering what amazing arrangements he was concealing. William had enjoyed it, pretending to give them clues about his plans, denying that he was spending Christmas with a film actress, or an aristocrat, or the Prime Minister, or a famous jockey, but making his denials with a minimum of conviction. At Victoria the girls had run from him and danced around waiting parents or gone off in their blue Burberrys to catch further Christmas trains, and he had been left alone on the platform.

There were rumbustious carols on the louspeakers, holiness in the heights. In his own depths he drank some tea and bought a newspaper which told him that the Abbey Castle Private Hotel, Bayswater Road (due to surprise cancellations) could still accommodate additional Christmas guests. So he went.

He thought he needed people. When he saw the people he thought he needed to be without them. So, on Christmas Day, withdrawn, clap-crossed, he walked by the indifferent river. He visited three public conveniences, cold and unfestive, before he found one with a notice and a number to ring. He went to a telephone box. The hospital was a long time answering. The person who answered had a mouth full of turkey and vegetables.

'Good gracious, no,' they said. 'Special clinic's not open today. It's Christmas. Don't worry, old boy – it'll keep.'

That was the trouble. The situation would not have been so terrible if he had known for sure, but there was the not knowing, the suspicion, the terrible soreness as it moved inside his trousers.

'What do you expect?' he asked himself as he walked, solitary, across Battersea Bridge. 'May I ask you – what do you expect? Of course you're sore. Any damn fool would expect to be sore after what you went through last night. After all, that nasty spot could have been caused by a fingernail.' He felt bigger, more assured, at the devilish memory.

'Be sensible. You can't expect to go to a gang-bang and escape unscathed. You chose this kind of life, boy. Nobody did that for you. You could have been quiet and ordinary, like all these men, gorged with plum pudding, stretched out behind these windows. But you're not like that, William Herbert. You're not the armchair type. You adventurer, you! To hell with it.'

It made him feel better addressing himself like that. Then he walked and worried more. 'I wonder if I threw myself under a car I could get it seen to?' He considered. 'After all, if they carry you into casualty they give you a thorough going over. While they are sticking on the plaster-of-Paris and splints I could ask them to take a quick look at my dick.'

The impracticability of the notion was forced upon him by an examination of the road in both directions. It was three o'clock on Christmas afternoon. There *were* no cars. No people either. Only smoke drifting tauntingly from complacent little chimneys and from the power station. The woolly smoke from the power station, like Santa's beard, was reflected in the unusual stillness of the murky river water. In the distance he heard a dog barking. He wondered if he could persuade it to bite him.

He went into Battersea Park, his steps echoing among the frozen trees. The flower beds were empty mud; like him, waiting for Christmas to go. It must be quite nice to be a bulb, or, better still, a mole, or something like that, which made its house in the earth. Around a corner he came upon three small boys playing cricket, wearing overcoats, gloves and woollen balaclavas.

'Just got it for Christmas?' he inquired like an amiable father. 'Wrong season, eh?'

They stopped their game and looked at him with hostility. 'Here you are,' he called, forcing the issue. The cricket ball was sitting gloomily on the sodden grass a yard away. William picked it up and bowled it at the boy with the bat. It half buried itself in the mud where it pitched making a human swallowing sound as it went in. The children looked at him with quiet bitterness. He dug out the ball with his fingers, laughing nervously and repeating: 'Wrong season, right enough!'

He felt them staring at his back as he walked on. Then one called: 'What did you have for Christmas, mister?' And they all laughed and went on with their game.

'What did I have?' he asked himself. 'If only you knew, lad, if only you knew.'

The path bent into the pleasure gardens, paralysed now by uncaring winter, the booths shuttered, the colours diminished and dead. A string of old lights, like fruit gone rotten, hung against a tree. Following it he saw that among the branches was the tree-walk, a wooden summertime causeway among the oaks.

The tree-walk interested him. It hung like a timber serpent through the creaking branches and its stepladder tail reached the ground by a faded yellow pay kiosk, stiff, like a sentry box. William went towards it and easily overstepped the piked and painted gate which had been bolted since the final summer day of the fair. He felt like a solitary child again climbing the close stairs. The wooden walk stretched invitingly and he followed it. He was in the trees now, looking through the irregular windows of their branches down to the world twenty feet below. On one side he could see the grey and thoughtless river and the offices sitting on its banks like dull packing cases. On top of one tall office building were panes of yellow light. Some caretaker and his family having a high old Christmas. He could look down on the roundabouts, still, stifled, and the dead hoopla stalls. Leaves were running in blind crowds, making a tinny sound, across the open spaces and huddling under canvas screens. There was no sunlight, only the dull wind in the park. He could hear the boys shouting and hitting the cricket ball on the other flank of the trees.

He walked up and down several times, a pleasure, he noted, which would have cost him a shilling three months before. He began to feel almost happy, almost free. Then he remembered what he had for Christmas and the thought made him morose and defenceless again. Fancy having it on Christmas Day. It was so sore. Generally and especially in that one place. Up there in the rattling trees the sharp inquisitive wind nosed into his trousers. Dispirited, he came down from the walk and took to the chilling path again. He came out of the park, under the painted arch, and wandered wretchedly across the next deserted bridge. It would have been nice to meet a tramp, he thought, or a drunk, or perhaps someone meandering with amnesia. The shifty afternoon light was leaving London. He walked on and, on the far embankment, he turned from viewing a statue of a patriot with a sword to see a police launch pushing conscientiously downriver. He ran to the embankment wall and waved.

William saw the launch hesitate in its passage and begin a wide swing against the tide towards him. In his increasing concern he waved again, motioning that they could continue on their voyage. But the busy boat came in close and slowed, treading water, while a river policeman shouted and asked him what the trouble was.

'No trouble, Officer,' William called back.

'Why did you signal us, then?' The policeman, who had the wind-pinched look of the river, stared truculently at him.

'I wasn't signalling. I just waved.'

'All right then, why did you wave?'

'Well . . . because it's Christmas. That's all.'

And, he thought, because I'm walking around in London by myself and you are the first people I have seen.

The policeman made a nasty face. He called to the man at the wheel: 'All right, Gerald. He only waved because it's Christmas.'

Gerald stepped up to have a look at the man who had waved because it was Christmas, and called roughly to his friend: 'If we had some mistletoe we could give him a kiss.' He went back to the wheel and gave the boat a quick kick forward. They droned off along the lead water. When they had gone three hundred yards, William danced up and down and waved both his arms frantically and shouted: 'Help! Help!' But they went on unheeding into the watery afternoon.

He found some deckchairs stored under a shelter in the embankment gardens beyond Charing Cross, appropriated one and defiantly sat in the middle of the wet lawn, folding his hands across his chest and staring up at the wide lights of the Savoy and the people moving across the flat warm windows up there. He remained seated resolutely for perhaps ten minutes, stretched back as though it were an August noon with the fullness of an English summer sun upon his face. Voices came through the deepening afternoon and two nurses in cloaks hurried through the gardens. He shifted in his deckchair. Perhaps he could ask them. Good girls, nurses. Good sports. Perhaps he could give them a quick look at it and ask them what they thought. 'Excuse me girls, I wonder if you'd know a case of clap if you saw one?'

No, my God, no. He must be out of his mind. They wouldn't be able to tell at a glance anyway, especially in this murk. Anyway they might not be trained for that sort of thing. They might be eye nurses or leg nurses. Specialists. He sank back in his incongruous deckchair, then half got up again and called to them through the cold: 'Merry Christmas, girls.'

They turned briefly but continued their flat-footed walk. They both called 'Merry Christmas' and gave him mechanical little waves and went on. William felt glad that he had not concerned them with his private difficulties.

He carefully returned the deckchair to its refuge and then continued his long stroll. It was four o'clock. There were round lights like big apples along his side of the river, the portholes of Captain Scott's *Discovery* tied against the bank. He read the notice telling him about the epic history of the ship and wondered whether perhaps he could go aboard and claim to be one of the Scott descendants on a quick, surprise, visit from India. They could hardly refuse to let him stay for a while under those circumstances. After all, he was perfectly respectable, apart from his syphilis, and by no means a tramp. But he shrugged and went on. There were two other ships idling there and an invitation, on another notice, to Join the Royal Naval Reserve. He wondered if it would be worthwhile joining for a couple of days and then deserting.

No, he most certainly wasn't a tramp. He was quite adamant about that. A wanderer, perhaps. But he had money in his wallet, more than one hundred pounds, his end-of-term pay from Southwelling. He had money, but nothing else. But he thought it was probably better than being a tramp, unless, of course, you had other tramps with you for company.

16

'BUT THE oddest bit of the day was me getting in the Seamen's Mission.'

'Oh, the . . . Seamen's Mission.'

'Certainly. And, I don't mind telling you, Rufus, I was very, very glad of it. Best thing that happened all over Christmas. In a way it made up for all the bother with the firemen afterwards.'

'Firemen . . . no . . . Tell me about the Seamen's Mission.'

'Are you sure it's important?'

'Well, we've done so much side-tracking that a bit more won't matter, Bill. Besides, I'm quite getting to like listening to what's happened to you. Down at the station they hardly believe some of it.'

'You *don't* go repeating it to the other coppers . . . policemen.'

'Oh no, don't you worry about that, Bill. Your secrets are safe with Rufus, old son. No, I just mention it in a very general sort of way, that's all.'

'Do you tell your wife about me, Rufus? Do you?'

'Yes, Bill. She was pretty upset about some things. About Louise and Mr Sherman, particularly. That sort of thing would affect a woman, of course. And she thinks that the girls were terrible to you. Up to now, anyway, that's how she feels.'

'You told her about the girls? *All* about them, I mean?'

'Well, again only in very general terms, Bill.'

'Good for you, Rufus. I'd like to meet your wife. She sounds very nice and understanding. And the new baby too,. Ha! Perhaps you could invite me to his tenth birthday party.'

'Now don't be going on like that, Bill. It's no use looking on the black side. You might only get seven or eight years. Tell me about this Seamen's Mission, for God's sake.'

'I saw them all going in the front door. It was near the docks, of course, and seeing them all trooping in, so cheerful . . . well, it was so refreshing after wandering about by myself all day. They'd all had a few drinks, I suppose, and they were calling out and shouting. So I just tagged on the end of the line and went in with them. Just for company.

'In the back of my mind, I suppose, I had some notion they might be able to help me with my trouble – you know – because, I remember thinking, sailors are always getting the pox, and they're bound to know something about it.'

'And did they?'

'I never asked them. To tell you the truth we had such a fine time that I just forgot my worries in that direction. It was amazing how they accepted me. They thought I was just another jolly jack tar, I suppose. Do I look like a sailor, Rufus?'

'No. I wouldn't honestly say you looked like a sailor. There's a touch of the wrecked yachtsman in you, I fancy. But a sailor, no.'

'A gang, a dozen or so, were going into the Seamen's Mission when I joined them, but there were a lot more inside. All sorts of sailors. All different nationalities. This was a good thing for me because nobody asks too many questions about you in that sort of company. A couple of chaps asked my name and where I was from, so I said the first thing that came into my head. I just said "Antwerp", and from then on everybody called me "Antwerp", just like that. It was as though they had known me for years. When I had finished singing, they all . . .'

'Singing?'

'Oh yes. I haven't got a bad voice, you know. And everybody had to do something to entertain. So I got up on the table and gave them some Gilbert and Sullivan, seeing as we had been doingi t at Southwelling. I did *Tit-Willow*, which went down very well with the sailors, and *The Flowers That Bloom In The Spring, Tra-la*, you know the sort of thing.'

'They liked it?'

'My goodness, I'll say they did. They went mad with appreci-ation, Rufus. They're not the rough bunch you might think. They kept shouting "Antwerp! Antwerp!" Quite truthfully, I've never felt so popular. I thought to myself, "I wish Louise could see me."'

'There are times when you really interest me, Bill. How did you manage, having a name like "Antwerp" and singing Gilbert and Sullivan? They don't really go together, do they?'

'Nobody asked me. That's what was so enjoyable about it. They didn't want to know all about you. We had a marvellous time, best Christmas "do" I can ever remember. And all men. There was lots to eat and drink, and a wonderful old chap with genuine wooden legs – you know, like the old sea dogs in pictures – did a sort of stumpy dance. He was fantastic. Very old and with wooden legs like that. I didn't think anyone wore them these days. What did they call him now? It was really suitable, I know. Yes, it was Wheeler – Wheelbarrow Wheeler. You see, when he sat down his legs stuck out straight in front of him like the handles of a wheelbarrow. Wheelbarrow Wheeler, that's right.

'The extraordinary thing about it was that none of it was rude or crude. You always think of sailors as being a very rough bunch, but it was all fun and there was hardly a bad word from anyone. A good few of them got plastered – well, it was Christmas after all. I had quite a few sherries myself, believe me. But there were no fights or anything.

'Mind you, there was one old fellow in a grey jersey who more or less sat by himself on one of the long benches. And I started chatting to him and he surprised me by asking me how long I had known Jesus. That sort of question always comes as a bit of a teaser, doesn't it, Rufus?'

'I'll say. Did you tell him? Were you able to give him a description?'

'Now, now. That's blasphemy, and from an Irishman, too.'

'I'll jot it down for confession. What happened after the Seamen's Mission?'

'It was getting late. I came out with some of the others. We were all shipmates by then. I was "Good old Antwerp". I don't think I've been so happy as I was when I was "Antwerp". Then I found a card in my pocket with the address of Mrs Lilley's hotel on it, and right away, up the street, came a taxi. My luck was changing, I thought.'

'And was it?'

'No. Mine couldn't change. I got back to the hotel and I saw this fire engine there, and quite a lot of people hanging around the front door. There wasn't any sign of a fire so I asked a man what was going on. He told me they thought some poor fellow

85

was trapped under the floorboards of the hotel. They'd been playing hide-and-seek that morning he said, and one chap had gone outside and had just disappeared. He said he'd been told all this by Mrs Lilley. He lived next door or something. Anyway, they looked around for this missing chap and couldn't find him. They thought it was a bit odd but they didn't worry too much, and they all went and had their Christmas dinner.

'Then, hours later, in the evening, Mrs Lilley thought she heard bangings coming from under the floorboards. Then she remembered there was a trapdoor that sometimes opened quite easily, but then got stuck fast and nobody could move it. It suddenly came to her that the chap who had gone out to hide might have gone down the trapdoor and not been able to get out again. They kept hearing these bangs, which could have been the hot-water pipes, but they were so worried, in the end, they sent for the fire brigade, who had arrived and were ripping up the floorboards.'

'That was awkward, Bill.'

'I was tempted to clear out then, Rufus. Just vanish and let them keep looking for me under the floorboards. But all my belongings were still in the hotel. So I walked in very casually, looking in a sort of interested way at the firemen. Then I wished Mrs Lilley a Merry Christmas and she nearly fell down in a dead faint.

'It was a very awkward interlude, as you rightly said. Everybody blamed me; Mrs Bloody Lilley, all the others, and the chief of the fire brigade, too. As though I'd given them the damned stupid idea to lug up the floorboards. The fire chief went barmy. Christ, only I could fall foul of the London river police and the fire service all on one Christmas Day.'

'You're what we call police-prone, Bill. That's your trouble. We've a fatal attraction for each other. If there were only the two of us left on this planet, you could bet your last quid I'd have to arrest you for something or other. Probably obstructing the footway, or holding an illegal meeting.'

'That's exactly how I feel, Rufus. Some of us are born to give the authorities something to do.'

'When did you go to the clinic? You know – about your bit of bother.'

'I had to wait until the day after Boxing Day. It was the longest time I can ever remember. Waiting for it to pass.

'God, I don't know how I hung on so long. I kept looking at it, staring at it. There was this really unpleasant sore place. I found a little toy magnifying-glass in the hotel – I suppose it had come from a Christmas cracker – and I had a good look at it through that. But it felt bad enough and it looked very red and waspish. I kept screwing my eyes up in anticipation, as it were, every time I went to the toilet in case it felt like broken glass when I went. That's one of the certain signs, so they say, don't they? But it didn't feel like broken glass. It just felt sore.'

'Were you still at the Abbey Castle Hotel?'

'Mrs Lilley's? Oh yes, I was there. She was pretty annoyed with me, but, after all, *I* didn't send for the so-and-so fire brigade, did I? Anyway, it would have been pretty difficult for her to fill my room just for Christmas night, and Boxing Day so she let me stay. It was very miserable, though. Nobody wanted to talk to me. For God's sake, you'd have thought it was my stupid idea to take the floorboards up.

'I couldn't wait to get out of the place. She charged me for Christmas dinner, too, although I didn't have it. Then I went to the clinic as soon as I could, the day following Boxing Day.

'There was only one other chap there and, quite truthfully, he looked too *old* to have it. My goodness, I thought, he looks too old to *do* it, let alone get anything from doing it. But it turned out he'd had it for years and years, and he'd been going there every day since to get an injection. Apparently he'd caught it before they had penicillin and what-have-you and he'd never been rid of it. Mind you, Rufus, he was very cheerful about it, but a bit coarse. I suppose if you go to a VD clinic every day it's bound to have a coarsening effect.

'Do you know, he'd even been to get treatment on Christmas Day. I'd got a bit annoyed about this, considering I'd been wandering about, worried out of my mind. But he said it wasn't the normal special clinic – that was closed – it was the casualty department of the hospital he had to attend. They gave him his injection there. Mind you, I have to admit he was amusing about it. He said – now I can't do the accent but it was really Cockney ... "Nar, I came jus' arter me Christmas dinner for the ol' jab. But I 'ad to 'ang abaht somefing shocking. Usually I get done right away, but I 'ad to get in the bleedin' queue. There was a long line of stupid buggers wiv turkey bones an' tanner pieces from the puddin' stuck in their froats."

'You can laugh, Rufus. I did too because it was so amusing, even though I was worried out of my life because of my trouble. But, mind you, he *was* uncouth. For instance he fell about laughing, cackling all over the place, when I told him I thought I had a dose on Christmas Day. Do you know what he said? He said: "Blimey mate, when all the others was looking in their stockin's you was lookin' in your trousers!" He thought that was really funny – and he told the orderly his joke and the orderly rushed off and told the doctor. You think it's funny, too, don't you, Rufus?'

'Well, Bill, it has *something* about it. The lads at the station . . .'

'You *won't* tell them!'

'No! Of course not. But I wish I could. They'd think it was funny. But I won't tell them. I wouldn't do that on you, Bill. I wouldn't even mention it in passing.'

'Honestly?'

'Honestly. Policeman's honour. There you are.'

'Well, thanks.'

'Did they tell you?'

'No, that was the terrible thing. They said I had to wait like everybody else. They said it would take a few days to get the blood test and the urine sample sorted out and I'd have to check with them then. They just said that – I'd have to "check with them", which made it very difficult as events went. They didn't actually say I'd have to *go back* there. I thought it was just a matter of phoning and they would tell you what was what.

'Mind you, Rufus, they fancy themselves as a real lot of comics in those VD clinics. It was bad enough, as I've just said, having this idiotic patient with his jokes about looking in one's trousers, but then this young doctor came in in his white coat and he had one of those bleeper things. You know what they are, don't you? If they want to call him anywhere in the hospital they send out a radio message and his bleeper bleeps.'

'What did he do with it, Bill?'

'Stupid idiot came up to me when I was being examined by the other doctor and passed his bleeper back and forwards in front of me – down there, you know. I suppose he must have been expecting them to call him just then, or perhaps they play this joke all the time. Anyway as soon as he waved it in front of me it started to bleep like mad. It gave me a hell of a fright, believe me. I mean, for God's sake, *I'm* not familiar with the things they use in hospitals, especially in *special* clincs, and for a moment I thought it was genuine. There it was going back and forwards in front of my dick and bleeping like mad. Hell, it put the wind up me. Then, of course, they all started to laugh like mad – just like I can see you're trying not to laugh. Yes, you can't fool me, Rufus. I can see you puffing out your cheeks. I suppose that's something else to tell the boys down at the policemen's canteen.'

'You had a copper's promise, Bill. Now don't worry. I won't tell anybody. But it is funny, now isn't it? You've got to agree that.'

'So it's funny for every other bugger. But it wasn't for me. After all I was in a state of acute anxiety. I didn't get the joke at all. It just seems to me that half the jokes in the world are on me. I'm always the one with his trousers down.'

'You actually were in this case.'

'All right. Even that's funny.'

'And they couldn't tell you there and then whether you were all right or not?'

'No. They said I'd have to wait for the result of the blood test and the wee-wee test and that would take a few days. They said I'd have to check back. Now they were the actual words, "check back". They didn't say I actually had to *go* back. Just check. I took it I could phone and they would tell me one way or another. It caused me no end of bother eventually, believe me.'

'Yes, you've told me that a couple of times now, Bill. I get what you mean, entirely.'

'Well, it did mess me up later on. When I was in Derby.'

'This is where you went after Christmas? This is where Connie, the American kid, was staying with the family?'

'Connie was never a kid, you know, Rufus. I wouldn't have made a kid pregnant. She was sixteen, every inch a young lady.'

'I bet she was. Every inch. Why did you go up to the place at Derby?'

'Truthfully, I didn't go just because the Ferbers lived there and the twins were there for Christmas and Connie was there. I *knew* Connie was staying there for the holiday, of course, but that wasn't the reason. I had to go *somewhere*. It was another three weeks until the term at Southwelling started again and I had to go somewhere. I didn't want to stop in London, particularly at Mrs Lilley's place. I had a lot of time to fill in so I walked to Derby.'

'Oh yes, I heard about this from our officers at Derby.'

'You've been making inquiries up there, eh?'

'Certainly. We've been talking to lots of people.'

'Miss Smallwood at Southwelling as well, eh?'

'You don't think we could keep her out of it, do you? She's the bloody headmistress.'

'I know, I know, Rufus. Don't get excited – please. It's a pity she had to know, that's all. She's such a decent old girl; her and her Gilbert and Sullivan.'

'Silly old twit. She's not fit to be in charge of a cats' home, let alone a load of kids. You didn't give her the odd shaft now and again to keep her sweet, did you, Bill?'

'Oh, Rufus, for God's sake! You really are appalling at times. Of course I didn't give Miss Smallwood a shaft or whatever you like to term it. She was a very nice old lady. For heaven's sake, where's your sense of proportion!'

'Shut up, Bill, before I start pulling your conk again. Don't rile me or I will, I promise you. These conk-tugging fingers of mine are itching.'

'Steady, Rufus. Don't start that again, please. You've been reasonable lately and it's been appreciated. My nose feels very much better. Let me tell you about Derby, shall I?'

'Tell me then, Bill.'

17

THE MINIATURE days after Christmas were fine and cold-edged. There was no rain nor snow in the south, clouds only gathered in time to catch the sunset and in oddments during the brittle blue days. The dry roads through the countryside to the Midlands made sharp sounds beneath the flints of his hiking boots.

William enjoyed the walk. He had undertaken it on impulse after he emerged unhappily and unsurely from the hospital the morning after Boxing Day. After gladly leaving Mrs Lilley's hotel, bracing itself for the New Year celebrations, he had left his suitcase at Marylebone Station. He liked Marylebone Station because it seemed so much smaller and more modest than all the big stations. The clerk at the left-luggage counter had, quite off his own bat, called him 'sir' and nobody had tried to play pranks on him, victimize him, or involve him in their lives in any way. He felt grateful and easy there.

After the hospital he had wandered through the indifferent valleys of London wondering how he should occupy himself before returning to Southwelling. All the people who passed, now they had been rooted out of their fat, warm holes where they had spent Christmas, were scowling and chilly. He had a quiet smile because of them. He felt like a veteran who had been fighting a lone action and now looked with some superiority on the relief troops. Ha! So you think it's tough now. You should have been out here on Christmas Day. Hell, absolute hell. Of course he knew that it wouldn't take the rest of humanity too long to come out of its Yuletide stupor and become once again its old braggart self. He did not intend to wait around and see that happen. He looked at the icy blue sky, remote and free, and thought his were probably the only eyes to be lifted to it that day. He began to feel stronger and more assured. He didn't even feel all that sore any longer. He probably had nothing of the sort. After all, when you're alone all sorts of funny notions come up on your mind.

They obviously didn't think so at the clinic. For God's sake they were so casual about it. They didn't seem the least worried. Fancy asking him if he'd been with a woman. That moron in the white coat, the one who had done the bleeper caper, had asked him quite seriously if he had been with a woman. What did they think it was – a friendly wallaby? Now *that* wasn't bad at all. A friendly wallaby! He wished he had thought of it at the time. Too late now. Mind you, old White Coat had done a bit of a double-take just after. He'd been filling up a card to give to William, with a number, something like 994,381 – there were a dirty lot of bastards in London, and that was only one clinic – and White Coat said in a bored sort of way: 'Prostitute?'

'Two,' William had said leaning forward slightly but challengingly.

That's when he did the double-take. 'Oh, *two* was it? At the same time?' He began to fill in a form.

What a damned fool. 'Not *exactly* the same time,' asserted William.

'More or less?'

'Well, first one and then the other.'

'Within minutes?' suggested White Coat, still writing.

'Seconds,' corrected William, a little arrogantly.

That had shown him. Come to think of it, Christmas *had* been eventful. Knocking off two beautiful women. Well, one wasn't that bad, was she? Drinking away with his shipmates on Christmas night, and having the fire brigade looking for him under the floorboards. My God, he'd have a story to tell if there was somebody to whom he could tell it.

There remained the problem of what to do with the next three weeks. He had a cup of coffee and bought a newspaper. The café was huddled with people, unspeaking or just muttering 'very quiet' when the ghost of Christmas just past was raised. The window had steamed up, as though to mercifully shut the world of reality away from them. Several people stared at William as he scooped away the white steam from his part of the cocoon and through the window watched a youth with a great hook of a yawn in his face, hanging up a skein of boots outside the shop opposite. Above the shop it said 'Surplus Bargains' and William, in his superior, buoyant mood, was pleased with the thought that it could be taken as a place where clergymen obtained cheap uniforms. But it was the boots which gave him his thoughts.

How far was it to Derby? Eighty, ninety, a hundred miles, he thought. It did not matter. The weather was sharp and blue; with a pair of those boots, now suspended like leather fruit, he could surely take to the road in the old romantic way, leave the city and walk. He would aim to reach the open country that night. He was fit, the cold air and these guileless skies of the last days of the year would be his journeying companions. He would stay at unconsidered inns and pubs, eat and sleep well. He would be a tramp with money.

After all, he asked himself logically, as the assistant in the surplus shop unhung the boots for him, why did people only hike in the summertime when there were great gangs of cars on the roads and dust and spoiling rain? He bought an anorak, warm and quilted as a bed, and a knapsack for his shoulders. He went to a garage for a road map.

The girl at the garage was another of the after-Christmas ghosts, ashen-faced, sticky-eyed and moving with a drifting indifference. She gave him the map in the little office and surprised him by inquiring if he wanted petrol or oil. He politely declined and set his boots in a northerly direction towards where the winter-resting fields lay under the sky. He felt more like a true hiker, purposeful, virile, aware, alive, walking briskly through all these suburban moles pawing their way about the shops; cold, hurrying to get home to their holes again.

He reached the first village out of London that evening, keeping to the broad main road of his map. At five o'clock he was the only customer in the village café, devouring plaice and chips sown with salt and splattered with vinegar. He had four slices of bread and butter, each as thick as a book, and three powerful cups of tea. The lady in the café turned the radio on for him and he listened to the tired disc jockey and the lively records. He felt free and good.

The lady said he could go on to a place called Radford where he was bound to get accommodation for the night. He stayed at a pub there, talking to the landlord in the abandoned bar, everyone having stayed at home that night recovering from the festivities. The landlord talked to him about politics and income tax and how much it cost him to keep his two daughters in school shoes. William felt like someone serious. He agreed sagely with the landlord and put in a few considered remarks of his own, not many, but enough to start the other man off on a new talking topic.

Just after ten, a girl in a shrunken sweater and a small skirt, came into the bar, a little furtively, William thought, and began to clear up. Her father returned to the subject of her shoes and instructed the girl to show William how quickly the soles wore away. She was about fourteen and not shy. She lifted her leg like a dancer and put her foot in William's hands. He inspected the bottoms of the shoes uncomfortably, feeling the shape of her foot in his hands, trying not to look up for an instant. Eventually, she blithely kicked her foot away and went on with her clearing up. William said he had a long road in front of him the next day.

'I'll get Kate to show you up the stairs,' said the landlord. 'Show the gentleman number three, Kate.'

They went up the crawling old stairs to number three, the girl's round and bouncing skirt just ahead of William's hesitant nose. She found a light switch on the landing and turned it on. She opened the door. Her eyes were more alive than any he had seen that day.

'We've had pop groups staying in this room,' she said to William triumphantly.

'All in one bed?' said William.

She giggled. 'No, daft. And we had Ricky Roland here once. He was fabulous. I took him his tea in bed in the morning. I was trembling all the way up the stairs, I can tell you. Fabulous ... There's a towel on the washbasin. The thing is along there, at the end of the passage. Goodnight, sir.'

It was cold taking off his trousers. He had a long look under his shirt to see if there was any news, but nothing had changed. He rolled into bed in his shirt, turned out the light, and lay there with the flickerings of an indifferent moon entering through the low window and sharing his eiderdown. He wondered how many rooms away she was undressing for her bed, whether she

94

would bring his tea in the morning. He patted the mattress like a familiar friend.

'Goodnight, Fabulous Ricky Roland,' he groaned. 'Goodnight.'

On his second day out he saw a galloping hare, heard the clank of winter ploughing and dogs barking across flat and empty fields. Several farm and country people greeted him and did not seem to think it odd that he should be treading the road at that cold time of the year. The sun shone all through the day, giving its orange touch to everything on the way, warming the serious stone of the barns, making the windows of cottages flash like signals, encouraging lucky geese who had survived Christmas to sit in barnyards and stretch beneath orchard trees. Smoke wandered in small coils from grandfather chimneys, and a village bus cheerfully arrived as though on order and carried him ten miles when he was tired of walking.

'Christmas and New Year,' the conductor informed him, 'are the peak times of the year for people cutting their own throats and sticking their heads in gas ovens. I'm always worried when New Year is on a Wednesday because that's the day the bus runs, you understand, and if there should be someone very depressed they might easily jump out in front of us. It's not on a Wednesday for a couple of years yet, though, so I'll worry about it when it comes. That's what I always say, worry about it when it comes.'

William's thoughts along the miles were tranquil and decent. He played, in memory, the best game of tennis he could ever remember, at Sutton Coldfield, three years before, when, he thought fondly, Louise was sitting at the courtside actually applauding him. At least, now he came to think about it, he *thought* she was applauding him. You could never tell with Louise, of course, she might well have been clapping his opponent. No, that was ridiculous; she was quite definitely for him. She had looked like a lily that afternoon, under the trees. It was just as he had always wanted it to be, almost Victorian in its gentleness, trees and ice-creams and lemonade, and Louise looking so cool and adorable under the chanceless Birmingham sky. He wondered how she was getting on with Mr Sherman.

You wouldn't find Mr Sherman pulling down a toilet cistern on his napper, that was for sure. They were not very far away, of course, from this very road he was walking. Just ten miles or so to the right once he had travelled another half a day north. Perhaps he could drop in on them! Just for old time's sake. After all, it was Christmas.

He was merely having a joke with himself until, at three in the afternoon, he saw the signpost with the words 'Midford-Pallant' spread out towards the east. He stood, very solitary and aware of it, looking at the sign. It was more like an instruction than a direction. He read it uneasily as though he thought they may have mis-spelt it. Then, as he was about to make himself move off on his original way, a bus with 'Midford-Pallant' illuminating its forehead turned the corner and stopped, questioningly, three paces away from him. Nobody got off and there was nobody to get on. But it waited, vibrating with patience, while the driver sat staring straight ahead and the conductor on the cross-bench seat cleaned his fingernails.

William's brain seemed to have gone stiff. He walked forward like a man with injured legs and boarded the bus. Even when he reached the step he nearly got off again, but the conductor looked up challengingly, as though suggesting he made up his mind, and William, hardly able to credit what he had done, tumbled forward into the nearest seat. The conductor gave every indication that they had only been waiting for him. He rang the bell and the bus moved off through the gathering afternoon.

'Sevenpenny to Midford-Pallant, please,' droned William miserably, reaching for his money.

'Ninepence now,' sniffed the conductor. 'Town centre. That where you want?'

'Yes,' mumbled William. 'That's it. Ninepence now is it?'

'Went up last September 15th,' said the conductor as though William should have been personally informed.

'Oh . . . well, you see I haven't been back.'

'Can't understand *anybody* going back to that dump,' said the conductor. 'Just can't understand them at all.'

18

'WHY CAN'T we carry on with our game today, Rufus? The Scrabble.'

'Sorry Bill, but I'm not fit for Scrabble. I'm fit for nothing. She brought the little perisher home yesterday, the baby. Cried all damn night. He's got a hell of a pair of lungs, believe me.'

'Oh, well done, Rufus! I'm so glad for you. All together again, eh? Isn't it funny how you get added-to like that. There are just the cosy two of you and off she goes to the hospital and – Whambo! – when she comes home again there're three of you. I bet you're glad to have her back again, aren't you, Rufus? I would be.'

'Of course, Bill, of course. But why can't they dish out a few quiet babies? I've known blokes in the station go right off their jobs because of a howling kid at home. Right off. They've either let some criminal get off the hook or they've been hard on some poor old innocent suspect. That's how it affects you.'

'Home pressures, Rufus, home pressures.'

'Exactly. So I'm a bit edgy today. Take warning, old friend. If I'm not my usual amiable, cooperative self, then you know why.'

'Ho, ho. That means I'll have to watch the nose, then, I suppose.'

'Keep your hand over it. I would. Boy, I feel really irritable today. Let me just put my fingers on it, Bill. It might make me feel a bit better, soothe me. No, don't worry, old fellow. I won't tug it or pull it or even give it a firm squeeze. Just let me get hold of it lightly. I won't do anything unpleasant. After all, you've done nothing to deserve it, have you?'

'No, Rufus. Are you sure you won't hurt it?'

'Sure. Positive. Look, I'll say, "*please*". There you are, "*please*".'

'All right, but you have promised. Copper's promise?'

'Policeman's promise, Bill. Come on, don't be frightened.'

'All right . . . now careful . . . careful.'

'There. I didn't do anything, did I?'

'No, I have to hand it to you, Rufus. You didn't hurt me, that time. Do you want me to go on telling you what I was telling you yesterday? I'd more or less like to get off the subject of my nose for the time being.'

'Carry right on with the story, Bill. If I doze off, just give me a nudge. My God, I'm tired. You just carry on.'

'All right, Rufus. Try not to go off to sleep though because it won't look very good for either of us if you're having a kip in my cell.'

'Nobody every worries about what goes on in here, Bill. Don't kid yourself about that. I could kick you in the balls every morning for a week and nobody would know anything about it. Although you could always complain to your Member of Parliament.'

'But you wouldn't, would you?'

'What? What wouldn't I?'

'You know. Kick me in the thingies.'

'No. You know that.'

'Well, in that case, I'm not going to complain to my MP!'

'Actually, Bill, I think I'll have a stretch out on your bunk. You can continue with the story; I'll just rest quietly here. I can still hear what you're going on about, don't worry. I may close my eyes but I won't necessarily be gone to bye-byes. So don't worry.'

'Are you sure you'll be comfortable? I mean, this is Wandsworth not the Hilton. You should see the trouble *I* have getting to sleep on that thing, what with my worries and my sore nose and with it being so flaming hard as well.'

'Worries? Do you really worry a lot, Bill?'

'Naturally I do. I worry about Connie and other things. I worry about Louise even, and that bastard Mr Sherman. And I worry about myself because, frankly, I sometimes get the feeling I've got less future than any of them.'

'Let me stretch out, anyway. Now ... ah, that's the stuff. Fancy a little kid like that screaming all night. I don't think that's much fun.'

'They're more fun when they get older, Rufus ... That is, if you see what I mean. Don't look at me like that. I meant that

98

parents always say they get more enjoyment from their children once they're running about and getting into mischief. Don't they now?'

'Tell me what happened when you went back to Midford-Pallant, Bill.'

'Yes, of course. Well, I simply got off the bus and started to wander around the town. Well, jog around the town. You can't exactly wander in big boots like that. I had a look in Woolworth's and then I had a look at the bank where I used to work and the soft drinks firm.

'The soft drinks firm had closed down, which was to be expected, I suppose. That old devil Thompson was a swindler. His cream soda was enough to give a navvy the guts-ache. Not that many navvies drank it mind you. Yes, I went and had a look around at all those places.'

'And the girls' school?'

'No. Of course not. It was the Christmas holidays. There was nobody there. I did have a glance out of the window of the bus, but it was all dark and deserted. I always think that's a bit sad, don't you, Rufus, when you remember a place so lively and all summery, and then you see it deserted in the middle of winter?'

'Nobody doing the high jump and showing their gym knickers, then?'

'Now, don't go on about that sort of thing, Rufus. Please. Like I told you, it was the holiday and everything was deserted.'

'Why did you go into Woolworth's?'

'I just like Woolworth's, Rufus. I like the smell of the floor polish. They always smell the same. Woolworth's, I reckon, is always one of the most cheerful places in any town. It's always warm, a bit garish and common, some people might think, but I like it. I'm one that wouldn't be stuck up about Woolworth's being common. Even after Christmas it didn't seem to have that depressed air that other shops seem to have. There were a few people in there buying presents for people they'd forgotten. You could tell that's what they were doing. There were these two girls trying to buy some tights for someone and getting in a pickle over the sizes. It was quite amusing. I said to them, "There're only three hundred shopping days to Christmas," and they both laughed because I had summed up the situation perfectly.'

'You spoke to two girls, then?'

'Yes, of course. Well there's no law against that, is there, Rufus? For God's sake, you just *make up* things about me, I think. After all, I'm allowed to bloody well talk to any-bloody-body I please, and when I pleeth. Oh no, for Godth thake, Rufuth. Lie down again. Jesuth it hurth ... Pleeeeeeth.'

'Well watch your language to a police officer, Bill. I take offence easily. Particularly when I've been up all night tending to my little baby son. Believe me, I don't want to have to get up from here and pull your hooter again, but I will do unless you cooperate. Now – did you speak to anyone else in Woolworth's?'

'No. Honestly, Rufus. Really I didn't.'

'Come on, tell Rufus. You can tell me.'

'No, Rufus, don't do it again. You rest quietly ... Now, let me get this straight, I hardly spoke to a soul, except the two young girls.'

'And that was just about the tights? COME ON! WAS IT? Come here you horrible perverted bastard. Come here ...'

'Christ! No, Rufus. Please, you rest! I'll tell you! You know I will. You know I can't keep a single thing from you. You're a hell of a good detective-sergeant, you know. I can't tell lies to you.'

'All right, I'll lie down. There.'

'Comfortable?'

'Tell me.'

'Well, it was just a bit of fun, that's all. I got on the weighing machine. I wondered how much weight I'd lost doing all that walking, so I weighed myself. And these two girls came up – the same pair – and started laughing at my heavy boots. Well they *did* look comical, I must confess. And I asked them if they thought they'd put on weight over Christmas, what with the pudding and all that. They said they'd get on the scales if I paid. So I did. It was just a laugh. Just the usual gag. I made the scales go up to fifteen stone for one of them and we laughed like mad. There was nothing more to it than ...'

'How did you do that?'

'What, Rufus?'

'Make them go up to fifteen stone. You stood on with her?'

'Well ... yes.'

'Behind her?'

'Yes. Yes, that's correct, Rufus. But it was only to amuse ...'

'*You*. To amuse you.'

'No. Honestly. To amuse ...'

'Did you touch her? Come on, did you touch her with your body? With the front of your trousers? With your genitals?'

'*Rufus!*'

'Did you? Come on, I want to know. Come on!'

'No. No, I didn't truly, Rufus. Honk! Honk! You're making me thound like a bloodith theal in the zoo. Leave it alonth! You're making me cryth again.'

'Right. I've let go. Did you touch her at all? Hold yourself against her? Did you, Bill?'

'Well, I may have just brushed against her navy-blue coat when she was on the scales in front of me. But it was an accident. Really it was! And, really, as for putting my trousers against her, or my ... well the other things you mentioned ...'

'Genitals.'

'That's right. Those. Well, Rufus, you make me blush.'

'All right, Bill. So you gave the little girls a thrill by letting them get weighed with you. Then what did you do, play leap-frog up a side alley?'

'No. If you want to know, after I'd finished in Woolworth's I went to see ... Louise ... my wife.'

19

FIRST HE turned on a detour, crossing through the early-dark streets until he passed their flat; the flat that had been theirs in the old days, the maisonette; the upper slice of a sandwich of three, with the street lamp's light just brushing against its bread-coloured face. He stood at the gate looking at the windows. It was complete night-time now. There was someone moving in the lambent window that he knew was the kitchen, the incumbent wife making a meal; and at the other two windows there was the blue acetylene glow of a television set. He stood on tiptoe by the gate trying to see the centre light of the kitchen. That was one of the few things he had ever been able to fix. He had put a plastic light-fitting, like an inverted bowl, to the ceiling in the kitchen. Louise had been pleased, for once, and had said that it looked very contemporary.

He was still on his toes when the upper door was pulled open. It still stuck, he thought. It opened out on to an outside stairway, half screened by a wall. He heard a boy's voice call: 'I'm putting him out, Dad. He wants to go out.' The door closed again and the cat trotted down the stairs and emerged around the corner of the wall. It stood and stared greenly at William who gave it the guilty nod he might give to a sudden policeman, and then continued his journey.

Eventually he went by the house where Louise lived with Mr Sherman. First he passed it at a casual gait, like a man out for an aimless stroll; then he walked back at a determined plod, like the hiker he was, lifting and dropping his boots heavily to the pavement; then he turned, craftily, and jogged by; dawdled back and hurried back yet again as though he had an appointment five miles away in ten minutes. There were lights in the big square house, blatant lights left on carelessly all over the place, that shone out on the tailored garden. He would bet Mr Sherman didn't do that garden. They must have a gardener, someone Mr Sherman had got from the council, probably. The ratepayers paid for that garden, for certain. William poked his tongue out at the house as he went by for the sixth time. On his way back he brazenly stood for a full minute just by the low garden wall, whistling, looking about him, hands in pockets, his left hiking boot drumming the pavement. He walked on and then returned yet again, looking up at the house as though he were a prospective buyer, snorting quietly as though he could see faults in the roof or he didn't like the way the drainpipes hung.

Why didn't he just go straight up to the front door and ring or knock? Why bloody well not? Go right in and give them a shock. Whoever came to the door, Mr Sherman, or Louise, he could wish them a loud 'Happy New Year', turn on his heel and walk off in the direction of Derby. That would shatter them. That would disturb their little love-nest. Or why didn't he get himself invited in and put on a lordly sort of act. 'You know, Louise, you and I parting was the best thing that ever happened. My God, I've been around since then.' He would put his hiking boots up on their furniture and spill their sherry. Jesus, they'd be glad to get rid of him.

He remained looking up at the house until a touch on the shoulder disturbed him and he turned guiltily and saw Louise. She didn't look so nice as when she was his wife, well, his real wife, he thought. A bit strained and thinner. But her smile was full and sweet. She was nice enough.

'I knew it was you, William,' she giggled. 'Why didn't you go up and knock?'

'Hello, Louise,' he muttered, looking uncomfortably at her. Then added: 'By the way, happy New Year.'

She giggled again and touched his cheek. 'We'll drink to that,' she said. 'Come on in.' She opened the gate and he followed her up the gravel path. That was council gravel, he knew. 'I was over the road at Mrs Harrison's,' she said as they reached the door. She had left it on the jar. 'We've been killing ourselves laughing, watching you from her front window. It was better than the television. Up and down, up and down, jogging and jumping, haring past, then back again. You're really funny, you know.'

'It wasn't funny,' argued William. 'I wasn't sure this was the right house, that's all. I didn't want to go into the wrong house, did I?'

They were inside now. They went into the sitting-room. There was a big curved green moquette suite, some shiny tables, and a cocktail cabinet which tinkled *Auld Lang Syne* when she got him a drink.

'That's clever,' he said conversationally. 'Can it play anything else?'

She ignored it. 'How *could* you pretend that you were not sure of the house, William?' she complained. 'You've delivered orangeade and soda enough times, and you spent long enough in the back of that delivery van spying on me through the hole.'

'I did not!' His sherry shook in his fingers.

'Come on now, you did,' she argued softly. 'Sit down anyway. It's marvellous to see you.'

'I *definitely* did not, Louise,' he said again, sitting on the green moquette settee. She sat opposite on one of the short, shiny tables. She was laughing at him again. 'I didn't,' he repeated. 'What would I want to lie in the van spying on you for?'

She wagged a thin white finger. 'I said nothing about *lying* in the van,' she said like a triumphant detective. 'I only said you were in the van looking through the hole. How you did it, only you know. So there, that proves it.

'Mrs Harrison used to watch you crawling into the back of the van from the driving seat. We used to kill ourselves laughing about it. George wanted to get in and drive you away or do something awful like that, but I wouldn't let him do it. You know, he even wanted to light a firework and toss it in on you one day. He's a devil.'

'Yes, he is,' nodded William.

She leaned back and looked him over approvingly. 'Still the same old handsome husband,' she said.

'Thank you, Louise,' said William. 'You look very attractive, too.'

She examined him further over the circle of her glass. 'But why the funny boots and that jacket thing? You look like one of those parachutists.'

'I'm a hiker,' explained William. Why did she wear her dress so short, he wondered. After all, she was a married woman. More than that, a one-and-a-half-times married woman.

'A hiker,' she nodded. 'Where are you hiking? Isn't it a bit early, or a bit late, for that sort of thing?'

'The weather's good,' he shrugged. 'There's no special time of the year.'

'Well, where are you going? You're not going to just hike up and down outside this place, are you?'

'Certainly not,' he said. 'I'm en route for Derby. I thought I'd hike there.'

'Derby?' she asked. Then, giving it up: 'Oh well.'

'Are you keeping well, Louise?'

'Okay,' she said, cocking the glass a trifle.

'How is Mr Sherman?'

'Drunk by now,' she said, glancing at the clock.

'I'm sorry.'

'Oh, don't get me wrong, William,' she said. 'He's not always drunk. It's just that the Christmas parties seem to be lagging over a bit this year. The council and the Rotary and all the other bits and pieces he belongs to.'

'You always wanted someone who was good at parties,' William pointed out mildly. 'I was never much good, was I?'

'No, I'm afraid you were hopeless, William,' She sounded much softer, sadder, now. She reached for his glass and he gave it to her obediently.

'Be careful,' he suggested cautiously. 'That was a big one last time.'

'You're walking not driving,' she said. She lifted the lid of the cocktail cabinet and it belled its tune. The sherry was longer than the last one, nearly touching the lip of the glass. 'There,' she smiled. 'That's a decent-sized one.'

'I'll say,' said William doubtfully as he took the glass. The red tongue of sherry was trying to roll over the top.

'I was hopeless at parties,' he agreed. He regarded his boots. For the first time he realized how round and big they were, sticking out from his legs like the supports of a bridge. 'Bloody hopeless.'

'You were at a lot of things,' she said uncharitably but quite gently. 'Tennis. That was the only thing. You were very good at tennis.'

'I was thinking the other day about that afternoon at Sutton Coldfield when I beat what's-his-name in the Midlands Championships. You had that hat on and you were sitting under the trees. It was very hot and nice. Do you remember?'

She laughed. 'I remember what's-his-name, Ronnie Robertson, if that's who you mean. The bastard. I don't remember anything about the day or the tennis though. Did you beat him?'

'Eight-six, six-four, eight-six,' William reminded her. 'It was a lovely day and you were sitting under the trees. In that hat.'

'I can't remember,' she shrugged. 'But if you got one happy day out of it all, then that's something, I suppose.'

'Louise,' he inquired. 'Are you happy now? With Mr Sherman?'

'Happy?' she asked. 'What's happy? He's got his faults. I'd like to know where he is sometimes. I'd like to know where he is tonight, for instance. Christmas parties after Christmas, and no wives invited! Personally, I doubt if we'll ever get married and we don't care all that much. We'll probably fall out before we're finished.' She drank and looked at him plaintively. 'But,' she said, 'he's not such a bloody fool as you.'

'Oh,' said William blankly. He drank his sherry and looked down at his big boots again. 'You know, these boots *are* a bit big,' he agreed. 'I've never noticed it before.'

'You were always too small for your boots,' she laughed, the seriousness immediately gone. She went to the cocktail cabinet and filled the glasses again.

'It's playing our song,' said William.

'Ha! That's not bad for you,' she said. She handed him the glass again. William thought the room had begun to feel warm. She sat and crossed her legs. He could see right up her flank. She had some bruises on the side, six inches up from her knee.

'Now,' she said. 'Tell me where you've been.'

'Around,' he said. 'All over really.'

'Well, where?'

'Antwerp,' he said recklessly. 'I was in Antwerp.'

'Antwerp! *You* went abroad?'

'Signed on a ship,' he boasted. He began to enjoy the idea. 'With old Wheelbarrow Wheeler. He's got real wooden legs. They stick out in front of him when he sits down. That's why they call him Wheelbarrow, see.'

'William, I don't believe you,' she said. 'You on a ship – in Antwerp.'

'Rotterdam, Hamburg, Las Palmas. All over.'

'What were you, the deck-tennis coach?'

'Deckhand,' he said simply. Then, as a romantic after-thought: 'Before the mast.'

'I can't believe it.'

'It's true,' William assured her smugly. 'Quite true.'

'Are you going back? To sea, I mean.'

'Might,' he answered. 'Could be the Indies next time. Singapore or Australia or one of those places. I've *had* places like Antwerp.'

'You're joking!' she said quite crossly. 'You're having me on.'

'Louise,' he said patiently, 'I'm not having you anything. I've been at sea.'

20

'SHE DID a rotten and damnable thing to me that night, Rufus. I don't know why some people have to be so flipping cruel. She just played about with me. And she wanted me to play about with her. She didn't cotton on that I loved her. I *still* did. Really. It was the same with Connie. She played around with me. They have a good laugh with you, these women do, even when they're only sixteen like Connie. They can't seem to get it into their senses that *I'm* genuine. They need men who only want to muck around like they do. The trouble with me is, *I* mean it.'

'Let's have a game of Scrabble, Bill. I feel like a game today. Maybe it will help me sort things out a bit. I'm shagged out, really I am.'

'The little baby?'

'The little bugger.'

'Keeping you awake?'

'Keeping the whole bloody street awake.'

'Howling?'

'No. Playing the clarinet.'

'I'm sorry about it, Rufus, but there's not much I can do, is there? Unless you'd like to move in here with me. It's quiet enough in the prison at night, except now and again you hear people coughing or crying. The man on that side cries at least once a week. But that's better than every night.'

'Maybe he doesn't get any fishcakes.'

'Ah, that's what I meant to tell you. We've had a glut of fishcakes, Rufus. God, you never saw so many. If we get any more we'll all be swimming out of here. Yesterday I even asked for their filthy soup I was so fed up with fishcakes.'

'What did you get?'

'Fishcakes. Naturally. I suppose they reckon you're in here for punishment so they make it as nasty as possible.'

'Now, Bill, don't forget *you're* on remand. You're still innocent until you're proved guilty at the Sessions. So don't you let them push you around too much. There's a limit, you know. At the moment there is anyhow.'

'No good, Rufus. I can tell you that from personal experience. I called them one night because that man was crying next door and what with my nose hurting I couldn't get any rest. And one of the warders just came in and gave me a really nasty push. Sent me right back against the wall there. It knocked all the breath out of me, believe me. So making complaints is a dead loss.'

'Still, I could reckon on a night's rest in this cell, Bill. I just haven't slept at all. It makes me feel so irritable – so watch out for your conk. I may want to start pulling it. It's a sort of therapy for me. Do you know, If I wasn't on this particular investigation I'd ask for nightwork at the station so that I could get some sleep in the day.'

'Doesn't he cry in the day?'

'Who?'

'The little one. The baby.'

'Oh, no. No, not that much anyway. Not as much as at night. And it makes Myra so difficult. She snores right through it. A bleeding great smile on her face. And when I wake her up and tell her he's howling again she gets so annoyed.'

'They are difficult, women, Rufus. I was telling you about Louise, wasn't I.'

'Oh, yes. You'd better go on with that.'

'What about the Scrabble? I'm afraid I upset it all last night when I went to the pot. We'll have to start again. Still, I was ahead on points, so I'm the loser. I'll get the board.'

'Wait a minute, Bill. Wait a minute. Let's hear about Louise. Come on – we might as well.'

'All right. What was I saying about her? Ah, yes, I remember. What I was going to say is that she's so cheap. So stinking cheap. There she is, living with Mr Sherman, and she knows I love her; well I did in a way, *then*. I wouldn't have been there otherwise, would I? I didn't go back to Midford-Pallant just to see the bank or Mr Thompson of the soft drinks firm.'

'Or Woolworth's.'

'All right. Have it your own way. Even Woolworth's. Although there was nothing in that. I've told you.'

'Sure, you've told me. Let's get on to Louise.'

'Get *on* is the word. Or *get off*. That's what she tried. She tried to *get off* with me. *Me*, her own husband. And in another man's bed.'

'And did you? . . . Get on?'

'I still loved her, Rufus. Looking at her across the room, so cheery, sipping her sherry and that cocktail cabinet lighting up her lovely face every time she lifted the lid. And the tune it played. Naturally I felt a lot for her. We had a couple of drinks and then we went upstairs. I honestly didn't know what to expect. After all, she'd left me for Mr Sherman and I couldn't think it possible that she could want me again. Even for a change.'

'Did she say that?'

'What – for a change? Yes, she did. That's the only reason she wanted me. But I loved her. I suppose I have too much respect for women. That's the trouble. Respect them too much and they just laugh at you for it. Even when you're crying. She was laughing at me, that Louise, when I was crying. She really is a rotten cow. I feel quite sorry for Mr Sherman.'

'Maybe Mr Sherman doesn't respect her so much, Bill.'

'Probably not. He knows how to handle her. That's the secret of women. I wish I had it.'

'Maybe one day you will.'

'Christ, Rufus, by the time I get out of here, or Dartmoor, or wherever they send me, I'll be too old to use it anyway.'

'Oh, I don't know. Supposing you get ten years. Eight and a half with remission, say. You'll *still* be in the nookey market. You'll be under forty-five. I'll bet you'll really feel like a bit then.'

'After ten years – all right, eight and a half with remission – I'll have probably forgotten all about it, Rufus. So it's no use counting on that.'

'Carry on about Louise. She got you upstairs.'

'That's right. She just said, "Come on with me," and went off upstairs. I half thought she might be politely showing me the house, but when we got to their bedroom she stripped off. Just like that. No fuss. She simply stripped off.'

'I bet that brought back some memories, Bill.'

'I'll say. She really is a magnificent woman, Louise. Very white and with these heavy breasts. She was laughing at my expression as she stood there. She made some remark about giving each other a Christmas present. Then she rolled across their bed on the quilt. And she started wriggling about, rubbing her legs together and then getting her breasts, one in each hand, and pushing the nipples against each other as though they were kissing.

'Then she let go of her left breast, no, tell a lie, her right, and she got hold of my hand. She giggled and said, "Give me a finger," so I stuck out a finger and she put it into her mouth and sucked it. She gave it one hell of a suck. I thought it was going down her throat! Then she let me take it out and she pushed her nipples together again and I put my wet finger in between them and sort of rubbed it up and down, flipping them to and fro.'

'Stop it a minute, Bill. You're giving me the horn.'

'I'm giving myself the horn, Rufus. I went bloody mad, I can tell you. I didn't give a thought to old Mr Sherman. Off came my anorak, after a bit of a struggle it's true because they're damn difficult to get off in a hurry what with the zip and the hood. But off it came, and my shirt and my vest. For some reason I was crying. I remember wiping my eyes on the tail of my shirt, which wasn't very hygienic, I suppose. But, honestly, Rufus, I truly thought she wanted me because she *loved* me. I loved her so much. I was rushing to get my things off like a kid going swimming in a river. I could hear her laughing inside my shirt. That is, I was inside my shirt and I could hear her laughing. *She* wasn't laughing inside my shirt.'

'I'd worked that out, Bill.'

'When I came out again. Out of the shirt, you understand, she'd moved herself across the bed and opened out her legs as wide as she could, like a pair of compasses. She'd bent them up and opened them out and she had her hand down there, sort of covering herself up. And then she slid it away and there it was. I'd almost forgotten what it looked like. Not just hers. Anyone's. And then, right away, I thought about Blanche – and Babsy! I stopped. Christ, I just stopped dead. I remembered what I'd *got*, or I *thought* I'd got. Suddenly I could feel it was as sore as hell. It was burning. I couldn't. I couldn't give it to Louise. Not my wife!'

'Bill, I give you up.'

'I couldn't, couldn't I now, Rufus? I stood there clutching my shirt and my vest and feeling that rotten dickie inside my trousers. God, I thought, oh God. And she stopped laughing. She could see my expression had changed. She propped herself up on her elbows and her breasts tumbled forward. You don't know how she looked!

'She gave a bit of an uncertain laugh again and said, "Come on then, slowcoach," or something like that. And I just started to stammer and I tried to put my vest on again. "What's the matter?" she said.

'Well, I had to make some excuse. I couldn't say I'd got the clap, could I? So I said, "It's these boots. They're too difficult to get off." She just gurgled out laughing and said, "Come on – don't take them off. Just take your bloody trousers off."

'I was in a panic. "I'll mess up the quilt," I said. "With my boots." She said she'd mess me up if I didn't get a move on. Then she slid across the quilt and made as if to untie my boots. She had rolled over like some kind of fabulous fish, Rufus, and her bottom . . . well, I could have touched her bottom. I could have put both my hands on it. It looked terrifically soft.'

'What did you do, Bill?'

'I sort of drew away and I told her not to take my boots off because I had holes in my socks. I know it doesn't sound very convincing now, but what else could I say? I backed away from her and said I'd have to be going on to Derby. I started to put my things on and she went berserk.'

'I'll bet.'

111

'My God, she went mad. She jumped off the bed and she screamed and spat at me and, while I was still trying to get my shirt back over my head, she hit me in both ears with her fists. Christ, she made me reel. Bang – in both at the same time! She brought them up together. Then she kicked out at me and threw a little alarm clock which hit me in the chest and went off ringing. I got out. I backed away and then turned and half fell down the flipping stairs. You should have heard her language. Filthy, that's the only way to describe it. The trouble was she looked so gorgeous. When I got to the bottom of the stairs I looked back at her and she was standing on a bend at the top, screeching and carrying on, but her breasts were stuck out, all flushed and thick, and her hair was falling over her face. Then she picked up the clock and threw it at me again, so I cleared out of the front door. I shouted back, "Happy New Year." I don't know whether she heard me but, anyway, she didn't answer.

'All I needed, of course, was to meet her husband . . . I mean, Mr Sherman, coming home from his party. Then we would have seen some real trouble. But, fortunately, that didn't happen. I saw the curtains across the road, at Mrs Harrison's, go aside as I went down the street stuffing my shirt into my trousers. I got into a shop doorway and sorted myself out. I was upset about the whole affair, believe me.'

'I bet you were, Bill. And that was all?'

'Yes, Rufus. It wasn't much of a reunion, was it?'

21

As though it had been anticipating his retreat from Midford-Pallant, the same single-deck bus nudged around the corner at the fringe of the town. He saw it turning the distant bend like an illuminated caterpillar. The same conductor was alone in the glowing inside, still staring at his nails. He acknowledged William morosely.

'Was it worth the ninepence, then?' he asked.

'Not tuppence,' sighed William.

'Nothing to get excited about in Midford-Pallant,' shrugged the conductor. 'I don't know anybody there that's even alive and kicking.'

'I do,' answered William. 'One anyway.'

'Well you're lucky.'

'No I'm not. How far does the bus go?'

'Ridchester.'

'All right, I'll go there.'

'You don't care, do you?'

The conductor turned the wheel on the cylinder held to his belly and sniffed.

William felt muddy inside. 'No, I *don't* care,' he said dismally. He did not want to continue talking to the conductor so he went to the tail of the bus and sat hunched and quietly truculent in the centre of the back seat. The conductor yawned and sat down and regarded his nails. They were thick and filthy. William had noticed them as the ticket had rolled out of the little machine.

It was five miles, all dark countryside with the occasional square lights of cottages going by like travelling lanterns. He thought moodily that if the bus drove on for ever through endless nights to Glasgow, Oslo, or Borneo, it would matter little to him or to anyone else. Perhaps it could travel on around the world until it had described the full orb and had arrived back at Midford-Pallant. The sherry from Louise's chiming cabinet, once warm and sweet on his lips, was lying in a cold pond within his stomach.

'You don't go around the world, by any chance?' he called to the conductor at the front of the bus. The man did not look up from his fascination with his funereal nails.

'Only on me holidays,' he muttered, then stood up in an official way and shouted: 'Ridchester. All change.'

William stumbled along the aisle and stepped down into the cowering street of the village, the studs of his boots striking the cold pavement like chisels. There was the scent of frost in the air. The two street lamps, one each end of the stumbling hamlet, were as bright as small flares in the hard air, but the middle of the street, where he stood, was dark as a hole.

The bus drove off with a grunt as though glad to be rid of him. He half waved to the conductor but the man did not glance up.

He began to feel a fever of loneliness. He thought comfortably of Louise. Even though she had thrown him out she was not to know his reasons for behaving as he did. She could not know it was for *her*. Damn Blanche and Babsy. That wasn't fair either. They could not have known what they were distributing. They were too good-hearted to willingly, knowingly, give anyone the clap at Christmas-tide. They had a lot of fun. Or they seemed to have. They enjoyed the life and they had that lovely little underground room, warm and enclosed, with the Indian restaurant next door, and lots of people moving outside their front door.

He tried to imagine Louise doing that sort of work and the thought made him shake and feel ashamed as he walked along the dumb half-mile of the village. On the other hand, Blanche, or better still, Babsy, could be wished on Mr Sherman with the greatest joy. By God, wouldn't Babsy, well stoned and blowing that blower thing, be marvellous when Mr Sherman was Rotating one evening.

But the thought comforted him for only a while. He was still isolated with the frost forming on his anorak and the last half-inch of his nose. He wondered what his sailor friends were doing at that moment. Good old Antwerp Herbert, the buccaneer of the Seamen's Mission, the singer of songs for sailors. Why couldn't he be Antwerp Herbert all the time?

The doors of the crouching houses along the street joined immediately on to the pavement. There were lights behind low curtains in the cottage windows and twice he stopped, guilty as a burglar, and put his ear to the glass so that he could hear the sound of the television set buried in there or the people's voices murmuring comfortably in the low rooms.

The street seemed endlessly lonely, hollow and black. He thought of Southwelling with sudden warmth. He had now firmly decided against running away from it. He would go back and try to begin again. Nothing would upset him and he would commit no more clumsy mistakes. Why was it that he stumbled into situations when a person like Major Prescod, who obviously liked young girls so much and in such a strange way, who blithely cleaned their shoes when they went to his house to tea, or washed their legs for them when they crept in from a cross-country race, remained safe and untroubled? Nothing terrible happened to Major Prescod. Providence allowed him to delight himself in his ministrations, his tin of Cherry Blossom and his brushes, not to mention the Brasso and the shoe buckles he polished with such gusto.

And yet at the very moment that William was feeling so sick over the horrific accident of walking in on Connie and Yum Yum and the others in the dressing-room, that final afternoon at school, there was the Major, dressed as Santa Claus for the end-of-term party, chortling over his teacup with pupils and parents gathered around his robes. He had called William over jovially and said from the corner of his whiskers: 'Heard you had an embarrassing adventure, old boy. Don't worry – could happen to the best of us.'

William had felt like replying: 'Or the worst,' but he mumbled, looking guiltily at the people around them: 'I felt terrible. Awful. Miss Smallwood was very decent about the whole thing, but there's no doubt it makes you feel a bit of a fool.'

Major Prescod had nudged him away from the crowd: 'My dear chap,' he said. 'Now just you listen to me. The girls just think it's a huge belly laugh. They've been laughing about it all the afternoon.'

'Everybody knows, then?'

'Went around the school like wildfire. What do you expect with three hundred young ladies? Walking in on the senior girls in the nude!'

'They weren't in the nude,' protested William. 'They were partly clothed. Mostly, in fact. And there were only two senior girls, Connie Rowan and Yum Yum – I mean, Pamela Watts – in any case.'

Major Prescod had treated him to a Yuletide beam through the spiral of steam from his teacup. 'Now look old chap, as long as Miss Smallwood doesn't get upset, what the hell does it matter? Miss Smallwood is inclined to blame the girls for leaving the door unlocked, anyway, and for not being ready on time. You've got nothing to worry about. You're on a good wicket here, you know. Or in your case it should be a good court, I suppose. Hah!'

'Hah!' William had replied.

'You're extraordinarily popular with the girls anyway. I don't suppose they mind if you walk in on a bit of bare backside now and again.'

'Major Prescod!' exclaimed William. He swung a worried glance about him. But the parents and pupils, standing with their tea and cakes, had heard nothing. Major Prescod patted him on the shoulder as though he had just revealed what he wanted for Christmas.

'It would be a miracle if a man in a girls' school didn't make a bloomer now and again, if you'll forgive the pun. It stands to reason. So don't let it get you down. As I say, the girls think you're marvellous. Some of the little devils were telling me only this afternoon that they're going to form a secret society next term called The Condominium and they're going to ask *you* to be president.'

'It doesn't sound as though it's going to be very secret,' said William, comforted nevertheless. 'Not if they're spreading it about in here. What's the object anyway?'

'God knows, I don't,' said the Major. 'You know how they love to form little cliques and secret societies and all that sort of rubbish. All I know is it's going to be called The Condominium.'

The Condominium. William repeated the words to himself as he remembered, and walked through the bare-boned street making for the village pub at its end. He did not know what the term meant, although it sounded impressive, and so the next day, renewed by another morning of wide winter sun over the placid land, he walked north again and decided to stop at the first town with a public library.

It was mid-morning when the road, as though suddenly tiring of its own climbing journey, dipped and curved into the market town of Barford. The public library was a beetle-browed building of solemn stone in the main square. There were old men crouched, as though in prayer, over the newspapers in the reading-room, and a large young woman, so rounded she looked as though she had been pumped up that morning, sat behind a desk. She observed William in his unseasonal hiking gear with suspicion.

'Do you think I could consult a dictionary?' he inquired.

'English?' she asked abruptly, as though indicating they had a gigantic foreign stock.

'Oh yes, of course,' replied William. 'I'm doing a crossword and I'm a bit stuck.' He saw her staring at his haversack and his boots. 'I do it in my head as I go along,' he explained. 'It makes it more difficult that way.'

'I can imagine,' she said. She showed him the dictionaries and stood by him while he consulted as though ready to prevent him ripping out any of the pages and absconding with them. He grinned unsurely at her and thumbed his way through the first entries. CONDOMINIUM. There it was. 'Government of a territory by two separate states acting in conjunction.' He acknowledged it with a puzzled nod. Then his glance caught the previous entry. CONDOM. 'A contraceptive. A sheath. Named after Colonel Condom who derived it from a sheep's intestine in the eighteenth century.'

William gave a dry little cry and let the bulky dictionary drop to the floor. The bang stirred all the bending readers who looked up irritably.

'Hush!' ordered the pumped-up lady as though she had known all along he would be trouble.

White-faced, William stared at her. 'Sorry,' he mumbled. 'It was just something . . . that's all.'

Her curiosity overwhelmed her. 'What was it?' she whispered.

'Nothing. Just . . . that . . . I've made a mess of thirty-three across.'

A few miserable miles north of the town, head down he walked, knowing they would never leave him alone, let him forget that French-letter day. He arrived at a signpost which threw its arms airily towards Derby and, at an angle to the east, towards Leicester. He stood head up at it as though consulting some thin wooden oracle. Why not forget Derby; forget them all? Why not travel to Leicester where, perchance, he might meet a rich and beautiful widow who would genuinely fall in love with him.

No, forget her being wealthy. That mattered nothing. Let her be beautiful and *kind*. Or not even all that beautiful. But kind, certainly. Perhaps she would have a little son and they could be content together. A thoughtful old man with a load of dung piled high on a cart coaxed his horse along the road and, after observing William carefully as though he was someone he might know, he manoeuvred the dung towards Leicester. William shrugged and turned along the Derby road.

22

'How DID it feel up there in the dock, today, Bill?'

'Very strange, Rufus. It's a funny sensation. A bit like being offered for sale.'

'Well some people look at home in the dock and others don't. I must say that you looked absolutely *right* sitting there. What did you think of the performance of poor old Decent? He's a stumbling old fool, isn't he?'

'Truthfully, Rufus, I didn't think he was too bad, although I haven't got a lot of experience of lawyers. Perhaps I was a bit biased because he was the only one in court who was on my side. He even tried to get me bail.'

'Ho! He'd have been lucky. With the charges over your head! Not a hope. Not with that bench, anyway. They're the toughest bunch in London, I should think. Tougher than most of the people in the dock.'

'Now I wouldn't have realized that, if you hadn't told me. The one in the middle, the chairman, seemed quite a pleasant man. And he was sorry he couldn't let me have bail. He said so. And Mr Decent got him to promise that it would only be another seven days remand and then they would hear the case.'

'That's just the beginning, though, Bill. That bench haven't got the power to pass sentence on a big case like this. It will have to go to the higher court, to the Sessions. They can send you down for just about as long as they like up there. Personally, just between ourselves, I think we're rushing it a bit from our side. We could build up a real blockbuster of a case, you know. A real maximum-sentence certainty, given a bit more time. But it will be quite strong enough anyway, and we can always add to our evidence, of course, between next week and when you come up at the Sessions.'

'I'm glad for you.'

'Oh, come on, Bill, don't be too despondent. Did old Decent have anything to say to you afterwards?'

'Yes, he gave me a few tips. He has some funny ideas. Heaven knows where he gets them.'

'Out of those kids' comics he reads, I should imagine. What did he say, then?'

'It didn't *sound* as though it came from the *Beano*, Rufus. It was quite psychological really. He told me to make sure I was wearing clean underwear and socks in the court and that while I was sitting there I should have a look around at all those who were ranged up against me and try to imagine that they were wearing old underpants or stale vests or that they had holes in their socks. He said that if I knew I was all clean underneath and they weren't then it would give me confidence and a sense of superiority.'

'That's straight out of *Chicks' Own*, that is, Bill. Surely even you can see that. Vests and pants and socks! Mind you, that's just like old Decent. Just about his mark. He once told a man to make sure he washed his neck because they were going to hang him in the morning.'

'Can we change the subject, Rufus. How is the little baby?'

'Not bad. Slept well last night.'

'How's your wife?'

'I was awake all night with her.'

'I envy you. I wish I could be awake all night with a wife.'

'Nothing like that, Bill. Well, not much. She was nagging. Asking me what I'd been up to while she was in hospital. Very suspicious sometimes, these women . . . Bill, you know the girl at Southwelling you called Yum Yum? . . .'

'Yum Yum. Pamela Watts.'

'That's right. You've no idea where she might be, have you? She's just vanished. We've been trying to get hold of her for a statement. Her mother doesn't know where she's gone.'

'Can't help you, Rufus. She's not here with me, I can tell you that. A lovely kid.'

'Yes, you said. All right, you can't help us there. We'd like to get hold of her, though.'

'Naturally. Every little helps. I may be doing twenty years before your lot have finished.'

'Not twenty. Twelve, I would say at the outside. I've got twelve in the sweepstake.'

'There's a sweepstake?'

'Just a little one. Just a few of us at the station and the solicitors' clerks and suchlike.'

'On how long I get in prison?'

'Yes, but it's the normal sort of thing we do among the lads. It helps to pass the time. As I said, there's only a few of us in it. We put a quid each in the kitty.'

'Oh, it's nothing big, then? I mean it's not government-sponsored, like the Premium Bonds or that sort of thing?'

'Now you're being sarcastic, Bill. It's just a private sweepstake that's all; just a few friends who'll be in court.'

'You mentioned the solicitors' clerks. Would that be *my* solicitor's clerks?'

'Yes, of course. Yours and ours. There's nothing personal in it, we just drew the numbers out of a hat. One of your solicitor's boys has got you going down for twenty years.'

'The judge isn't in it?'

'No.'

'Or the jury?'

'Well, not as far as I know.'

'I wouldn't like them to fall out among themselves over something like a few quid in a sweepstake.'

'Forget it, Bill. It's nothing. Just a side-issue. You'll get a fair trial.'

'I wish I could be certain.'

'Oh, you will, there's no need to worry yourself about that. People nearly always do.'

'What do you want to talk to me about today, Rufus?'

'Well, thinking things over, I was getting a bit anxious about this pox of yours.'

'No more anxious than I was. I rang the hospital from

Loughborough on the morning of New Year's Eve and asked them if they could tell me if I'd got it and, if I had, what it was I'd got, and what I ought to do about it. They gave me a nasty shock, believe me, because they were quite offhand and said they couldn't give the results of blood tests and urine tests over the phone. They'd never said that before. They'd said I'd have to check, that's all. They were the very words. I got pretty hysterical and I started shouting down the phone at them, saying I had a right to know if I was carrying anything around, and, if so, what. But they were really snooty and said it was all confidential and it could be anybody ringing up. I'd have to go back to their clinic if I wanted to know, otherwise I'd have to go to another clinic in whatever part of the country I happened to be. I got a bit desperate. I told them I was up in the Orkneys; I even tried to make a noise like the sound of the wind and the sea. The man went away for a minute and came back and said that a sort of travelling pox doctor goes regularly around the Orkney Islands and I ought to report to him.'

'So you'd got to New Year's Eve and you still didn't know? How did it feel?'

'Well sometimes when I didn't think about it too much, it seemed to be all right. But it was still very sore on occasions. I thought perhaps it was the wind blowing through my trousers when I was walking. I thought perhaps it was getting ... chapped. You won't believe this, but I even bought some cotton-wool and made a sort of bird's nest around it in my pants so that it wouldn't get cold.

'It proved something of an embarrassment. I got a bus from Loughborough to Derby, because the weather clouded over and I wanted to get into Derby for New Year's Eve. There was a fat woman sitting right opposite me with a snotty little kid and she kept staring at me. She got all red in the face and the kid kept ogling. When they got off, the woman just jabbed her finger towards my trousers and I looked down and there was this curly bit of wadding sticking out through my flies.'

'What happened in Derby?'

'All sorts of things. I went to the post office where I used to work, and walked in one door and out the other. Strangely enough, I felt very powerful doing that – simply crashing through one of the swing doors and tramping right through and out the other. All those stamp-licking idiots looked up at me, and all those poor benighted prisoners stuck behind the grilles. I'd escaped from that, anyway. Then I went off down the road to the Ferbers' house where the twins were staying. And Connie.

'Frankly, I did the same trick as I did outside Louise's place – I just walked by, then walked back again. I kept it up until the twins suddenly appeared on bicycles. You should have seen them. A couple of little beauties, exactly the same round faces, and well-shaped tops.'

'Tops? What d'you mean, Bill?'

'Their tops. The tops of their bodies, of course, Rufus. You know . . .'

'I'm not always familiar with the technical terms, Bill. Tops. That means above their waists? The opposite to bottoms.'

'Now, Rufus. Upper parts, that's what it means. The bits that their blouses and sweaters would go over.'

'Right, I've got it.'

'I'm glad. Anyway, they made a gigantic fuss, putting their arms about me and all that type of embarrassing thing. They asked where I was going, and I pretended to be astonished at the coincidence of arriving outside their parents' house. I said I was hiking to Newcastle to see my grandfather who hadn't long to live.'

'That's a bit of a slow way of getting to somebody who hasn't got long to live?'

'I hadn't thought of that. Anyway, they were so excited they pulled me into the house and Mr and Mrs Ferber were just as overjoyed to see me. They insisted that I should stay that night for their New Year's Eve party, and I forgot all about my poor old grandad, dying in Newcastle.'

'The American girl was there?'

'Yes, Rufus. She came in with some ridiculous twerp in a rugby scarf and beatnik hair. For heaven's sake, you've got to be one thing or another! You either play rugby or you're a hippie. You can't play rugby with bloody hair like that. They'd tear it out by the roots.

'He had a car and he brought Connie to the house in it. I really didn't take a fancy to him. And she sat all very prim and American. That might seem strange but that is how she was. Her voice was that sort of beautifully soft American type; not a drawl but something extraordinary. And she always looked so Victorian, so sweet-faced, and with this magnificent hair dropping over her shoulders. On this afternoon she wore one of these maxi-skirts, the long things, and I've never seen anything so elegant and . . . fetching. She looked like a photograph I remember seeing of my grandmother when she worked on munitions in the Great War. She had a long skirt and boots like Connie, and that sort of hair.'

'Very dangerous.'

'What is, Rufus?'

'Wearing long hair in a munitions factory.'

'Yes, Connie thought of that, too. Grandmother was something to do with airships, I think.'

'Maybe she was a mooring rope.'

'Rufus! Now you're taking the piss out of my dead grandmother.'

'Sorry, Bill. Anyway, Connie.'

'Connie. Yes. She sat there looking at me in that splendidly relaxed, superior way she had. She kept looking at my boots and smiling to herself. And my anorak. And my haversack. She was quite impressed, I think, with the whole outfit.'

'It's just as well she couldn't see your cottonwool balls.'

23

SHE WAS like a young Victorian. The slow, incandescent, honey of her eyes, watching him with a seriousness only a trace removed from laughter; her hair drifting calmly behind her straight back; the long demure skirt she wore that day and the jaunty puff of the sleeves of her linen blouse.

'You look like my grandmother looked when she was working

on munitions in the First World War,' William said when they were alone in Mr Ferber's front room, sitting primly opposite each other.

'I don't quite know what you mean by that,' she said.

'Oh, I mean it in the best way,' said William, deepening his voice, sounding more fatherly, retreating under the caution in her eyes. 'We had a photograph at home once, gone all brown like a potato, and there was my gran and some of the other women munitions-makers posing. And they all had these long skirts and long hair.'

'Don't you suppose that was maybe a little dangerous if they were in a plant?' she pointed out. 'The long skirts and the hair. Didn't they get caught in the machinery or anything?'

'Well they looked all right. In perfectly good shape. That's an Americanism, isn't it? "In good shape".'

'I guess so,' she said.

There was a dusty silence between them; a long gentle silence. William fidgeted and broke a smile at her. She remained sweet and composed.

'Really,' he said. 'I *like* these new old-fashioned skirts. They're very elegant. You look as though you could be leaning against a bicycle, oh, sixty years ago.'

'I thought we were making munitions.'

'Well, you're on the way to the munitions factory on your bike.'

She laughed at him. 'Sometimes, Mr Herbert, you are strange, strange, strange.'

'Some people do have that opinion,' he said soberly.

'Why?' she smiled. 'Tell me why – and truly . . .'

'Well, what?'

'Why were you marching up and down outside this house, this afternoon?'

'I wasn't!' William protested. He felt his face swelling.

'Hush. There's no need to shout. *I* say that you were. Up and down, up and down. It was like you were on guard.'

'No, no,' he hesitated. 'I wasn't sure this was the correct house, that's all. I'd look pretty silly charging into the wrong house, now, wouldn't I? I merely was not sure . . .'

'Oh, boy, you looked pretty furtive to me. Anyway, just

where are you supposed to be going all dressed up like that? Those boots must weigh pounds.'

'They are pretty heavy. They've asked me to come to the party tonight. So make sure you don't dance with me. I'm a killer with my boots.'

She giggled. 'You still haven't told me – where were you going?'

'For a walk,' he insisted. 'Just for a walk around the country, that's all. There's no law against it and the weather's nice.'

'How was your Christmas?' she inquired quizzically. 'Was it a film star, or a politician? I can't recall. You were sure going somewhere exciting.'

'Great, great,' he mumbled. 'It was an actress. She was tremendous fun. And her maid.'

'Her maid? My, my, Mr Herbert, that sounds very intriguing. Are you going to tell?'

'There's nothing I *can* tell,' answered William swiftly.

'Did she give you a present?'

'Yes, she did. In a way.'

'How d'you mean, "in a way"? Either she did or she didn't.'

'She sort of gave me something to remember her by.'

'A secret?'

'Very much so.'

'I won't ask you, then.'

'Don't.'

'The party looks like it's going to be just fabulous,' she said. 'They've been really kind to me here, Mr and Mrs Ferber. D'you know, Mr Herbert, there would have been *nowhere* for me to go at Christmas, nowhere at all, if I hadn't been invited here. Can you imagine having nowhere to go at Christmas?'

'I can,' said William.

She said: 'My folks have gone to Cambodia.'

'That's a funny place to go for Christmas.'

'Sometimes I just can't guess if you're joking or if you're serious.'

'I'm serious. It does seem a funny place to go.'

'They didn't go only for Christmas. They're just trying to get peace settled somewhere on earth. I don't know how they're going to manage that because they're always hollering at each other. But they get these ideas. It amuses them.'

'Will you be here until you go back to Southwelling?'

She shrugged gently. 'No, that's just the very worst of it. I have this aunt, this pretty-dead aunt, and she's in London and she wants me to go and stay. I guess I'll have to go.'

'I'm going to walk back,' he said. 'To Southwelling. It's very good for you, this walking. Excellent for tennis.'

'That's a long, long way.' She shook her head. 'How long will it take?'

'To be truthful, if I get tired, or it starts to rain, I just get on a bus. So I think I'll be there in a week. It will give me another week to get the courts and the equipment ready for the beginning of term.'

Suddenly, girlishly, she said: 'Tell me about the adventures you've had. All the things that have happened since you left the school.'

William swallowed. Her face was open and interested.

He laughed uncertainly. 'There wasn't very much,' he said. 'I met a man with wooden legs, real, genuine wooden legs, like the ones you see in the pictures of old sailors. He was a sailor. He was called Wheelbarrow Williams.'

'No!'

'Yes. Wheelbarrow Williams. You see – because his legs . . .'

'Certainly!' she exploded. 'Because they projected out when he was sitting down!'

'That's right. They stuck out. Do they have wooden legs like that in America? I wouldn't have thought they were very modern legs.'

'Nowhere! Nowhere in the world! Tell me more.'

He found himself embroidering the story of his Christmas sailors, how carefree he had been, how they had called him Antwerp and he had accepted it and been Antwerp for a while. And how he had gone to the hotel and found the firemen looking for him beneath the floorboards. It seemed that he had never before talked to anyone for so long, and with such enthusiasm.

She bent towards him, listening with all the eagerness of a young girl, her hands at her mouth. When he told her about Mrs Lilley and the floorboards she shouted with laughter.

'William! Oh, William, what a fabulous thing! Imagine them getting the fire cart! And where was your actress while all this was happening?'

'Oh, her. She was resting.'

'Tired, huh?'

'No. But she had to start in what we call a pantomime – a Christmas show – the next day.'

They sat, not awkwardly, but unspeaking, for a few moments. Then she said: 'It's time I left. I have to call Verney. You saw him this afternoon. We came in together.'

'Yes, I saw him.'

'That's Verney,' she said.

'He looks like a Verney,' mumbled William. 'He's coming to the party, of course.'

'Oh, of course. He's my date. I'm not crazy about that long scarf he wears.'

William nodded: 'I didn't go a lot on that myself.'

'Anyway, he's *it*. My date. Is Mrs Ferber getting your room prepared?'

'Yes, that's why I'm waiting.'

'Well, I'll be seeing you. Try to get something else to put on your feet. Then maybe we could have a dance.'

'I'll come barefoot,' said William.

He should never have telephoned the hospital during the party. It was the foolish drink again. During that few weeks, it seemed to him, he had become a sherry addict. Hooked on Bristol Cream, he told himself bitterly. Or that Cyprus stuff, the pale friend that led him astray. There it was, looking with its appealing limp eye from his glass and the next moment he was doing something ridiculous.

They gave him a lot of sherry at the party. There were at least seventy guests and William, established in one corner by the telephone, thought each one must have been instructed upon entry to ply him with as much sherry as possible. It came to his hand in all its sunlit shades.

'William,' invited Mr Ferber hospitably, 'have a schooner. Keen on a drop of sherry, aren't you?'

William, who had already drunk seven, said: 'Ha! A schooner!

Sailed before the mast, you know, Mr Ferber. Antwerp Herbert, I was called.'

The twins leaned, hands on knees, each side of their father. They looked with their indulgent and mocking eyes at William, wearing one of their father's shirts, which gripped tight at his Adam's apple, one of his suits with the middle jacket button undone and the zip fly jammed irrevocably three-quarters up its climb, and a pair of patent-leather dancing pumps from the nineteen-thirties which bit vengefully at his feet like a pair of small hunting dogs.

Connie came to the chair. Young Connie in a white trouser suit and her hair coiled up like a finely baked harvest loaf. 'May a mere pupil dance with a member of the staff?' She curtsied and William jolted from his chair, heavy with sherry, and sudden uncoordinated happiness, and went with her towards the glad people and the lively music. She danced a yard away from him, moving like a girl from a Balinese temple, her hands following the pattern of her body, her body the guidance of her feet. But her face was separate from the dance, as though set in its own frame, serene and removed as ever. He felt, however, that her smile was possibly for him.

'You make such little steps,' she said.

'It's the shoes,' he nodded down. 'I can't do this modern sort of stuff anyway. I'm a bit of a fox-trot specialist myself. But these shoes are like mousetraps, especially after walking for a week.'

She gave a brief laugh. 'The necktie looks as though it's just attacked you.'

'That as well. It's like a damn python.' He felt well and proud to be dancing with her. He could almost keep with the music and he didn't mind all the close people. 'Feet and neck. I think they're trying to get me both ends,' he said. 'But I don't care. It's the New Year in a couple of hours. Everything will be all right then.'

'For you?' she asked.

'For you, too,' he said. She looked away from him, so he added: 'For everybody.' She continued her solo dance while he paddled his feet.

'Where's your rugger-bugger?' he inquired amiably.

'Mr Herbert!' She admonished him quietly with no seriousness. The white suit continued to move before him until the music ran out. Then she touched his hand as though she were really sorry and said she was going to find her rugger-bugger. William went back to his corner chair. His sherry glasses were arrayed in a long line on the telephone table at his arm like the keyboard of an antique musical instrument. The twins approached him together and produced a bottle. He selected a glass and they poured.

'Cyprus sherry,' said Tina.

'The Revenge of Archbishop Makarios,' intoned William. 'Bet you don't remember him, do you?' They shook their heads together. 'We're only fifteen,' said Tina.

All the sherry tasted the same to William now. He put the glass alongside the others. Claire said it looked like the test-tubes and the retorts at the science laboratory at Southwelling. William squinted at the lined glasses, then looked into the crowded party and picked out the leg and one slim arm of the white trouser suit. Verney had his arm about her.

William said thoughtfully: 'I've got to make an urgent phone call. Nobody will mind, will they?'

Tina pushed the instrument along the table to him. 'Is it private?' asked Claire.

'Very,' he leered unconvincingly.

'To your actress? You want to wish her all the best for the New Year?'

'Almost right,' agreed William. They went into the crowd, holding hands, and William felt in the pocket of Mr Ferber's suit for the telephone number of the hospital.

He grunted, poured himself another pale sherry, and left it on the table while he winced his way upstairs in Mr Ferber's spiteful dancing pumps. He found his special-clinic card in his anorak.

Returning to the chair and the table he heavily dialled the London number. He lifted his long glass and studied the column of liquid with a narrow hospital squint. 'Clear as anyone's,' he muttered with a minor swagger of the shoulders.

The hospital operator answered.

'Special clinic,' William grunted.

'Closed. I'm sorry. Opens nine tomorrow. Won't it keep?'

'No, it won't!' snarled William. 'You always say that. Give me a doctor. Let me speak to a doctor. Get one of them on his bleeper.'

'It's New Year's Eve,' sighed the operator.

'Christ,' said William, whispering angrily very close to the mouthpiece. 'Does the entire medical profession pack up every time there's something to celebrate? Get me a doctor – I don't care if it's Michaelmas or bloody muck-spreading. You *do* have a doctor somewhere, don't you?'

'Just a moment. I'll put you through.'

William nodded his head with a small jerk of savage satisfaction as he heard the click on the line. The phone was picked up again and a voice bellowed: 'What d'you want?'

William hurriedly withdrew his ear. Then he advanced on the mouthpiece. 'A damn doctor,' he said emphatically. 'That's what I want.' He could hear music and shouting going on in the background, quite distant and separate from the sounds of the company around him.

'Go to bed and keep warm!' shouted the man.

'Rubbish,' threatened William. 'You've got an orgy going on! I shall report this to the newspapers. I'll have the *Daily Mirror* around there in a bloody trice.'

'Look old boy,' said the voice more patiently. 'What is it?'

'I want the result of my blood test from the special clinic, that's all,' whispered William immediately pleading. 'Be a friend, will you?'

He could hear the man howl coarsely at the other end and then call to the others to come and listen to this. He heard the distant stampede towards the receiver.

'All right,' said William. 'Make a great big joke of it. I don't give a damn. All I want to know is whether I've got it or I haven't. I don't want to go into a nice brand-new year with a dose of syphilis. That's reasonable, isn't it?' He went nearer the phone. 'Listen,' he pleaded, 'I'm at this party and I've got a whacking great red-head sprawled across a bed upstairs. But I can't move until I'm sure whether I'm okay. Don't you understand that?'

'You're a sportsman,' the voice said with a drunken attempt

at being sober. 'Sportsman of the Year, that's you. Fear not, sir. I myself will unlock the special clinic and have a look at the diagnosis. What was the number they gave you, and what's your name?'

'Herbert,' breathed William. 'That's the surname. W. Herbert. And the number is 994,381. It's on the card here. No, it's not the telephone number, nor the date. It's my special-clinic number. H-E-R-B-E-R-T. That's right. And thank you very much.'

'What's your phone number there?' said the man. 'It'll take a few minutes so we'll call you back.'

That was the first moment that William thought something could possibly go wrong. But he gave them the number. 'I'll stay by the phone,' he promised.

He would remain there, he resolved, as immovable as a faithful guard dog until they came back with his news. To be honest it was not hurting him any more. It was probably nothing more than a scratch from Blanche's fingernail. He had been blaming good old Blanche and Babsy for nothing. But he would wait. He would be sure.

Again he raised the sherry glass and examined the elongated pond. First one eye, then the other; against the light, away from the light.

'The examination of an expert.'

William lowered the glass guiltily. Then he smiled at the woman. She was elderly, puffy, and beaming. The New Year lights shone festively on her white hair.

'Not really,' replied William modestly. 'Merely examining the texture. Always have a glance at that.'

'The sailor is always the expert at everything,' she nodded. 'They tell me you sailed before the mast.'

'On and off,' he smiled thinly.

'My late husband was one of the Cape Horners. Yes, one of the good old Horners.'

'Remarkable,' said William. 'Was he good to you?'

'What a strange thing to say. Treated me well, I must admit. Very well. Where did your voyages take you?'

'Antwerp,' volunteered William. 'That sort of place.'

'Oh,' said the lady, the smile flooding away. 'Not the Horn?'

'No, not the Horn. Not yet.' He kept switching his eyes to the telephone. How long they were taking to come back. Suppose they didn't. Suppose that was merely to put him off while they continued their party. No, they wouldn't do that. They had called him a sportsman, after all. Then he saw Connie separating from the crowd and coming towards him.

The old lady nodded pleasantly at Connie. 'Home is the sailor,' she incanted. 'Home from the sea.' She tottered off. Connie regarded the crouching William.

'Why are you stuck away in that corner, Mr Herbert?' She turned her head to one side and regarded him. 'Are they *all* your glasses?'

'No,' William shook his head. 'I'm testing the drinks for everybody else.'

She smiled. 'Maybe you ought to test your feet again,' she suggested. 'I'll have to go just after midnight because Verney has a big day tomorrow.'

'What's that? His big day?' He was trying to remain in the seat by the telephone for as long as he could. She was holding out her slim arms for him.

'Some football game,' she shrugged.

'I thought perhaps his mother was going to knit him another scarf. Anyway, why do you have to go? You live here.'

She giggled. 'I'm staying with Verney's folks tonight, because the Ferbers have so many people staying overnight. Are you going to dance with me?'

He still kept to the seat, but her young hands touched his on the arms of the chair and she brought him to his feet. They danced, close this time and slowly.

'Can we stay more or less in this vicinity?' he asked. 'I'd like to be near the blower – the telephone.'

'Sure,' she said. He was aware of the feel of her touching him all the way up his body except for the area of no-man's-land around their stomachs and immediately below. Her smell, the softness of her breasts lying against him and the brushing touch of her ear, which he thought was probably accidental, brought a gigantic feeling of indigestion to his body.

'Is it your actress?'

'Who?'

'The person who's calling.'

'Oh, no. Not really.'

'Is it a message from her?'

'You could say that.'

'Wishing you a Happy and a Healthy New Year?'

'Yes, you could say that, too.'

They danced in tight, slow, whirls, William watching the white fist of the telephone receiver at every turn. He felt Connie stiffen.

She said: 'I guess she must be chic.'

'She's all right,' nodded William.

'You're getting pretty up-tight about somebody who is just "all right".'

Mrs Ferber, dazzling in a fat, silver trouser suit, gained the centre of the floor like a popular and colourful wrestler lumbering into the ring. 'A game!' she hooted. 'We're all going to have a game! Two teams. Form up in two lines, Indian file. Come on everyone!'

'Oh, crazy,' said Connie softly. She was holding William's willing and yet unwilling hand. 'You stand behind me, William. Ah, there's Verney. He can stand in front.'

Backing away like a nervous horse, William said: 'I'm better in my own corner there. I'm hopeless at games. Really, Connie.'

'A tennis coach, hopeless at games!' Connie laughed. She tightened her grip and pulled him. He knew the telephone would ring at any moment. He could not allow anyone else to answer it.

'I'd honestly and truly prefer to sit down,' he insisted, trying to be calm. Mrs Ferber was pushing him fussily into line behind Connie. 'For Christsake,' he kept protesting at a mutter through closed teeth. 'For Christsake.'

'For nobody's sake,' said Connie coolly, half turning around. 'You join in and feel free to enjoy yourself. Forget your actress. Forget the call.'

'Now everybody!' encouraged Mrs Ferber. 'This is an absolutely marvellous bit of fun. We have two lengths of tape – two long lengths – here they are, and to each of these ends we are tying a teaspoon . . .'

William watched in prophetic misery. He could see what they

were going to do. But Connie was trailing her left hand behind her like a short tail and she lightly held his fingers. Her piled hair was like a splendid cushion just at his chin. Cautiously he moved forward a fraction and touched the hair with the point of his nose. But very lightly, so she would not notice it.

He felt an awesome inevitability as he watched the silvered Mrs Ferber ritually tying a teaspoon to the end of the long tape which was to be his team's. Never had he seen the game performed, but he could hear Fate sniggering close to his ear. Once more he shiftily tried to move from the expectant line, crouching a little as he shuffled to the side. Connie, who was looking towards Mrs Ferber with what he thought was childish excitement, was not so occupied that she failed to see his attempted escape. Her hand darted after him, brushed against his leg and captured him, second attempt, at the fingers again. He realized that he had pushed his hand towards her automatically to prevent her probing fingers touching him anywhere else.

'Hold it, William,' she whispered, without turning around, meaning both the hand and his escape. He obeyed and, hunched like an uncertain tortoise, he moved back into the line again. Mrs Ferber was explaining.

'Now the gentleman at the front puts the spoon down the front of his trousers ... Stop it now! Cease! No unseemly laughter ... Hoo ... hoooo ... down the front, yes, Mrs Reynolds, that's correct ... and then, of course, the tape follows – and whoops. Out of the bottom of his trouser leg comes the spoon. The lady behind picks it up and puts it down the front of her dress or her blouse – or whatever – and wriggles it down until the tape comes out at the hem. Yes, Beatrice ... right down the front, dear ...'

'For Christsake,' mumbled William. They were all jolting about him like children, brimming with anticipation and party delight.

'Then,' gurgled Mrs Ferber. 'The gentleman behind the lady picks up the spoon and ...'

'PUTS IT DOWN HIS TROUSERS!' they all shouted hideously.

'Exactly,' beamed Mrs Ferber. 'And then the lady, and so on, to the end of the line. The members at the end of each team must rush around with the tape and tie up all the members of his team in a nice neat parcel. The first team home is the winner.'

Connie turned to him slowly. 'This,' she announced quietly, 'looks like it could escalate.'

'Only the English could start an orgy with a teaspoon,' said William. 'I don't *want* to play. That call will be coming through. How the hell can I answer it with a spoon and three feet of tape dangling inside my tousers?'

Connie put her hand over her mouth, a gesture completely girlish, and her eyes laughed at him. 'You've got to stay, Mr Herbert. Nobody will *love* you if you don't stay.'

He looked at her quickly when she said that, but she had turned away again and was giggling over Verney's shoulder in front of her. Verney was half bent as though tensed for a scrum or a heavy tackle. Mrs Ferber shouted: 'They're off!' and the game began. Hysterical laughter hooted from the front of the teams, shouting and jumping up and down under the party decorations. William stood in morose and helpless anticipation. Once more he tried to sidle out, but this time Mrs Ferber, parading like a ringmaster before performing seals, rammed him unceremoniously back into line with a powerful thrust of her fat silvery arm. 'No, you don't, Mr Herbert,' she bellowed. 'No, you jolly well don't!'

Verney had gained the spoon and the attached tape now and had vigorously forced it down the front of his trousers. He wriggled like a muscular young elephant and Connie squealed as the spoon appeared from his trouser leg. She crouched and picked it up and Verney and the others to the fore leaped and squawked as the tape ran along between their outer and inner garments.

William watched Connie with a sort of mesmerized misery. He realized that his hands were shaking. She had put the spoon down the front of the tunic of her trouser suit and was wriggling with enchanting violence within touching distance of his trembling fingers. The white material she wore quivered as her tall body moved. Then the spoon dropped from the flared trouser leg.

'Mr Herbert!' The order came from Mrs Ferber. She gave him another push with her butcher's hand, and he dropped

135

down and bashfully picked up the spoon. How warm it was from Connie.

'Down your trucks, Mr Herbert! Down your trucks!' Mrs Ferber bawled. All confusion, William put the spoon into his trousers and felt it fall like the clapper of a bell down to his groin.

'Wriggle!' All the team were shouting. 'Wriggle, Mr Herbert!'

He wriggled and fed more tape into his trousers, the spoon descended the right leg and he felt it grabbed by the woman behind him. Like a sailor pulling a hawser she tugged at the spoon and William jumped at the speed of the tape travelling down his trousers. The woman, throbbing with sweat and excitement, tugged violently and uncaringly, and all the team, from William to the man at the front, bobbed like buoys on a line as the tape travelled sharply on.

The tape had reached the ultimate member of William's team, which was leading in the race, when the telephone rang. William gave a little ashen cry and tried to get out of the line to reach the receiver.

'It's for me! My call!' he whimpered as he tried to break from the game. His attempt at exit resulted in the tape being pulled tightly down the trousers and dresses of those on either side of him. Connie sat down heavily and the throbbing woman behind William screamed and tipped forward. He still tried to get out. The tape in his trousers went as taut as a tuna line, each time he lunged out so he was angrily pulled back by his team mates.

'*For Christsake*!' William thundered. 'Let me out! It's for me. The call's for me!'

Someone had picked up the receiver a few yards away and he fell into a blind panic at what they might be hearing. '*Get off*!' he called violently as Mrs Ferber tried to push him back into formation. 'Scissors! Get some scissors!'

He kept lunging out of the line and being pulled and tugged back again. Connie was rolling on the floor and Verney had fortuitously fallen across her. The throbbing woman was on her knees, scrabbling about as though she had dropped something from her purse. The entire team, all hooked on the long, tight tape, were disarrayed. Shouts came vaguely to him. 'Steady on!' 'Dammit, look here, old boy!' He heard their blame as the tightness of the tape on his trousers pulled him forwards and he sank pitifully on his knees in the centre of the other fallen. The other team were exultantly being tied up by their last man and they leaped in the air as they claimed their victory.

William's team were now all sitting on the floor panting in their line like a beaten boat-race crew. He glanced at Connie and could see she was laughing wickedly inside. The others observed him balefully.

'The telephone,' William explained pathetically as he looked at them. 'It was ringing – for me.'

'It *was* for Mr Herbert, most certainly.' The woman whose husband had been a Cape Horner strode firmly through the debris of the game. 'A very nice lady called you, Mr Herbert – with a lovely little poem.'

'A poem!' Mrs Ferber came forward like an armoured knight. 'How absolutely romantic!'

'No,' pleaded William. 'No, please.'

'Mr Herbert,' she said laughing at him and threateningly waving her doughy finger. 'You have scuppered the game, and so we must read the poem. Fair is fair – right everybody?'

'Right!' they called at once. 'Fair is fair!'

'Dear God,' mumbled William to himself. He looked and saw Connie staring at him strangely. 'Oh, dear God.'

Mrs Ferber had gained the piece of paper from Mrs Cape Horner's hand. 'How odd!' she beamed. 'How very intriguing.' Then: 'Here it is, everybody.'

William crouched like some wild creature trapped among a warrior tribe while she read from the paper. He seemed to hear the words from miles away:

> *'A Happy New Year,*
> *We wish you today.*
> *Please tell Mr Herbert*
> *His sherbert's*
> *Okay!'*

After they had welcomed the year, Connie left with Verney. 'That was a cute poem,' she said to William who was sitting on the stairs. 'Was it in code?'

'Yes, in code,' he replied. She had put on a warm cape and a hood with a rim of fur. Verney was starting his sports car.

'Did you get the message?' she asked.

'Yes, I got it, thanks very much.'

'I'm real glad. Goodnight, William. Happy New Year.'

'Happy New Year, Connie.'

24

'OH, RUFUS! It's you. You gave me a bit of a start opening the cell door like that.'

'Like what?'

'Suddenly. I didn't hear you. I just felt the draught.'

'I see. I only popped in, Bill. I won't be coming to work today. I'm taking the wife out. It's her birthday.'

'Fine, Rufus, fine. Wish her all the best from me. I'd better take the day off, too, I suppose.'

'You haven't got a lot of choice. Anyway, have a good day.'

'And you, Rufus. Tomorrow?'

'Yes . . . Oh, Bill . . .'

'Yes?'

'Have you and old Decent thought up a defence?'

'A defence?'

'Yes.'

'No . . . not really. He keeps asking me about my mother and father.'

'I think you'll need to think of something better than that. Don't tell him I said so, but you will.'

'Thanks for the suggestion, Rufus, I'll try and think of something.'

25

HE BEGAN walking south again on New Year's Day; a mild morning with mixed cloud and some quiet January birds squatting in the turned fields. In the distance, as he took the winter road, the helpful sun turned a silver light on to the remote rising countryside. It beckoned him hopefully. In imagination he decided that the distant sunlit places would lie under sudden and miraculous summer when he arrived. Winter would immediately be gone. The grass would be full and the trees fat; there would be soft places of tar on the road, and the air warm against his face. Perhaps a party of schoolgirls would be out picking wildflowers in their cotton print dresses. He looked up guiltily from his thought and saw at once the Midland spire of a church held straight like an admonishing finger. He quickly transformed the schoolgirls into old-age pensioners.

But there would be a girl with them. Just one. He would allow that. And not all that good-looking, either. She would be a calm young girl, as Connie was so calm, but not as slim and elegant as Connie, not so composed. Connie had so much of a woman about her. But this girl with the old people would be about fourteen. Perhaps she would have a July straw hat and her fair hair would show underneath its rim and brim; and a print dress, of course. A blue and white print dress, such as they wore in the hot days, with a belt of the same material, and ankle socks and single-button shoes. The dress would have its hem just over her fat knees and her legs would be a bit chubby and have some light hair, like down on them. Her arms would be brown from the long days of sun and the games she had played under it. Her eyes would be blue and inquisitive, laughing, excited, trusting and unknowing. Were there girls like that? Of course. They didn't all fix condoms on to innocent men's motorized bicycles. She would know of nothing like that. Her talk would sometimes be solemn and sometimes silly. Sometimes she would blush and occasionally cry. He could not imagine Connie crying. She would be very kind to the old-age pensioners picking the flowers from the banks. She would make pretty hats for the ancient women and let the wrinkled gentlemen pinch her and pat her bulky buttocks. She would be a kind girl.

A blue lorry, its broad back empty except for some tarpaulins blowing like a mane as it travelled, went by him and stopped a hundred years beyond.

William was thinking of the girl he had made and her skinny herd of elderly people. He hardly noticed the lorry until he was alongside its cab. The driver was leaning on his door like a farmer across a gate.

'Thought you'd never get 'ere,' said the driver. 'Want a lift?'

William blinked. The girl and the ancients vanished. 'Thanks very much,' he returned vaguely. 'How far do you go?'

'Oxford,' said the driver. 'Any good?'

'Yes, thanks very much.'

He climbed into the cab. It was like a small room with a curtain at the back and a little bunk where the driver could sleep. There was a teapot and a kettle and a small oil lamp, a pile of paperbacks, and a transistor radio.

'All modern cons,' said William.

'Believe in it,' said the driver. 'Like a snail, me. Carry me house with me. Every comfort. I've even 'ad a bird in that bunk, and she wasn't no lightweight, either.'

He was a young, rough man, bulldog-faced, fat-armed, with a complexion like red pepper. 'Giving lifts,' he said. 'Funny business. Always risky, but full of interest. You never know who you'll get. Take you, for instance. How do I know I'm safe with you?'

'You're safe with me,' William assured him.

'You could murder me.'

'I won't.'

'I'm not saying you *will*, mate, but you could. Some of the boys won't give lifts. But I like to take a chance. I had a clergyman once what had been kicked out of his work for putting a beef sausage in a choir lad's hand. He reckoned he only did it as a joke; came up behind the boy and did it. But he got chucked out for it and I reckon they did quite right. I reckon he was definitely a bit on the turn. Definitely. Then there was this dirty old man, he must have been seventy, who kept on about all the goings-on in the old folks' home where he lodged. Do you realize that if you ever get put into an institution like that you'll find that there are about six old birds to every one old boy. It's because us blokes nearly always pop off first, so there's a lot of old dears left over. An old chap in one of them 'omes could be in paradise providin', of course, that he's kept his health and strength.

'Mind you, he was a dirty old pig. What he said he did to some of them in the local pictures. You know they get in very cheap in the afternoons, the pensioners, and he used to have a right fine old time. He reckoned that he always took his bowler hat with him and took his sexual tool out under cover of the hat. How about that! And then he used to lean over to the old dear, whichever one he was with, and tell 'er if she wanted it then it was under his bowler.'

The young man bellowed with laughter at the memory. 'Sat right there, where you are now, and told me it all. Enjoyed telling me too, the old hog. He said there wasn't much point in doing these things if you had to keep it to yourself.'

'He didn't believe in keeping it under his hat,' said William.

'No, he didn't . . . Hey, that's funny! Under 'is hat!'

They drove on through the dun-coloured country. A handful of rain was thrown against the windscreen of the cab. The young man grunted and switched the wipers on for a moment to disperse it. It was a timid shower and they were soon through it.

'Lovely this time of the year,' said the driver. 'Everywhere's fabulous and clear, especially the road. That's what I like.' He paused and sniffed as though savouring the highway. 'You been hiking, then?' he asked eventually.

'In a way,' said William soberly. 'Keeps me fit.'

'Where you heading?'

'Southwelling, Sussex.'

'What will you do when you get there?'

'I'm a master at a school.'

'Oh, a teacher. What's it you teach?'

'Sports.'

'Thought you looked in good trim. What is it – football?'

'Tennis,' said William. 'It's a girls' school.'

141

The driver did not take his eyes from over his wheel. He seemed to be trying to think of the road. But a prolonged nasal whistle escaped from him.

'Gawd,' he murmured. 'That can't be bad.'

'It's all right.'

'I bet you don't half have yourself a time.'

'How do you mean?'

'Well, come on. *You* know. Don't you?'

'They're children,' said William huffily. 'The oldest is only sixteen.'

The driver seemed to be smiling like the man smiles at the prospect of something he knows he can never attain. He put the windscreen wipers on again as they ran through another shower and moved his head dreamily back and forwards in time with them. He gave a little kiss at the top of each stroke, right, then left, then right again.

'Only sixteen,' he said. 'They ain't children at *fourteen* these days, mate.'

'These are,' said William stoutly.

'Well maybe they're high class. I suppose they would be, going to a school with a tennis master. But generally speaking they ain't. I'll tell you something – and it's the dead truth, too. About a month ago, I picked up these couple of kids just outside Altrincham. Boy and girl. Still in their school gear, the pair of them. Shouldn't have done it normally, I suppose, but it was tipping down and they were trying to shelter under one coat. They said they was going to the girl's aunty's about twenty miles from there at Fellington. So they got in the cab, but on the way I stopped for my dinner at a café and they said they'd stay in the cab. I've got that little transistor and I said they could have it on.

'Have it on! They was having it *off* when I got back!'

'Never,' said William.

'I mean right there. On that bunk back there.'

'What did you do?'

'I stood and watched,' said the driver soberly. 'I was going to chuck them out. But I watched instead. She could have only been fourteen and she had her leg dangling over the side of the bunk and her pants around one knee. He wasn't much older.

God believe me, he had muddy football shorts under his trousers and he'd pulled them down and he was giving it to her good and she was loving it. They looked strange, I can tell you. Ever so strange. Tell you the truth, I was a bit frightened. Funny feeling, really, but I didn't dare go in.'

He stopped the wipers because the rain had flown over again. He kept shaking his large doggy head. 'It was marvellous to watch. I've never watched anybody doing it before, let alone a couple of nippers. Marvellous. You could tell it was so bloody enjoyable for them. When he came, she laughed like mad. I could see her laughing through the window. And her leg was going back and fore like a pendulum. Afterwards I couldn't help thinking to myself that I didn't enjoy it my first time nearly as much as that. I was nineteen and I was in the Army at the time, and I'd paid for it. That's how most blokes seemed to get their first shags in those days. It's different now, ain't it. Looking at them made me think I'd started much too late. You know I was most impressed with those kids. Laughing all the time! I'd never thought of it as anything to laugh about. I couldn't disturb them. I didn't have the heart. I left them to it and went back to the café. Quite honestly, I didn't know whether to have a wank or a sausage roll and a cup of tea.'

26

HE SAW Southwelling as, after four days, he left the road and walked down through the black rheumaticky trees and on to the forehead of the rise that overlooked the school. It was comforting to know it was still there. He was glad he had decided to return.

Red-bricked, it looked so hale, permanent in the faded fields; afternoon lights amber in two small windows, and a dab of smoke hanging about one of the old corkscrew chimneys. Its roads ran out through the grounds to the perimeter like sprawled limbs. The river, he could see, was gorged with winter rain and the outdoor tennis courts had big dull plates of water on their surfaces. He sighed gratefully that at last he was home and his journey was accomplished. He still had fifty pounds of his wages. It had been a cheap Christmas.

Now he would go down, light the fire in his own room, tidy up a bit, have a look at the indoor court and the equipment, and sit that evening with the television.

He moved one foot forward to descend the path that joined with the school road on the flat ground. Then he paused, for a bicycle had run around the ash trees by the main quadrangle and was travelling towards him down the long right extension of the road.

Miss Smallwood did not ride a bicycle as far as he knew. Miss de Berenger and Miss Whitefriar, the science mistress, did but they would not have returned yet nor would the other teachers. It was still a week to the beginning of the term. It might be one of the domestics. But he knew it was not. He moved the second step down the slope and then continued until he had reached the level. The bicycle rider was coming fast through the spaced trees of the avenue, where the road yawned out into a long bend. He could see her riding, appearing, vanishing, reappearing, like a picture in an old cinematograph show. He stopped and waited. There was now no doubt or mystery about her. She was wearing grey trousers and a bright blue sweater. Her hair flowed as she pedalled. She rounded the last of the curve and came clear of the parade of trees. Then the cycle wobbled as she slowed towards him.

'Did you guess?' she laughed.

'I had more or less a good idea it was you,' he answered carefully. Only Connie could look as she looked then on that vacant January afternoon. She dismounted the bicycle and turned it in the road. They began to walk towards the school.

'You walked a long way very quickly,' she said.

'I didn't walk all the way,' he admitted. 'I didn't *have* to walk, you know. There were no rules and I won't lose my amateur status. So I had a lift or two and I took a couple of bus rides, too. I was only on my feet for part of the way.'

'I was *so* surprised to see you. I calculated that Wednesday would be the earliest you'd make it.' She was silent, expecting him to say something, but he remained quiet. 'Don't you want to know why I am back early, also?' she asked.

'I was trying to work that out, Connie. What happened to the aunt in London?'

'Well, I guess she and I didn't really get on too well. So I quit. I told her I was coming back to school and she sure looked relieved.'

'Miss Smallwood is back, of course,' he said casually.

'Sure. She was really pleased to see me. This place is a little heebie-jeebie when there's no one around. We had dinner together last night in the big hall. It was real strange just the two of us there and nobody else. Now, there'll be three for tonight.'

'More staff than pupils,' he laughed unsurely. They walked on around the wide armful of trees. Some steely sunlight broke the clouds and projected thin shadows over the road before like the rungs of an old worn ladder.

'It's so quiet,' she said. 'You wouldn't think it could be *that* quiet here. Without all the voices. I heard some crows outside the dormitory window this morning. They were having a real big quarrel in the trees. I've never heard them before because of all the noise that normally goes on.'

'Did you mind sleeping alone in the dormitory?' he asked.

'Not really. It was a little scarey at first, but I sang a few songs. Like *God Bless America*, *Yankee-Doodle* and *We Shall Overcome*. Loud songs. I felt okay after that.'

They were nearing the rosy buildings now. The trees were opening out to show the long lawn and the terraces, cut and subdued at this time of the year. The air was mild but darkening.

'Connie,' he said. 'Perhaps I could ask you a favour.'

She continued walking, looking straight ahead, but she slowed a little.

'I understand,' she said. 'You don't want Miss Smallwood to know you were in Derby over the New Year.'

'That's more or less it,' he mumbled.

'Only more or less?'

'If it were possible, and in this place I very much doubt if it is, I would prefer everything that happened up there to be kept quiet.'

'Okay,' she said easily. 'Nobody will know. If I tell the twins to forget it, they'll forget it.'

'Thank you.'

'It's nothing.'

'Connie ... was anything said up at Derby – we say it *Darby*, by the way, not *Derby* like you say it in America?'

'I know that already, Mr Herbert. It just takes a little getting used to, that's all.'

He was relieved that she still called him Mr Herbert. 'What did they think?' he repeated.

'At Derby?' she said, continuing to pronounce it her way. 'Well, what did they say? Not a whole lot. They just think you're crazy and funny, like I do. Gee, when you got caught up with that tape and the phone was ringing. Oh boy, Mr Herbert, there's been nothing like that since the Golden Oldies.'

'What's that? The Golden Oldies?'

'The old movies. The silents.'

'Thanks. So I was like Harold Lloyd or Ben Turpin.'

'You were terrific. You always look so darned serious.'

'I was *serious*. So would anyone have been in those circumstances.'

'It was an important call, huh?'

'Important to me.'

'Some of those people really thought it was all an act. Truly. They wanted you to go and do the same things at their parties. Mrs Ferber said you were not available.'

'Well done Mrs Ferber,' he breathed. 'My God, you'd think I was a Punch and Judy man. Nobody in this world is more serious than I am, and with good cause, believe me. I have some very serious things happening to me. All the time.'

27

THIS WAS the occasion when you first had sexual intercourse
... relations ... with Connie? ...'

'Pardon, Rufus?'

'For God's sake. This was the time when it all really started,
wasn't it? The time when you first screwed this girl, before you
screwed the others?'

'Rufus!'

'Well, was it?'

'Yes, I suppose it was, Rufus. But what's happened to you?
That's not a very pleasant way to put it, is it? You were all
right yesterday, going off to take the wife out on her birthday ...
Oh, is that it? Trouble at home, eh?'

'Do you want me to tug your hooter, Bill?'

'No. You know I don't.'

'In that case, let's get on with it. Never mind about *my*
problems. You're the boy with *real* problems. There's a big
high wall staring you in the face. And written on it in bloody
great letters is "Ten Years".'

'Don't remind me of that, Rufus. Have a morsel of thought.
Don't you think I *know* ... there, you're making me cry like a
little kid now. But surely ... You realize? ...'

'Wipe your eyes. Stop booing or I'll give your nose a nasty
pull. That's right. Have you got a handkerchief?'

'They take it away from you with the bootlaces and your
belt. How anyone but a genius or a gymnast could commit
suicide with a handkerchief defeats me. It doesn't prevent you
killing yourself, it only stops you wiping your eyes. Thanks,
Rufus. That's a nice handkerchief. Your wife obviously does a
good job on them. That's better. I don't mean to cry, but,
frankly, there's not a lot for me to laugh about, is there? And,
if I sometimes seem abrupt when you ask me questions like
that, Rufus, it's because I'm a bit shaken by them. You've been
very patient, one way and another, I'll admit, but I do want to
tell you the *whole* story. Everything. It puts it in perspective.

To be truthful, I look forward to telling you *exactly* what happened. In a way, I suppose, I like hearing it all again myself; I can remember the happy things about it as well as all the other stuff.'

'All right, Bill. Now, what happened when you got back to the school? Don't let me rush you into it. Just tell me what took place during that next few days.'

'With pleasure. One thing – just one before I start telling you – how did the birthday go? How is she, by the way?'

'Who?'

'Your wife, of course . . . Myra.'

'Oh, Myra. Fine. It was a nice day out, Bill. The weather is really settled out there now. Oh, yes, everybody enjoyed it. You would have enjoyed it. Nothing fabulous; just a bit of shopping and a meal. Very modest.'

'How old did you say she is now?'

'Twenty-eight.'

'Nice age for a wife and mother.'

'Sure. Now let's get back to Southwelling in January this year. The only people who were there, apart from the domestics and the gardener, were Miss Smallwood, you and Connie. Miss Smallwood was sleeping at her cottage, I take it, and that is some distance from the school. And you were in your normal room on the ground floor and Connie was in the dormitory which is also on the ground floor.'

'They're some distance apart, of course, Rufus, and, although they called it a dormitory, really it was quite small. There were only six girls accommodated in it. They were senior girls, you see. The juniors had about twenty or more to a dorm.'

'Right. Now describe what happened on that first night back at Southwelling.'

'For a start, that evening, we had dinner in the big dining-room. It was really unusual, uncanny almost, just the three of us sitting at the top table and all the other tables bare and empty. We found it very difficult to talk normally because there were all sorts of spooky echoes in that hall that you didn't notice when the rest of the school was there. I suppose, really, it would have been far better to have our meals somewhere else. Over at Miss Smallwood's cottage, perhaps, but she was a strange woman, to say the least – what with this Gilbert and Sullivan kink and one thing and another – and she insisted on us eating in the dining-hall. Apparently even when she was by herself in the school – which quite often happened because she never took long holidays and the school was more or less like home to her – she had her meals there.

'But we found that we were conversing in hoarse whispers. That was something of a strain, too. You found yourself in two minds whether or not to ask someone to pass the cruet. Miss Smallwood didn't seem very conscious of it but she kept whispering to me, asking about the holidays and what I had been doing. I got a bit annoyed with Connie because she kept sniggering. I always felt disappointed in that girl when she behaved like . . .'

'Like a girl?'

'Yes, I suppose you're right, Rufus.'

'What happened after dinner?'

'It was a little awkward. Normally, in term time, the staff would go into the common room for coffee and have a chinwag for a while before going to their own rooms. The girls were never allowed in there, of course, but Miss Smallwood suggested that Connie should join us. That dreadful girl acted up and made out she was thrilled with the honour and that sort of nonsense. I could *see* she was doing it. Personally, I thought she over-acted it quite a bit, sort of jumping up and down like a little kid wetting her knickers with excitement. Miss Smallwood believed her, of course, and quite a ceremony was made of it. The headmistress led the way in and then Connie and I followed. And Connie went around that common room as though she were in some bloody Aladdin's cave. "Who sits here, Miss Smallwood?" And, "Who sits here, Mr Herbert?" The little bitch. Miss Smallwood fell right in, head first, of course, and went through the names of all the teachers and which chairs they sat in. It seemed to please her no end.

'We sat around for a while and had some coffee and Connie put on some records of *The Gondoliers* which thrilled Miss Smallwood. She honestly was a little bitch that evening, laughing up her sleeve the whole time. And she *could*, you know, Rufus. She laughed more inside than she did outside, as I came to realize.

'After a while I said I'd be off to my room as I wanted to watch television and I left Miss Smallwood and Connie together. I knew it would not be long before Miss Smallwood went over to her cottage and I had some stupid idea of asking Connie if she wanted to come in and watch the television with me. It was strictly against the rules, of course, and in the end I decided against it. No point in sticking my neck out.'

'Or anything else?'

'Anything else?'

'Skip it. So you watched television all on your own.'

'Yes. It just seemed a trifle pointless that three people should be inhabiting a big building right in the middle of Sussex on a winter's night – and that they were all separated from each other.'

'Why didn't you go over and keep Miss Smallwood company?'

'I didn't think of it, to be honest.'

'No. Well you wouldn't. Did Connie come to your room that night?'

'No, Rufus, of course not.'

'Don't give me this "of course not" crap, Bill. Tell me what happened. You're like a great fairy dancing around a circle of shit. Something *happened*, Bill. *Now. Tell me!*'

'No! Yeth, I willth. Oh donth, pleath. Thith is ridiculoth.'

'Right, tell me, then. I want to know about you laying that young girl.'

'I didn't! Not that night, Rufus. Christ, my nose is bleeding. Look what you've done. Fancy doing that again. Give me a hankie, will you.'

'You've still got mine, Bill. From when you were crying. You put it in your pocket. That's it. Don't worry about a bit of blood on it. It will wash off. There. It wasn't that much, was it.'

'No, it's stopped now. Thank God. It would have been a bit silly if you had needed to put a key down my neck to stop it. That's the usual way, isn't it? The only key we've got is the key to the cell! That would have been a bit of a joke. Now, *please*, Rufus, leave my nose on my face, will you. Look at the mess that hankie's in. I hope it will come off.'

'What about Connie?'

'It wasn't that night. Anyway, as far as "laying" her is concerned – as you put it – I think it was more like she "laid" me. Connie never let anybody actually lead her into anything.'

'What happened that night?'

'I just watched the television.'

'What was on? Tell me the programmes.'

'Oh, Rufus, how can I remember now. It was months ago.'

'Bill – you went up into the loft, didn't you?'

'The loft? No, honestly, I didn't go up there, Rufus. You've seen the loft, have you?'

'Oh yes. We're pretty thorough, us detectives, you know, Bill. I've been up there in the loft. The trapdoor is only ten yards from your room and there's a stepladder thing in the next small room.'

'It's not a stepladder thing. It's an umpire's chair. We use it on the tennis court in the season. In the winter it's kept in that room with all the other tennis equipment. There's nothing remarkable about that. I'm the tennis coach and that room is simply my storeroom.'

'All right, Bill. I stand corrected. It's a tennis umpire's chair. But it makes a bloody fine stepladder. I got up into the loft quite easily with that. And it's pretty quiet down at that end of the building. Nobody would see you. And you crawl carefully along the rafters and the joists and you come eventually to a wooden wall. That wall juts on to Senior Girls' Dormitory A. That was where Connie slept, wasn't it, Bill? Wasn't it? Answer me.'

'That's where Connie slept, Rufus. You're quite right. At the far end.'

'And in that wall was a hole. *Another* hole, Bill. Like the one in the soft drinks van at Midford–Pallant. You're like a little mouse sometimes, aren't you? Making holes. If Mr Herbert looked through that hole – what could Mr Herbert see?'

'The dormitory, I suppose.'

'You *know*, you don't *suppose*! And just to make things homely there is a pillow on the rafters, Bill. What was that for?'

'I don't know. It wasn't me.'

'What was it for, Bill? For resting your knees or resting something else.'

'God, that's disgusting! What are you trying to say, Rufus?'

'It's been to the forensic laboratory, that pillow has, Bill. If it was for resting your knees on then you're in real trouble, son. You've got semen coming out of your legs.'

'Shut up! Shut up you dirty copper pig! You can't speak to me like that. Rotten bastard that you are. Go on, pull my nose . . . here it is . . . oooooooooooh!'

'There. Now I've hit you. Get on your feet, Bill, and pull yourself together. One of the things they teach us police officers is the value of the surprise element. You were sticking your nose out at me and I punched you in the guts, didn't I. There, now sit on your bed. How about a game of Scrabble now, then Bill? I bet you couldn't think up many words just at the moment.'

'I want to be sick . . . Rufus . . . Move the Scrabble board from the pot . . . will you, please.'

'Oh God, Bill. You've done it now. Right in the middle of the Scrabble board. It just shows that I don't move as quickly as I did once. My goodness, that's buggered up the game a bit, hasn't it. How many points for s-i-c-k? Or s-p-e-w? That's more points, I bet.'

'Try v-o-m-i-t, Rufus.'

'That's my boy. Come up smiling.'

'Why hit me like that, Rufus? I ask you . . . was that necessary?'

'Fifty-fifty, I'd say. It was and it wasn't. Just tell me about going into the loft.'

'You'll hit me again if I don't, won't you?'

'Yes, old chap, I will.'

'Let me get my breath back.'

'Certainly. Take one, two, three, deep breaths. In through your nose – out of your mouth. That's it . . . one, two, three . . . now again . . . and another three. There, that's fixed you. Now tell me about the loft.'

'All right. I will. I did go up there that night. I admit it. All I wanted to do was to see her, that's all. Nothing dirty. I only wanted to see her in her bed. You don't know how I tried to fight it off. I was all cringed up in front of the television, just as though I had a stomach pain. I was certain I was going mad. In the end I got the umpire's chair from the room and got up into the loft.'

'You already knew where it led? You'd worked that out?'

'Yes, I had worked it out previously. But I hadn't been up there before. I'd never given in before. Never.'

'Go on.'

'But I did this time. It's no use. I've got to admit it.'

'Yes, you have. Or I'll belt you again.'

'I thought you might. I'm getting so I can read your thoughts. All right. I went up there and I lay in the dark, lying on the beams. I didn't crawl along to the wall for a long time. All I did was lie there and feel afraid and ashamed of myself. God, I was *so* ashamed.

'Then I thought, as I was up there, I might as well go and have a look. I was crawling along the beams, getting splinters in my knees, and suddenly I heard her. She was singing. Just like she had said. She was singing *We Shall Overcome* and *God Bless America* and all sorts of songs. I lay across the beams again. She was singing about *Yankee-Doodle Dandy*, something about "With the girls be handy". I knew that there would be nothing indecent in it then. Nothing wrong. I knew she was undressed and tucked in her bed. All I wanted to do was to see her – just as I told you.

'I got to the wall and there was this hole between two of the planks. It was already there. I didn't have to make it. By now I was trembling. I was terrified and excited and feeling dreadful. It was all I could do to force myself to look through the hole.

'She was sitting up in her bed at the end of the room. Her bedside lamp was on and she was brushing that beautiful hair. She had a pink winceyette nightdress, which was the school regulation nightdress. I sat and watched her while she brushed her hair and she sang all those songs. Even the Whiffenpoof song, you know, Rufus, about the poor little lambs that have gone astray.'

'I know the song.'

'And then, after some time, she put her light out and settled

153

down in her bed and I went back along the loft and climbed down and went to my room.'

'What did you do there?'

'I took the splinters out of my knees.'

'When did it happen, then?'

'You mean the sex.'

'Yes. I'm getting impatient to hear about it, Bill.'

'The next day. I didn't want it to happen. I did all I could. Please believe me, Rufus, I had a cold shower in the morning – they advise you to do that, don't they – and I put a tracksuit on and went for a long run. It was a freezing morning and I thought it might get it all out of my system. I even wrote a letter of resignation to Miss Smallwood, well half a letter, anyway. But, it all happened before I could actually get the thing finished. And after that, of course, I was really in trouble. There didn't seem any point in resigning.'

'Or you didn't want to.'

'I feel so miserable about it. But you're right, you know. If I'd cleared out right away that morning none of it would have happened, or if I hadn't gone back to the school at all. If . . . if . . . It's just a load of ifs. But, cross my heart, I had every intention of packing my bags after lunch. But I fell to the temptation of wanting to see her just once more, just once. I made the excuse to myself that I needed my lunch so that I would be stoked up with food for the rest of the day and I would just be able to get on the old phut-phut bike and drive as far away from the place as possible by nightfall.'

'Why didn't you?'

'Why didn't I, indeed, Rufus? The whole thing was sabotaged from the very first. I had my cold shower, and bloody icy it was too at that time of the year, and I was just jogging out in my tracksuit, when she called from the window and I hadn't gone half a mile before she was pounding along after me across the fields. She was wearing a bright red tracksuit and she had tied her hair in a sort of bunch behind her. I tried to be light-hearted, just normal and friendly, with her and we had a race up the slope to the road. Of course, she was fitter than me – that just had to be – and we ended up with her offering me her hand at the top of the slope.'

'And you took it?'

'No, Rufus. I wouldn't let myself touch her. She was so . . . so . . . vivid that morning. The fields and the woods were just dead and the road was empty. There was no colour in anything, not even in the sky. But she was so bright, so beautiful and alive in that red tracksuit. She seemed like a little fire. She kept laughing at nothing and in the end we slowed up a bit and walked through the trees. We were both panting by then, and she kept huh-ing, blowing out her breath, and saying we were like a couple of dragons. Truthfully, Rufus, if I hadn't been so worried I would have been deliriously happy. The whole place looked different. She kept finding spiders' webs all wet from the dew and she swung on an old branch and it cracked like a shotgun going off. Then she picked up a bit of old dry cow turd and threw it at me in fun, and started off running again wanting me to chase her.'

'And you chased her.'

'I pretended to. But I made sure I never caught up with her. She kept slowing down, but I said I was puffed out and I had to walk for a bit. Actually, it wasn't far from the truth. I'm nothing like as fit as I was when I was playing regularly. In all we must have run about three or four miles. Her hair across her forehead was sticking to her with sweat when we got back into the school grounds. I was rolling with it, all down my body. She was steamy and rosy-faced. Her eyes seemed quite pale. We walked the last couple of hundred yards and I couldn't help noticing the way the jumper of her tracksuit was sticking to her body . . . you know . . . at the top. She knew I was looking because she gave a small giggle and she pulled it away from her.'

'We went back into the school and I had a shower and went in to lunch with Miss Smallwood and Connie, and everything seemed to be all right, except I was in hell.'

'And after lunch?'

'As I said, I went back to my room to write this letter of resignation and after about twenty minutes Connie came into the room.'

'And that's when it happened?'

'Yes. That's when it happened.'

IT WAS raining against the panes of his window, hard gusts of rain, and the afternoon had become closed-in and dark. He was sitting at the desk by the window with the green table lamp switched on. She entered the room, just brushing her fingers against the door as a knock.

William looked up. She was wearing the long red skirt he had seen her wear at Derby. And the same white blouse with the delicate and beautiful sleeves to her wrists. He stood in front of the desk, in front of the notepaper so he concealed it.

'What are you doing?' she asked.

He said: 'Writing a letter.'

'To your actress?'

'To Miss Smallwood.'

'What is it?'

'My resignation.'

'Oh.'

She was standing just in front of him, looking past him out of the window. 'Would you like to go for another run?' she joked quietly.

'I think the weather has changed,' he answered. His hands were trembling. He clutched the sides of his trousers tightly with his thumbs and index fingers.

'Sure,' she said solemnly. 'It's like night out there.'

Without another word she stepped one step and pressed herself against him, her breasts and her lowered head sighing against his shirt, her hands still not touching him, just idle at her sides. He felt as though someone had thrust a sword into his body. Sickness and fear shook him and he tried to look over the soft curve of her hair to the door of his room as though it were some sort of salvation. The knowledge of her engulfed him then, overtook him. His aching arms and hands, moving like a robot's metal limbs, moved up stiffly and then lost all their resistance. He threw them around her and hugged her to him wholesomely, his cheek to her hair, feeling the great stifled desire expanding within him. Her girl's hands came up gently to him and touched his arms, lying softly against them.

He felt her move and her fragile head turned again to the window and the rain: 'It's like somebody throwing pails of water,' she murmured. 'You're not going away, are you, Mr Herbert?'

William wagged his head speechlessly. 'I think you'd better pull down that blind,' she said coolly. 'There's nothing to see out there this afternoon anyway. Pull it down, then close your eyes.'

Still not trusting himself to speak, he did as she said. He had never been able to pull the blind first time. It always stuck in the middle and he invariably had to climb on the desk to free it. It jammed now. He tugged at it angrily, then climbed up and jerked it loose. He descended, grimacing apologetically. She watched him, her amber eyes laughing.

'Now,' she said, as though it were a nursery game, 'you have to close your eyes.'

He obeyed her blindly. The room seemed very warm to his face and he knew she was moving only a few feet away from him. For a terrible moment he thought she had played a trick on him and had gone out of the door leaving him standing with his eyes shut. But she continued to be there. He could sense her smell and hear her movements.

'Open now,' she said.

He did. She was standing about three feet away looking at him quizzically. She was naked to the waist, red skirt hanging elegantly to his floor. Her warm skin, her stomach, her grown breasts; her hair lying on her shoulders; her hands idly by her sides. The light on her skin, the shadows of her body, the sureness of her face. He could not believe he was seeing her. The terrible sickness brimmed up inside him.

'Connie,' he whispered. 'Please, Connie. You're a girl at school.'

'Don't believe it,' she said quite firmly, moving up to him again. 'I'm older than you, Mr Herbert.'

Her slim arms ringed his neck and her breasts collided with his shirt. Her face was lifted towards him and his helpless hands, resigned, freed, went about her running madly up and down her long back, from the waist of her skirt to the gentle flats of her shoulderblades. He kissed her savagely, mouth, and then neck, and then her pale, sleepy nipples; and, hurriedly too, as though she would vanish in the next moment. He bent to her, collapsed, pressing his head to her small flat stomach. Her hands, at the back of his neck, stroked the bristly hairs.

On his knees, like some odd knight, he held her about the waist and she confidently pulled the zip of her red skirt and let it fall. She stepped from her shoes and her skirt at the same time, pulled her tights impatiently away from her legs, and the pink gingham pants with them.

William had risen and looked at her with stupid wonder. He stood free of her now, his eyes all over her, his pleading hands stretched out.

'You're slow,' she whispered. 'I've finished.'

'Yes, I can see,' said William. 'I won't be a minute, Connie.'

She laughed at him and took his shirt and singlet off for him. It seemed to William that the room was revolving. He tried to take his shoes off without undoing the laces. One came away after a fight, but he almost wrenched his ankle trying to tug the other loose. The lace had tightened and was biting into his instep. He pulled fiercely again. It hung on to his foot like a tenacious puppy.

'I'll need a penknife,' he said wretchedly.

'I haven't got one with me,' she said taking his fingers and running them down her naked stomach.

'There's a safety razor over there on the washbasin,' he pleaded.

'Just a moment.' She walked to the basin and came back with the razor. He began to unscrew it.

'I know what is going to happen,' he said to her. 'I'm shaking so much I'll cut a main artery with this blade and I'll ruin everything. I know I will, Connie. I always do the stupid thing.'

'Let me,' she said calmly. She took the thin blade and knelt before him at the side of his bed. She cut the lace efficiently.

'I'll put it back in the razor,' he babbled. 'I'm a bit short of blades at the moment.'

'And cut an artery?' she smiled. 'Let me put it back.' She slipped the blade into the razor and carefully screwed it together

again. She returned it to the washbasin and on her way back she pushed the bolt of the door home. She returned to him. He had taken his trousers and underpants off.

'I managed those,' he grimaced.

She looked at him. He thought that her body had gone a soft pink.

'*Someone* has been expecting me,' she said, touching him. They stretched along the bed together. He continued to let his hungry hands run all over her, her bottom and her thighs, her back and her indolent breasts. She put both her hands, the elegant hands he had so admired, between his legs and cradled him gently there.

He still could not believe that she was there. 'It hurts, you know,' he whispered.

'What hurts?' Her eyes were closed and she moved her fingers.

'You know. What we're going to do in a minute. Well, what I *think* we're going to do.'

'Why should it hurt?'

'If you're a virgin.'

'I'm not this year,' she answered, opening her eyes. 'Why don't you climb on top of me now, Mr Herbert. I have a feeling for you, darling.'

He raised himself above her. He prayed that he would not spoil it as soon as he touched her. He was as stiff and trembling as three-ply wood but she lay gently, as though sleeping. She moved her legs for him, smiling encouragement at his nervousness, brushing a thread of hair from her serene eyes. She watched him intently as he closed with her, her honey eyes fixed on his steaming face. Gradually she closed her lids, very gradually, a fraction at a time, until his mouth was against her hair, his chest to hers, and her eyes were completely shut. They moved together tenderly, all the fear gone from him, all the arrogance from her. The rain rattled the window as though it wanted to get in with them.

'It's still pouring outside,' he said.

'Tell it to go away,' she whispered.

'Clear off, rain,' he said.

'Move a little to one side, darling,' she asked him. 'To the left – ouch! – no, *your* left, crazy. That's right. And the legs go like that, one over, one under, and you hold my bottom, and we can study each other's expression.' They continued to move unhurriedly.

'You look serious,' she murmured. 'Do you have problems?'

'A few. I'll take it out before it happens.'

'That's what the English girls call Battersea Park.'

'Why Battersea Park?'

'That's the railroad station before Victoria. It's nearly the end of the journey.'

'Oh, I understand. Well, I think I'm nearly at a signal box.'

She laughed. 'Not yet. And don't worry about the last but one stop with me, honey.'

'But I *do*, Connie.'

'Don't worry. Please. It will be fine.'

His control had surprised him. He loved her so immensely; his concern, his anxiety were all for her. Her girl's body took him and gave him the softest comfort he had ever realized. They made their love for a long period, laying across his bed in patterns, turning and trying, until they knew they could delay no longer. The journey had to be accomplished. They went headlong into it with giving and receiving, a violent sobbing coming from William and a beautiful peal of laughter from the young girl. They rolled and swam on the bed and, as she laughed, she cried out finally: 'Choo ... choo ... choo ... Victoria!'

29

MISS SMALLWOOD sat between them at the table. 'Having you back early, Connie dear, makes it seem as though the term has already started. And you, of course, Mr Herbert. In a few days they will be spilling back. All of them. The place will be full of sounds again.

'I always like to think that the spring term arrives in such drabness and departs in Easter sunshine. It's a reassuring thought, don't you agree?'

'Yes, Miss Smallwood, I feel exactly the same,' said William. His body felt hollow, drained and cleansed from the afternoon, and yet he knew he would want her again very soon. Connie sat composed and demure.

'You're reticent tonight, Connie,' observed Miss Smallwood. 'Are you well, child?'

'Very well, thank you, Miss Smallwood,' nodded Connie from above her oxtail soup. 'I was just thinking of all the good things that are going to happen this term.'

William closed his eyes over his plate. Miss Smallwood held her spoon aloft like a tennis racket and served an imaginary ball. 'Tennis!' she hooted and her voice volleyed about the empty hall. 'This year is going to be Southwelling's year. Isn't that so, Mr Herbert?'

'I really hope so,' blinked William.

Miss Smallwood swept her spoon down for a swift ace. 'I'm more than confident,' she asserted. 'We'll get that dashed Clifton Cup back from St Margaret's this year. We've got the capable players and we've got a splendid coach. In July it will be up there on the shelf where we've had a space waiting for it for the last twelve years. I want Southwelling to be remembered for its tennis, Mr Herbert – and for Gilbert and Sullivan, of course.'

'Will you remember Southwelling for its tennis?' William asked her. Connie lay passively beneath him in her bed in the dormitory.

'No,' she said drowsily. 'I guess for its Gilbert and Sullivan.'

That night, he had sat in his dark room after dinner staring out into the garden. A chilly January moon loitered above the black trees and surveyed the soaking countryside without interest. William had left his door open and he could hear her in the distance singing her American songs. Her brave, but off-key voice travelled through the ground-floor corridors to him. When she ended, he rose hesitantly and stood with his fists on his desk for a moment, then went along the passage to her.

The door moved at his first contact and he stood in the

opening. There were five empty beds, striped with insipid moonlight, and in the sixth Connie sat, her bedside lamp shining orange, brushing her hair. She stopped brushing when she saw him.

'Help,' she whispered. 'There's a man in the dorm and I know he's come to do me some harm.'

'Is that the loudest you can shout?' William asked, walking easily between the counterpaned beds.

'It is,' she replied quietly, moving the brush through her hair again. 'I have a very low shouting voice. What kept you?'

'I waited until you'd finished singing,' he said.

'It's just a sop to my patriotism,' she shrugged. 'You wouldn't know those songs? Yankee-Doodle is the greatest. That's the old original version I was singing. It says "and with the girls be handy".'

'I heard that, but I don't think Miss Smallwood would appreciate a duet coming from here.'

'Correct,' she agreed. 'I'm afraid it's a narrow little bed, but there *is* room if one of us lays on top of the other.'

'My bed is big,' he pointed out.

'You can't play all your games at home,' she said. 'Take your robe off and get in. I'd sure like to lie on top of you for a while. I'd like to talk.'

She slipped out of the small bed on the opposite side. She was wearing her winceyette nightdress, her hair long and passive on her shoulders. She watched him watching her and invited him into the bed with a graceful wave of the hairbrush.

He took his dressing-gown off and stretched himself between her sheets. She tapped him playfully with the hairbrush.

'You're a monster,' she laughed.

'That has occurred to me,' he answered.

'Poor old monster,' she sympathized. 'Can I come into my own bed now?'

They surveyed each other very carefully when she climbed into the bed and lay her body along his. Their eyes holding on to the moment when they felt full contact with each other and still while she settled herself. She reached up and put the hairbrush on the locker and then turned the lamp switch. The room became solemn with lemon moonlight.

He could feel the rough, young nightdress, against his naked chest and legs. His hands went to it and he rubbed the material and the stirring body beneath it.

'Do you want me to take it off?' she said secretly. 'Or do you like it?'

'I like it,' he answered just as quietly. 'I like the rough feeling.'

'A sexy woman wouldn't wear a thing like this,' she pointed out.

'You're a little girl.'

'And you are a dirty old man.'

'How will I be able to see you when the rest of the girls come back?'

'Don't worry, there'll be ways.' She giggled as he ran his fingers easily down the parting of her small bottom. 'Gee, what if they were all here now, in these beds! That would be really something, huh?'

'Can you imagine what a screaming there would be,' he said. He continued to caress the nightdress. Then he bent his hands up so that he could cup them under her breasts beneath the winceyette.

'You're wrong,' she said. 'I think they'd all be like mice, just listening, and then you'd have to go to *each* bed, one by one.'

'Connie,' he whispered into her ear. 'These are children ... and so are you, for that matter. A child, that is.'

'Wow,' she breathed. 'But such randy children! You should hear us talk sometimes when we're in the dark.'

'That's little girls' talk,' he said.

'It was the same little girls who got you into the bathroom that night, darling. Remember when Mary Bosham was supposed to be drowning?'

William was bewildered, then shocked. His hand went to her chin and he lifted her face up firmly and stared at her in the uncertain moonlight. 'She wasn't drowning?' he said.

'Oh, William,' she laughed. 'It was so crazy! It was all *so* crazy. When you were giving her the *bouche-à-bouche* I had to get outside. There were girls in the corridor in tears they were laughing so much.'

'And I, bloody fool, thought they were crying with relief

because she hadn't drowned,' he said. 'How rotten. What a lousy thing to do to a man.'

'You *liked* it,' she teased. 'We talked for weeks about how you couldn't take your eyes off poor Mary Bosham even when you were trying to resuscitate her. Oh boy, it was so beautiful. She'll be a star some day. A great tragedian. That night, after lights out and prayers, we were rolling on the beds here in hysterics.'

'I'm pleased I caused such amusement,' he said seriously. 'It didn't seem so hilarious to me.'

'You loved it,' she accused him again. 'All those girls. Come on, admit it.'

'I admit nothing,' he said. She suddenly sat up on him, one leg either side, then leaned forward and kissed him. 'Poor deceived tennis coach,' she said. 'All those naughty naked little girls.'

'Connie,' he said patiently, 'I am a grown man.'

'Yes, I can tell that.'

'None of your American double-talk, young lady. I'm not only a grown man – I'm a *married* grown man. You may like to know that you, well, *we*, are committing adultery. You're pretty young for a co-respondent.'

'Not at this minute; we're not committing anything,' she smiled. 'I am only sitting astride you.' She moved a fraction down his trunk and suddenly, very easily for they were ready, they touched and found each other. She lifted the front of her nightdress without fuss and sighed as she lay on him. She began to move to her own, slow time.

'Now we are,' she said.

30

'JUST A moment, Rufus. Don't come in yet.'

'Why not? Are you committing suicide?'

'I'm having a wee.'

'Would you credit it? All right, I'll wait.'

'Thanks. I may be a little while.'

'What, just doing that?'

'I'm probably the longest wee-er in England, Rufus. They call it bladder-retention.'

'It sounds impressive.'

'Bladder-retention?'

'No, the volume. Is it always like that?'

'It goes on for minutes at a time. The girls used to be astonished.'

'They knew about your trouble.'

'Not exactly, Rufus. But when we were on the island it was all very communal. Connie said I ought to be in the Olympics. She said I should piss for England.'

'You really must tell me about the island, Bill.'

'Oh, I will. I'm getting towards that bit now. I don't mind telling you, at all. As I said, I *like* to hear it myself. It's just such a great damn pity it has to come out in court. You can come in now, Rufus.'

'That's certainly fantastic, Bill. I wouldn't have thought you would have got that much to drink in here.'

'I'm not too badly off like that. That man in the next cell sends me in a bottle of light ale every night, you know. The warder brings it along for a bob. Where it comes from originally, God knows.'

'That's extremely neighbourly of him, Bill. I should watch it though. That man next door is on a charge concerning defiling Post Office Telegram boys. You mind he doesn't bring in a little pill-box hat and suggest that you wear it.'

'You don't think he'd do that, do you? Mind you, I heard he was sexually funny. In fact the warder – confidentially – advised me not to walk in front of him in the exercise yard. So I get behind him now. Actually, it's quite laughable because the word gets around in here, as you can imagine, and *nobody* wants to be in front of him in the exercise yard. You'll find he's always the one leading the crocodile.'

'Right, Bill. Let's get settled. Put the Scrabble board over that pot, will you?'

'I'm sorry I asked you to wait outside, but there's no privacy in here, you know. I can't bolt the door. *They* can, but I can't.

All the bolts and locks are on the outside. It looks a nice day out there, Rufus.'

'Forecast said there's going to be some rain spreading from the west.'

'What a pity. Not that it makes much difference to me, of course. I don't have to run for cover.'

'No, you're very fortunate like that, Bill.'

'I'm going to miss a whole batch of summers, I suppose, Rufus. It's a bit difficult in here to tell what time of the day it is, or what time of the year it is. You only notice the difference in the exercise yard. The old lags tell by whether it's the spider season, or the caterpillar season, or the ladybird season.'

'Strange hobby that.'

'You've got to do something, Rufus. Life seems very long in here. I read that book they brought in – *Little Women* – but, to be honest, it's a bit young for me. And you can't help feeling that it's all slightly old-fashioned and dusty. Girls aren't like that now; just take it from one who knows and is a bit wiser. They're not like that at all. The lorry-driver who gave me a lift opened my eyes to that. And he was right. Mind you, I took quite a fancy to Jo in the book. But I couldn't keep with the story. I reckon my only occupation in here, apart from talking to you, is thinking. I think a lot. Some nights I think until my brain hurts.'

'What about?'

'The usual. My situation. What it is, what it has been, what it might have been with a bit of fortune. When I think that the persons I have loved, Louise and Connie for instance, have been the ones to hurt most.'

'Who else have you loved?'

'Ha! Now I know this sounds very silly, and I want you to take it in the right spirit – I mean, I'm not the man next door. But when I've weighed it up, I've come to the conclusion that I'm *very* fond of you, Rufus. It's a strange thing to say, I know, what with my nose and the way you punched me in the guts only yesterday, but I'm probably closer to you than anyone I've ever known. For one thing, I've never talked to one person for so long, and I've certainly never had anyone listening to me for so long. You know more about me than any other person in the world. Now, as I said, I don't want you to take that in the *wrong* spirit, because it's not intended that way. But that's how I feel about you, anyway.'

'I'm very touched, Bill. In all my years as a detective I've never had a man on a serious charge like this say such a nice thing to me. Let's shake on it.'

'My hand, Rufus.'

'And mine, Bill.'

'It's a pity we can't drink to our friendship. But until tonight I don't get another bottle.'

'Never mind, Bill. When I get outside I'll have a drink for both of us in the pub across the road. What would you like?'

'Well . . . er . . . a sherry, I suppose, Rufus. That's my usual. That's the stuff that gets me into trouble. Yes, make it a sweet sherry.'

'And I'll have a double scotch, straight. I suppose you'll have to owe me for them.'

'No, it's all right, Rufus. Let me pay you now. As you know, we're not supposed to have money in here, but I'm learning a few tricks. I mean, I've got to have a few dodges to make the next ten years bearable, haven't I? I've got a ten-bob piece tucked away here. Take that for our drinks and bring me back the change.'

'You're a clever bugger, Bill. Fancy hiding money like that. Ten bob! You'll be bribing your way out of here next. But there won't be a lot of change from a sherry and a double scotch. In fact, I think it will only just cover it.'

'Oh, I see. Well, not being a hard-stuff man I don't know what whisky costs. Anyway, if it's not enough let me know next time. There *could* be more where that came from.'

'You old rogue. All right, Bill. But as we'll be drinking with you not present, perhaps we'd better say "cheers" now. Let's imagine we've got our glasses.'

'Of course!'

'Right then – cheers, Bill!'

'Cheers, Rufus.'

'Now, back to business. We can't spend all day boozing, can we?'

'Indeed, no. Where do you want me to start?'

'Tell me something which has been interesting me ... well, bothering me. You know when the police found the silver cup in your suitcase ...'

'Ah, now. I'm glad you've brought that up, Rufus, because I want to explain about that. It was the Clifton Cup, of course ...'

'Now, wait a tick, Bill. Steady. I hadn't finished. You go off like a rabbit sometimes. We don't want to spoil a nice morning like this – what with our friendship pledged and everything – by having anyone's nose pulled, do we?'

'Sorry, Rufus. Certainly not. I just wanted to explain about the Clifton Cup, that's all.'

'We'll come to that. The cup is the subject of a separate charge. No, Bill, what I wanted to know was about the other things the coppers found. The little pairs of embroidered things.'

'Now *you* steady on, Rufus. Please don't jump to conclusions. They're not all that they seem.'

'They looked straightforward enough to me. Five pairs of navy-blue knickers. And under the crotch of each – what the advertisements in the Sunday papers call the gusset, I believe ...'

'The gusset. Yes, I understand that's correct.'

'... under the gusset, embroidered in red, pink, blue, yellow, and lime-green thread, the names of five girls.'

'Connie started it. God, the trouble that Connie has put me in. She gave me a pair of her pants just at the beginning of the new term. She put them under the pillow in my room and when I tackled her about it at tennis coaching she just whispered something about them being a memento.'

'But *you* didn't like them?'

'It's no use me saying that, Rufus. They were Connie's. They had been on her. I was touched ... excited, I suppose. But I *didn't* want the others. I wasn't a flaming Redskin collecting scalps.'

'Connie got to your room easily, then? Frequently?'

'No, that was the trouble. It would not have been difficult, but she didn't choose to. While I was lying there at night, starving for her, feeling terrible, with an erection up to my chin just about, she would be giggling in the dormitory with those other little bitches. Sometimes she wouldn't come near me for nights on end; three weeks it was once, three weeks and one night to be exact. Then, in the middle of one night, I'd feel someone getting hold of me, a hand under the bedclothes. And I'd open my eyes, hardly daring to hope it wasn't only a dream, and she'd be standing by the bed. She would look just like a sleepy child in her nightgown. She would nod to me to move over and she'd climb in with me.

'Now, when at night I'm lying on this horrible little bed they provide here, I think about her all those miles away in America, and me, all these miles away here. It makes me cry like a kid. I'm so worried for her. About our baby and everything. And I dare not let myself think that she's gone for ever from me. I think if your people, Rufus, the authorities, would bring her across and let her come into this cell with me for one night, you could take me to the bloody scaffold the next morning and I'd smile at the hangman.

'It was so luxurious. My bed was quite big and we could both sink into it, deep down like kids in cottonwool, and her arms would go about me and that nightgown would be against my skin and I'd feel her small toes down the bottom of the bed. Sometimes, the terrible girl, she would seem to go off to sleep as soon as she got into the bed, as though she had been sleep-walking from the dormitory. As a matter of fact, I thought that would be a convenient excuse if on the off-chance anybody ever caught her in my bed.'

'What? That she walked in her sleep and climbed in with you? It wouldn't convince me, Bill.'

'Well, you're a trained detective. You're not Miss Smallwood. Anyway, that's what I thought would do if it ever came to a last-ditch excuse. But, as I was saying, she would appear to go off to sleep and I used to be scared stiff in case I went to sleep, too, and we stayed there until the morning. So I used to force myself to stay awake. And then, after a bit, she would put her hands down to my thing and start to rub it, and I'd know she wasn't really asleep at all.'

'Good deduction.'

'I'll ignore that. I know when you're taking the mickey. And when she started that sort of business the whole thing would begin. She used to eat me, consume me, I suppose you'd say, but never in a fierce way, always sleepily, as though it was true that she had walked in her sleep.

'She hardly ever said a word. All the time while it was going on she would make little grunts and squeaks, like a baby pig, and dull sort of movements, except at the last part when she would get terribly screwed up and excited and she'd start that laughing again. Not very loud, just quietly as though she was having some private joke, and then after it was all done she would get up, just as sleepily, and walk out of the room without a word. And then it wouldn't happen for days. Three weeks and one night it was once.'

'You mentioned it.'

'Twenty-two days – nights. I counted it. Every minute. And I was afraid to ask her during the day in case I upset her and she never came again. But I used to have a terrible time of it.'

'Did you go up into the loft at those times, during the intervals, Bill?'

'The loft?'

'Yes, the loft. Don't ask me which loft or I'll hit you.'

'Well, yes, I did find myself up there once. I had to see her, Rufus. I couldn't stand not seeing her.'

31

IT WAS dark in the loft, dark and hung with cobwebs for his face and splinters for his knees. Little glow-worms of light showed in a few places where there was some kind of parting in the wood, sufficient for it to filter up from below.

William crawled along breathlessly, like a miner in a shaft, moving towards the face of the wall that looked into the dormitory. All the afternoon he had watched her. It had been a freakishly fine day for January, with pleasantly surprised birds singing, and the trees suddenly stretching and shaking themselves in the mild air. The river moved by the school like mercury and had receded from its winter frontiers enough to allow the outdoor tennis courts to be used. After lunch, William had four of the red-surfaced courts in use. Connie had come out with Susan Belling at two-thirty. They had walked towards the courts from the school, swinging their rackets and laughing in conversation. They were both wearing white nylon tracksuits.

He adjusted the net for them, watching Connie through the mesh as he measured it up. She was playing a ball against the side netting and made not a sign that she even knew he was there. He made something of a performance of fixing the net and then asked them seriously if they would like some balls. They declined, and as he walked away he could hear them sniggering. He watched them at a distance as they moved well across the court. They were both good players and their game flowed in the unexpected sunshine. He watched them stop after their warm-up and strip from their tracksuits. They played in white shorts and white woollen sweaters.

Although he was supposed to be coaching the ten-year-olds, little lily children with large rackets, he eventually walked across the courts again and stood outside the perimeter netting watching Connie and Susan. He tried to give the impression that he was on hand if either of these senior players should need advice or assistance. But they continued their game without a glance in his direction, talking only to each other, and laughing at the personal jokes.

When they had finished, they carefully sheathed their long legs into their tracksuits again and walked away, close together, still chattering, without even acknowledging him. He was left to lower the net.

He waited until nine-thirty before he climbed up into the loft. All the evening he had sat hunched on his elbows in his room. He had written three letters to Connie and two to Miss Smallwood, each one revealing that he was about to resign from Southwelling. As he completed each letter he read it and tore it up. Desolate and furtive he took the spare pillow from his wardrobe and went out to get the umpire's chair.

Even when he stood on the seat of the tall ladder chair it was some distance to the trapdoor. He pushed it aside into the dusty head of the loft and heaved himself up into the blackness. Once more he lay for an interval across the rafters and joists, panting more with apprehension than exertion. Like an animal in a secret hole he remained prone. The blank wall of the dormitory was yards ahead, but he could hear the girls' voices filtering along the triangular tunnel.

Eventually, like a marauder, he moved forward. He used the pillow to protect his elbows against the vicious splinters of the old savage wood. He grunted, then rested to silence himself. The slivers of light that escaped from below gave some minimal illumination for his low journey. Then he saw the wall and the yellow streak that was the spying hole just ahead. He paused again. The girls' voices seemed to call him on like sirens.

Reaching the wall, he leaned against it for a moment and then pushed his face towards the crack. He pulled the pillow beneath his knees.

The full lights were on in the dormitory. He had meant to look for Connie first, but immediately in his view, a few feet beneath his eyes, Susan Belling was stretched inelegantly on her bed. She had taken off her gymslip and was lying in her black stockings and white silk blouse. One leg was crooked up and she lifted the other and rested it on her knee to examine a toe poking through the hose.

William felt himself begin to tingle. She half moved about, clumsily, and he looked down the jet backs of her stockings to the sudden pink and white of her flesh. Her knickers were tight in her exposed valley and as he watched she began to take them off, carelessly yet taking a long time about it. Like a stripper. She half pulled them down over her stockings, then changed her mind and undid the stockings from a little belt and pulled the whole lot down together. She rolled on to her stomach, pushing her white buttocks into the air.

Crazily he stared at her from his dark place. His excitement was making him feel sick. She remained still, her backside projecting pertly. He tore his eyes from her and looked at the rest of the room, Connie was in her bed reading, Julia Summers was also in bed sewing a sampler and the three other girls were all sitting on one bed giggling at a book. William looked back at Susan. She had stretched across the bed towards her locker, the narrow white sweep of her back, her bottom and her legs showing to him. She was trying to get something in the locker.

He saw her retrieve a box tied with ribbon and she called something to the others.

The girls sitting together on the one bed dropped the book and, giving small squeals, hurried towards Susan. Two were wearing dressing-gowns and the other was still in her school uniform. Connie and Julia Summers looked up from their beds but did not move. He saw that Susan was holding up a blue garment.

'Put it on,' said Avril Spring. 'Let's see.'

William swivelled his eyes to Susan. She was unbuttoning her blouse. She took it off, and then, with curious shyness, turned away from the other girls. She was facing him, facing the wall, and she took off her vest and small brassière. She shook her hair beautifully and the small noses of her breasts quivered as she did it. She was very smooth; as she lifted a blue night-dress over her head he could see her ribs impressed on her skin. She wriggled the nightdress over her body. It was short, to her thighs. The others, with their school nightdresses to the shins, stood admiringly as she paraded like a fashion model between the beds.

'Let me try it?' asked Avril. She was a dark-skinned girl, short and wide, with a cloud of black hair. She was quickly out of her dressing-gown but she turned from the others before lifting her nightgown free of her head. William saw that she had a thick bunch of hair below her stomach, and staunch little breasts. She tried the nightdress. Then the others, all except Connie, began passing it from one to the next, stripping with their strange shyness of each other, then parading and laughing. He was surprised to see that Mary-Ann Adams had such grown breasts, full and mellow, while Jeanette Keen had little berry nipples and gingery pubic hair.

He was sweating heavily as he leaned against his peephole. He had opened his trousers for relief. Susan had put the night-dress away in her locker and now lounged directly beneath him. She began to rub some white cream into the tops of her legs. William watched her touch herself gently and without haste. Laughingly she called to Connie: 'If I can get rid of this hair on my legs I'm going to be so beautiful for some lucky boy.'

Tightly, William tugged the pillow from beneath his knees

173

and pressed himself into it. He clenched his eyes and hugged it. When he could breathe again the lights were going out in the dormitory. Connie's was the last to be doused. He watched the darkened room for movements. The girls called their goodnights and then began to sleep innocently.

Uncomfortable and despising himself he backed away along the loft. He left the pillow there against the wall knowing that he would be back. The splinters still attacked him and the cobwebs loitered around his ears. He came to the trapdoor and lowered himself into the void towards the darkened landing. His feet moved to find the umpire's chair. It was not there. First this way, then that, pendulum fashion, to the right, to the left; in a little circle. 'Oh Christ,' he said. He moaned and kicked out. He could not touch it. His arms were aching from the suspense. Once more, desperately, he circled and kicked out into the emptiness below. Then he half slipped, half dropped, fifteen feet, hitting the wooden blocked floor heavily and biting back a cry as he felt his ankle twist.

The pain jumped through him. He gave a quick squeak and then scuffled on his knees guiltily back into a dark corner in case he had been heard. The umpire's chair was leaning against the wall there. He crawled along the passage to his room, then, remembering the trapdoor, reappeared with a broom and, standing on one leg, stork-like, manoeuvred the trap into place.

He returned to his room and lay on his bed, cursing; his ankle and his mind throbbing. It could only have been one of the girls. It could only have been Connie.

'The low-down, sneaky bitch,' he cried to himself.

32

'SHE DID it right enough, Rufus. Oh boy, that little trick had Miss Connie written all over it.'

'She told you?'

'Eventually she admitted it, but she didn't have to tell me

174

anyway. The way she creased herself laughing when she saw me hobbling around on a bloody stick. That was enough to tell me it was her. You should have seen that ankle. It was terrible – swollen and bandaged up. It looked like a damned great bag of laundry stuck on the end of my foot.

'I made excuses to Miss Smallwood and the other staff that I'd fallen down some steps, and, fortunately, Connie had the decency not to tell the other girls that she knew I was in the loft.'

'How did she know you were there?'

'My luck again. Apparently she had slipped out of the dormitory to come and see me in my room. She had never before come so early in the evening like that. I must have just gone into the loft because she told me she could hear me breathing and panting up there. My room was right at the end of that part of the school, so really there wasn't all that much risk that the umpire's ladder would be spotted. But she saw it there and just took it away. She wasn't very sure what I was doing up in the loft, but she worked out the geography pretty quickly. But she never told the other girls. In some ways, I suppose, she was quite a sport.'

'Ah, that reminds me, Bill. Talking of being a sport. *You're* a sport. You really are. All the lads in the pub thought so yesterday. They all wish you well and they insisted on joining in and having a drink with us. Your round came to thirty-two and six. So you owe me twenty-two and six. That's right, isn't it? Ten bob off thirty-two and six?'

'Oh, I see, Rufus. Well ... I certainly hope the boys all enjoyed our drink.'

'Oh they did that, right enough.'

'Can I ask you something?'

'Sure.'

'Are these the same boys, the policemen and the solicitors and their clerks and suchlike, who were having a sweepstake on how long I'd get in prison?'

'The very same, Bill. They'll be glad that you remembered them. But, mind you, don't get the wrong idea about these chaps. They're good lads. As I told you before, there's nothing at all personal in this sweepstake business. It's just a mild gamble, that's all. It could be a bet on *anything*. It's just that you're a convenient subject, if you understand.'

'Well, truthfully, Rufus, I've only got another ten bob hidden and I was rather hoping to keep that for any little luxuries. But I suppose you'd better have that. Here.'

'That leaves us twelve and six short, doesn't it? You can give it to me some other time. Maybe I can have a couple of free tweaks of that nose one day.'

'No, I'd rather give you the twelve and six. You may have to wait ten years until I get out, so don't put the interest rates too high, will you?'

'I'll keep them in line with the Bank Rate, Bill. I promise.'

'I was only making a joke, Rufus.'

'Oh, I see. That's the trouble with you, Bill Herbert, you're so subtle that people misread you completely. That's half your trouble with these young girls. They think you won't *do* anything, and damnit before they've got time to clutch their pants to their bottoms, you've *done* it!'

'Now *you're* joking. You *are*, aren't you?'

'Yes, all right, if you say so. Anyway, the boys enjoyed our drink. I suppose I'll have to put my hand into my meagre policeman's pay packet for the money that's short.'

'I'm sorry I've only got this ten shillings. If it had been ten pounds then the boys could have all had a good lunch – couldn't we?'

'Now you stop putting ideas into my head, young Bill. Let's get down to business, shall we. What were we on yesterday? Oh, yes, before the thing about the loft and you twisting your ankle, you were telling me about the girls' pants that were in your suitcase. The ones with the names embroidered on the gullets.'

'Gussets, Rufus. G-U-S-S-E-T-S. The piece of material that fits between the girl's legs.'

'Sorry. It's all so new to me. Anyway, what about the others? Were they sort of mementoes as well, like Connie's?'

'The same type of thing.'

'What – they gave them to you after you had seduced them?'

'I don't like this word "seduced", Rufus. It makes it sound as though it were all my fault. They had it all spaced out and

176

planned, believe me. By rights, I should have been handing my Y-fronts out as souvenirs of their conquests. Just take that little devil Susan. I couldn't sleep, I was lying there with it throbbing away like billy-o . . .'

'What?'

'What d'you mean, "What?", Rufus? Oh . . . I get you . . . for Christ's sake . . . no . . . my ankle, I meant. It was giving me hell, but she still put in her appearance at eleven o'clock at night.'

'An early bird, eh?'

'Exactly, and there was a good reason. You can bet your life on that. I might have guessed she was up to something because that afternoon she complained of cramp on the court and she came over to me for treatment. I couldn't even walk with my ankle being so bad, so she had to sit on the stool opposite me and I had to work on her leg like that.'

'Did you always get rid of the girls' cramp?'

'Only the little ones as a rule. The senior girls used to work it off themselves and only the juniors used to come to me.'

'What did you use on them, liniment?'

'Liniment and hands, usually.'

'The magic fingers, eh?'

'Well, it usually worked.'

'I bet.'

'Rufus, there are times when you look at me in the strangest way. You give the impression that you don't believe me. For heaven's sake, I'm trying to assist you as much as I can. I tell you a damn sight more than I tell Mr Decent and he's supposed to be working for my defence.'

'Ha! That reminds me, Bill. Old Decent was in the pub yesterday when we were having a drink with you. My God, you think you're hard done by! Poor perisher. You won't believe this, but it's true. You'll just laugh.'

'I hope so, Rufus.'

'He was supposed to be defending some bum bandit who'd given a boy sixpence for an ice-cream – then taken him up a dark alley. The last hope of the defence was the man's mother. If she would only weep a bit in the box and say what a good chap he was at home, then the sentence might not be so bad.'

'And Mr Decent couldn't get a single tear out of her. Don't tell me.'

'Worse, much worse, Bill. The old girl, who didn't know what the hell was going on, couldn't find anything good to say about her son. Poor old Decent was desperate. Then the mum said that one thing she could say – he was occasionally very generous. He used to give the little boy next door sixpence for icecreams!'

'That's terrible. Is he the best counsel they could get?'

'He's the best *you* could get.'

'Oh.'

'That reminds me, Bill. Now I come to think of it, Decent had a drink, too.'

'With me?'

'That's right. A gin and tonic. Cheered him up a bit, poor sod.'

'Well, you'd better add it on to the twelve and six I owe. I'm glad I bought it for him, though, Rufus. I hate to see people down on their luck.'

33

HIS FOOT throbbed rhythmically like an outboard motor. He lay in his bed feeling its revolutions. On the previous night he had slept for only two or three hours. Now he dozed against the pain until it had diminished and it purred sombrely at the end of his leg.

She did not touch him, but he sensed her waiting there through his thin sleep. His sticky eyes saw the form at the bedside and he smiled appreciatively in the dark and caught her hand, shuffling back at the same time to make room for her in the bed. She rolled in with him warmly and with no hesitation, immediately closing with him like a girl performing a familiar movement with a partner in some horizontal dance.

He felt then that there was something unfamiliar about her.

First her movement into the bed was not the same as Connie's movement. His right hand moving under her nightgown and up her flank told him that the skin was different, a cooler texture, and the breasts he found were fuller, better nourished, the nipples softer, more diffuse, not like Connie's fine round buttons.

He moved his injured foot with his surprise and winced. In the close dark his eyes zoomed to her face. She was smiling at him confidently, half under the sheets.

'Susan,' he whispered. 'Is that you?'

'Yes, Mr Herbert,' she confirmed. 'I had that awful cramp again; the same as this afternoon. I thought you might be able to treat me.'

'Connie sent you.'

'Don't worry. We're best friends. But she's stricken with the curse and she thought you might be lonely, and desperate. You poor Mr Herbert.'

She felt delicious against him. Her hair was more curled than Connie's, her face much more animated. The body beneath the long school nightgown made dancing movements. Her knees collided with his thighs and her open toes were fixed like brackets to his hard shins.

'You should not be in this bed at this hour,' he whispered severely.

'I'm here now.'

'I know.' He bent to her, hesitated, and then kissed her face with a resigned shrug. She returned the kiss to his lips with amateur thoroughness.

'What about your cramp?' he asked.

'I think this treatment will improve it – gradually.'

'Just this once, then. But you must not come in here again.'

Giving in to it completely he allowed his hands to travel around her waist and dip to the mounds of her backside. She was more fatty there than Connie, more mobile, more massage-able. Wickedly he rolled his palms across the bulges and then sent his fingers suddenly, like slim divers, between her legs. He sensed her relaxing slightly, obediently.

'You're in a terrible state, Mr Herbert,' she pointed out. 'That – that feels like there's some third person in this bed.'

'It is apt to get in the way,' he said. He felt hot and hurried, still astonished at her presence. He rolled on top of her and let out a soundless squeal as he unthinkingly moved his huge ankle.

'Let me take this off, first,' she suggested, tugging at the nightgown. He half lifted his weight from her and she smiled through the dark.

'Pull the curtains back,' she suggested. 'We can see each other.'

William, conscious of his ill-balanced state, left the bed and hopped to the window, injured leg and penis swinging free but straight, like the derricks of a ship.

The night he viewed from the window was full of ragged roaming clouds, but the bloodless moon was still there, freeing itself and shining into the occasionally open sky. He watched it only briefly then went back to her. She had taken off the nightgown and it was lying like a shrivelled pink skin on the floor. The bedclothes were pulled playfully over her head.

He caught the sheet and turned it back until the top of her was exposed in the insipid light.

Easy and unworried she smiled at him. She lay fully on her back with her hair curling across his pillows. He examined her expression of mischievous triumph, then stared at her breasts, round as spinning tops. He put his fingers forward, first to one and then the other and felt them give and quiver. She remained passive and he trembled and choked as he turned the sheet and blankets back farther to expose her round stomach, the slightly spread hips and the cornet of fair hair. Then another fold of the bedclothes and the sight of her legs, lying carelessly.

'What's the time?' she asked him.

Surprised, he bent and peered at his alarm clock. The luminous figures were never very clear and he had to move close to them.

'Are you due somewhere else?' he asked as he climbed above her again.

'No, I just wondered.'

'Eleven-thirty,' he told her. 'It's better to come about three o'clock, Susan. Everybody's asleep then.'

'I would be, too,' she answered. Then: 'Where are you

putting *that*, Mr Herbert? I'm not terribly experienced but I'm almost certain that's the wrong place.'

'Sorry, Susan,' he fumbled. Then he found her quickly and fell against her, making a look of surprise touch her face. She was different from Connie again. She was very small inside and she did not love sleepily as Connie did, but urgently and without any true feel for the rhythm. He attempted to pull the sheet about them but she could not spare the time. She darted at him, demandingly, pushing her body upwards. His ankle protested at each change in direction although he tried to keep it anchored to one corner of the bed, pushed outwards like a supporting strut.

He attempted to keep pace with her, but she was running off on her own. She screwed up her face and bit at her lip as though something had upset her and then her face cleared and she lay and let him continue at his own elder pace.

'What's the time now?' she asked eventually.

He sighed and edged towards his clock again. 'Twenty to twelve,' he said. 'We didn't hang around, did we?'

She smiled and kissed him, this time like a grateful child. 'In twenty minutes,' she announced, 'I will be sixteen.'

The significance did not immediately occur to William. 'Many happy returns,' he said politely.

'That's why I came early,' she said brightly, getting up and pulling her nightdress over her head. 'I decided that when I slept with *you* it would have to be a *crime* or nothing. And it was. *You* have committed a criminal offence.'

'Oh God,' said William quietly. 'It didn't dawn on me. You came purposely for that? Just that?'

'It wouldn't have been the same after midnight,' she pouted. She moved towards the door. She patted his foot and then kissed the bandages. 'Any fool can do it when she's sixteen,' she said.

34

'DONTH ... DONTH, Rufuth ... Oh ... ooh ... ooh ... oh ... oh, Rufus ...'

'Pinch, punch, first day of the month, Bill! And no returns! Come on now, don't say a little pinch on the nose and a tiny prod in the guts hurts you.'

'Christ, Rufus. You *did* hurt me. Maybe you didn't mean to ...'

'It was only a joke, Bill. Didn't you ever do the old "Pinch, punch, first day of the month" when you were a kid?'

'Yes, I expect I did when I was a kid. Or, more likely, they did it to me. But I sort of haven't done it for quite a time. So I'm a bit short of practice. It was so unexpected you coming in the door like that and pinching and punching me. It's easy to forget these funny little sayings.'

'My grandmother in Coleraine, always came down the stairs backwards saying "white rabbits, white rabbits" on the first of the month.'

'Couldn't you have walked in here saying "white rabbits" instead of attacking me?'

'You'd have thought I'd gone potty, Bill. You know damn well you would.'

'Well it hurt, that's all.'

'Ah, look at you, William Herbert. August the First – in a few days you're before the magistrates. A remand to the Sessions – and the Sessions are on, let's see, September 28th.'

'Oh, I'll be well settled in for Christmas, then.'

'Certainly. You couldn't have timed it better. Just think how you were last Christmas, wandering aimlessly about, nowhere to go.'

'Well, I'm more or less fixed for the next few Christmases, aren't I?'

'That's true. Ah, Bill, I've been thinking about you quite a bit recently. Even in my off-duty time.'

'That's most kind of you, Rufus. What sort of thoughts?'

'Your power over women fascinates me. That's an honest fact.'

'It's very good of you to say so, very good indeed. On the other hand, of course, it could be argued that they were not *altogether* women. Nearly – mind you.'

'Now you're letting modesty get in the way. It's not just the schoolgirls I'm talking about, though, it's grown women. My wife, my *own* wife, wants to meet you more than any other man in the world. Every night she asks me about you and about what you've been telling me.'

'Good gracious. You don't tell *her*, do you?'

'Not down to the little details. Don't worry about that. Sure, she's never met you but she thinks you're intriguing. Hell . . . Well, I don't know whether I ought to tell you this . . . you won't repeat it, will you?'

'No, Rufus. I don't get much of a chance to repeat anything in here. We live a very quiet life in prison, you know.'

'I know . . . but . . . all right. Promise though?'

'Promise, promise.'

'She bought herself a pair of schoolgirl knicks yesterday. She had them in a Marks and Spencer's bag on the bed when I got home.'

'No!'

'Absolutely true, Bill. I'm just waiting until she puts them on.'

'Christ, that's a bit perverted, Rufus! You start on that sort of business and you'll end up in here having some bastard like you interrogating you. THAT WAS ONLY A JOKE!'

'I'm glad you mentioned it. God, my fingers were halfway to your snout, old friend.'

'I could see.'

'Well my advice to you is to steady up with the jokes. Or *tell* me it's a joke *first* before you come out with it. It could save you quite a lot of pain. Anyway, what I was going to say is my mother-in-law wants to meet you too. She gets damn well near to tears about the state you're in and she threatened me with every curse in hell if I'm the least bit cruel to you.'

'But you *are* cruel to me, Rufus. You pull my nose and you punch me in the guts.'

'I keep forgetting to tell her about that.'

'Yes, I suppose you do.'

'But it's something, isn't it, that they want to meet you so much? Myra's mother wants to make you some more fishcakes and both she and Myra are going to be in the public gallery when you eventually go for trial. They've promised to wave when you go down to do your ten years.'

'I shall watch out for them.'

'I would if I were you. Just think, my wife and my mother-in-law will probably be the last two women you'll see for a long, long time.'

'Well, it's very comforting to think that somebody in the audience will sympathize with me. There's no chance of getting them on the jury is there?'

'None at all, I'm afraid, Bill. Anyway they wouldn't let their personal sympathies blind them to justice. They both think that screwing schoolgirls is a terrible thing. It's just that it *fascinates* them, that's all. That isn't to say they agree with it, or that they'd have liked to have been screwed by a schoolmaster when they were little girls. Anyway, I've got to come straight with you over this . . .'

'What?'

'Well, the sweepstake was so popular . . .'

'You've extended it.'

'Absolutely correct. We've issued another ten tickets because of the demand.'

'And your wife and your mother-in-law have got two of those ten.'

'Right again. Remarkable. D'you know, Bill, I'd swear you're developing some sort of . . . what do they call it? – extra-sensory perception – since you've been inside.'

'I could be. I do enough thinking about the outside and all the people out there.'

'Anyway it boils down to this – the sweepstake, I mean. If you get eighteen years my mother-in-law gets a holiday in Majorca.'

'I will try. Promise.'

'Oh come on, don't lose your sense of humour over it, Bill.'

'All right, I won't. That's one thing I should hate to be without – my sense of humour. I don't know what I'd do.'

'Anyway things are going along quite quickly now, Bill. We've had people going to see the various girls for statements, and over in the States they've been working on Connie.'

'Working on her? What's that? What do you mean?'

'That's the way they put it in the message from Chicago. It's only the way Americans talk. It doesn't necessarily mean they've given her the third degree or anything.'

'What *have* they given her, then? "Working on her" sounds sinister enough to me. I hope no big bugger of a G-man or whatever they call them has been doing anything to her to make her talk.'

'Apparently they didn't have any trouble with her.'

'Oh, she made a statement, then?'

'She made a statement.'

'Is there any chance of knowing what she said, or even a bit of it? Can you give me some idea?'

'Mr Herbert! You're asking a police officer to give you information which will be used by the Crown! Don't you realize what that means!'

'Sorry, Rufus. Don't get mad. I'd just like to know, that's all. If I had any money I'd offer you a bribe, but you've had my last ten bob. Can I ask you this – just one thing without perverting the course of justice and all that sort of trouble? Can you tell me anything about her? *Anything*, Rufus. Did the American police say how she was. After all, she's pregnant. Anything at all. I worry about her so much. She's so bloody far away.'

'Have you ever seen a police report, Bill? Better still, have you ever seen an *American* police report? No, well I thought you hadn't. If you had, you wouldn't ask such a lot of hooey. They're not letters from mummies, you know. They don't tell you how people are, how they're feeling. They're full of *facts*. They're very expensive things, police reports, and they have to be filled with *facts*. After all it's the taxpayers' money you're using up.'

'Who?'

'You, for God's sake. *You*, William Herbert.'

'I suppose I am really. Now I've got that on my conscience,

too. It's not from choice, though; I don't want to use up anybody's money. Least of all the poor old innocent taxpayers'. Frankly – and I suppose you've come to this conclusion yourself, being as you are a detective and you observe human nature pretty closely – frankly, I don't want to give anyone trouble at all. I'm not the trouble-making type.'

'How did you get the other pairs of knickers, Bill?'

'The ones in the case?'

'Right. The knickers we found.'

'Hey, your wife hasn't embroidered her name on the crotch of hers, has she? ... uuuuuugle ... uggle ... uggle ...'

'Get on with it!'

'You pulled my tongue! Oh, that hurt! Oh ...'

'Leave my wife and her knickers out of this, Bill. Your tongue just happened to be sticking out. That's why I tugged it.'

'You ... you are rotten ... I ... I thought it was coming out by the roots.'

'Now you know me better than that, Bill. If I pulled it right out how would I get the rest of this yarn. Don't worry, it was only a momentary urge. I didn't like it much anyway. It's nasty and wet.'

'It's made all my eyes water again. That was agony, Rufus. Don't do it any more, please.'

'Where did it hurt most?'

'Right at the bottom. Where it joins up to the back of my mouth. It's still stinging.'

'Oh, by the way, before we go on with the knickers business I must tell you a joke that was going around the canteen last night.'

'Good, I'd like to hear a joke.'

'It all came out of that kid Susan wanting to get bottled before she was sixteen. And this joke ...'

'You *told* them about that – in the canteen! After you'd promised.'

'Only in the most general way, Bill. Do you want to hear this joke or not?'

'All right, tell me the joke.'

'Well, there was this copper walking his beat at night and

he comes upon this car. In the front is a chap naked like he was born and in the back seat is a girl, also stark nude, see. The copper asks them what's going on, and the chap nods over his shoulder and says: "I'm waiting until midnight. She's sixteen then!".'

'Ho! Yes, I can see the funny side of that all right, Rufus. Very amusing, Of course, he *knew* she would be sixteen at midnight. With Susan I didn't know until it was too late. Then I'd done it.'

'That reminds me. Susan. Now why did she want you to open the curtains? Was it to let the sweet romantic moonlight into the room? Or did she want to get a good look at that big love-hook of yours? Or was there something else?'

'Something else. You're good at picking up the clues, aren't you, Rufus.'

'Why don't you tell my inspector that.'

'If I get a chance I will.'

'What was the reason?'

'Connie was outside the window, and two of the other little bastards. They watched the whole performance. Connie told me some time after. She seemed to think I ought to be pleased, but I was so embarrassed. I used to feel such a damned fool when I'd fallen into one of their traps.'

'The bait wasn't bad, though, was it?'

'Not bad. But Susan didn't mean anything to me. I only did it due to the fact that I was all sexed-up and she said that Connie had sent her because she was worried about my being depressed. And, naturally, I believed it all. But I only really wanted Connie. The others were just to please her. I was just sacrificing myself. It was Connie, Connie, Connie, on my mind all the time. I couldn't imagine her being so cruel as to watch through that window while I was having it with Susan. And with two other girls as well. The funny thing was, I actually turned around once and I must have seen their heads sticking up over the sill. But you know how it is when you're busy. I just thought it was three of the garden shrubs.'

'Easily done, I suppose. Now, let's get back, once and for all, to those knicks. They're exhibits A to E as far as our case is concerned.'

'Oh no, Rufus! You're not going to show those things in court, are you?'

'They're part of the prosecution's case, Bill. It's difficult to see how that can be avoided.'

'But everyone will see them. And the embroidered names. Oh, this is terrible. I didn't realize ...'

'Well you do now.'

'All right. You win, Rufus.'

'I know.'

'Rufus.'

'Yes?'

'I don't want to *pry* or anything. Finding out about the Crown evidence and all that stuff again. But ... what else will they be showing as exhibits?'

'All sorts of things. All the usual. Anything that might help the prosecution's case.'

'The usual? Well, what?'

'Let's see. I shouldn't tell you, Bill, because forewarned being forearmed. If you know what we've got in mind, you understand, you might be able to make some crafty moves to block our case.'

'Like committing suicide.'

'Now don't talk in that defeatist way. You've got your whole life before you. You're only thirty-five – well forty-five if you take your sentence into account – and that's not at all old in these days.'

'Tell me what they'll show in court.'

'Your pillow, for a start. You know, the one from the loft and they'll produce a forensic report with that. You remember I told you they found the semen.'

'I think I *will* commit suicide. Christ, think of that coming out. The newspapers gobbling it up. What will Miss Smallwood think, or Louise, or, God forbid, Connie? She might read it in America.'

'She will I expect. The case is getting a lot of publicity over there. They don't have the same idiot laws as ours about protecting criminals before they're tried.'

'They're very advanced like that, I suppose, Rufus. Connie's been in the papers over there, then? She must have been.'

'Now you remind me, yes. Do you know, Bill, now I come

to think of it I've seen her photograph in one of the American newspapers. Somebody showed it to me at the station.'

'Rufus ... Rufus ... you've seen her photograph! And you didn't tell me, Rufus!'

'Hell! I've just told you.'

'Rufus, tell me something about the photograph. Anything. Was it full-length or just the top of her?'

'I can't remember. I have a funny idea she was in a swimsuit. No, that was Miss World.'

'You're torturing me, aren't you? I can tell you are. You like to make me squirm. You do it on purpose.'

'Bill.'

'Yes, Rufus?'

'Do you want me to become official and unfriendly? Or do you want us to go on sociably as we've done so far? It's up to you. I don't *have* to be reasonable with you. Just understand that.'

'I understand, Rufus. No ... I'm sorry ... Please stay friendly. I couldn't stand it if the only bloody visitor I get turned nasty on me. It's just that I wanted to know about Connie, that's all. You know how anxious I get about her. It probably seems unreasonable to you.'

'Well it does when you expect me to remember every little thing I see in the paper.'

'I've said I'm sorry, Rufus, and I am.'

'All right. Let's, once and for all, finally, get back to the knickers.'

'I'll tell you everything you want to know about them. But would you try and find that picture from that American newspaper? Could you have a look for me, please?'

'All right. I'll see. Now tell me how you came by the other pairs.'

'Dribs and drabs. Jackie MacAllister was on the island.'

'Ah, yes, the island. I've been wanting to hear about the island.'

'It was very nice there. I had a marvellous time. And so did the girls.'

35

WHEN HE recalled the island during his worried days in prison, staring at the uncompromising wall, he remembered the freedom and the spacious hours, the white calling of gulls, the songs of seals and sea, the noble, abandoned, lighthouse, so phallic according to Connie, and Miss Smallwood's accident on the cliff.

It was Easter and the island was called Downsley Isle, four miles off the Pembrokeshire coast, so isolated by the occasional combination of heavy weather and a ten-knot tide race, that they had to take Miss Smallwood off by helicopter. What had worried William was the way the girls had cheered.

'Were they cheering the helicopter men?' he asked Connie when they were lying by moonlight in the huge empty glass dome at the pinnacle of the lighthouse, where once the light had been. It was like being enclosed in a gigantic display case.

'Guess again,' she suggested, leaning up on her elbow to look from the great curved window over the freshly moonlit sea. 'Maybe they were giving three cheers for Miss Smallwood *going away*. Now we're all snug together here. You and me, twenty other girls and Miss Tilling; so everybody is just fine.'

He had not fully realized about Miss Tilling then. Since his worry over the way she had given the unnecessary and vibrant kiss of life to Mary Bosham in the bathroom, he had not given any thought to her oddities.

'The headmistress did have an *accident*, didn't she?' he asked Connie.

'Sure, sure,' said Connie, kissing his neck. 'She slid all the way down the cliff on her ass and right into that nasty old cold sea. It was just fortunate, I guess, that the cliff is all shale there and not very steep. Just crazy for a toboggan ride.'

'But it *was* an accident?'

'Oh you bug me sometimes, Mr Herbert. She was too brave, that was her trouble, going so close to the slippery grass at the edge to see those dear little iddy-biddy puffins with their cute faces. And whoosh! A—way she was gone, sliding down like something from the Golden Oldies.'

'That's the old films, isn't it? You mentioned it before. About me and that tape up at Derby.'

'I did too. Gee, you and Miss Smallwood should have been in one of those movies together. You'd have been just great.'

William looked at her. The round room was like a bowl and the moon blazed in. They were lying on a sleeping bag thrown down upon the massive cast-iron platform which fifty years before had been the mounting for the light. She was wearing her jeans and about her shoulders was a heavy sheepskin coat. The coat and her arms formed a cave or a tent, he thought, and inside she was naked, her breasts eyed him. Satin moonlight made smudgy shadows on her face and touched her long gentle hair. William was wearing a heavy fisherman's sweater but she had taken his trousers off.

Connie leaned back on both elbows so that the coat moved back and she looked down through the shallow channel of her breasts to the pale face of her stomach. 'This is certainly strange up-here,' she said. 'Lying out on this big disc thing, with the moon screaming in all these windows. You know – it's just like being a human sacrifice. All tied up and laid out for the chief of the tribe to inspect.'

'Your imagination,' he muttered. Then he said: 'Are you sure Miss Smallwood wasn't a sacrifice?'

'She *slipped* down the cliff,' said Connie emphatically. 'Can't you understand that? She was edging up on her buttocks to get a look at . . .'

'I know, I know,' he nodded. 'The dear little iddy-biddy puffins with their cute faces. But that was all? When she lay moaning and shivering on the stretcher she said something to me about the girls being all so eager and keen to see what you call those iddy-biddy puffins with their cute faces that she thought someone may have accidentally given her a push.'

'Oh God, William, did you *see* her when she was up to her armpits in the ocean? She was splashing about like one of those mythical seabirds we made up.'

'The long-booted khaki-faced crap-nibbler?'

She giggled. 'That was a honey,' she said. 'Sure, she looked like one of them.'

'You forget I had to go down and pull her out,' pointed out William. 'She was thrashing about more like a damned pelican.'

'Oh, if only you could have been there to see the beginning of it. The descent!' She smiled serenely at the memory and lay back on the sleeping bag. He bent to her and touched her nipples with his mouth. Her hand went to his hair and she pressed his ear into her breast.

'I would rather have watched than taken part, believe me,' he said, moving eventually then lying alongside her.

'Dear Christ,' she breathed. 'She went down the slope so exquisitely, arms and legs in the air, whooshing down, yelling out, and then that gorgeous splash when she went in! The girls were hysterical, rolling all over the grass.'

'And then I came along,' he sighed.

'And *did* you come along! It was like Robin Hood, Ivanhoe and Batman all at once. My God, I just ached. You went down that cliff on your poor old ass, zooming down, and splash – *in you went, Willie boy*!'

'You still haven't answered my question,' he said pushing himself up on his elbow. 'Did anyone give her a nudge? I shall be bloody annoyed if they did. She could have drowned.'

'She wasn't drowned,' pointed out Connie. 'And, anyway, it gave those terrific airmen in their helicopter some rescue practice.'

'Thank God they came. Two broken ribs, a nasty wobbly leg, and probably exposure and pneumonia as well. I thought she was very courageous to shout out, "God bless you. Enjoy your holiday!" as they carted her off.'

'Some of the girls were pretty disappointed that the helicopter actually landed and picked up Miss Smallwood,' said Connie. 'They thought that those flyers would put down a rope or a cable, or whatever they do, and haul Miss Smallwood up to them. Can't you just see her waving as they pulled her up on the winch, and, maybe, slowly, majestically, revolving around and around as she went. What a sight that would have been! Gosh, some of those girls are really gruesome. They were getting real excited about what would happen if poor Miss Smallwood slipped off the cable and plopped down to the ground again.'

'Did somebody give her a push?' persisted William.

'How do I know? Everybody was crowding near the edge of the cliff to see the puffins and I guess it was easy for someone to strain over too far and accidentally launch Miss Smallwood.'

'Monsters,' sighed William. She had him cupped in her hands now. She ran them around his aching lower parts and up to his stomach as though she were washing him. He reached, unpulled her zip, and she wriggled out of her trousers. The moon flooded in on them from every side.

'In you go, Willie boy,' she repeated, but this time softly. Eventually she whispered: 'Splash.'

They lay, writhing slowly, on top of the wide cast-iron plate. The curved windows, looking out on the island and the sea from all sides, were like a cage all about them. When they had finished they hung together, letting their mingled sweat cool, in the sleeping bag.

'Hemingway said that until you'd had sex in a sleeping bag you didn't know what it was about,' she said eventually.

'I bet he didn't think of a sleeping bag on top of a disused lighthouse in bright moonlight,' yawned William.

'We couldn't do this so easily if Miss Smallwood was still here,' she pointed out.

'She wouldn't come up here,' said William. Then he looked at her. 'I bet you *did* give her a push,' he said.

Connie said nothing. Then she shrugged. 'It's going to be more fascinating without her,' she said. 'I feel that observing the greater ruffed ringed short-assed urine wader all day and Gilbert and Sullivan around the campfire at night has certain limitations. We'll just have to remember her last words as the great bird whisked her away, "God bless you all. Enjoy your holiday" – and live by them.'

'What about Miss Tilling?'

She regarded him quizzically. 'Surely *you* know about Miss Tilling?' she said.

He did not know about Miss Tilling. But he said: 'Oh, of course.'

'Just think,' whispered Connie. 'An island miles from anywhere. No Miss Smallwood, and Miss Tilling going about her own interests. William, my boy, you could be having a field day. There's me and there's Susan and some of the other girls. There's that cute Jackie . . .'

'Connie,' he pleaded, 'I wish you wouldn't . . . There's that cute *who*? Jackie?'

'Jackie,' she nodded. 'She likes you, haven't you noticed?'

'That kid with the broken teeth and the boils! I *thought* she'd been looking at me in a strange way. Connie, for God's sake, you just cannot keep fixing these girls up with me. Darling, don't you know it's *you* that I want. You can keep the others . . .'

'You didn't send Susan back unopened,' she observed.

'It was only . . . It was just . . . Oh, for Christ's sake. All right, I didn't send Susan back. But Jackie. She's so terrible, Connie. I swear she's got a cast as well. I know she has.'

'Only if you stare at her for a long time. Several minutes. I know they try it in her class. All the girls do it. She's probably very sexy, William. And she's very keen.'

'Clean?'

'Clean and keen. And her boils aren't nearly so bad at this time of the year. I wouldn't wish her on you in early March. But the cherry harvest is past.'

He was about to say: 'You make me feel like a prostitute,' when there was a sound from the lamp room below. The trap-door issuing from the narrow, curling, lighthouse stairs, made a gritty sound and amber light flowed into the area below them, beaming up through the wide openings at the sides of the metal plate on which they stretched.

A stiff cold came over William. Connie seemed relaxed and did not move. He looked at her anxiously but she only blinked both eyes at him carefully, reassuringly. Someone was in the room below them now, the light was wandering about.

Miss Tilling's voice echoed in the enclosed lamp room as though she were speaking in a tomb. Connie smiled at William and confidently pulled her sheepskin coat closer to her breasts and stomach. William was fearfully trying to creep back into his trousers.

'At last – at the top,' said Miss Tilling with a whispered heartiness. 'We could be at the top of the world, dear. Let's put it here, shall we. It's just as well it's a wind-up isn't it? We wouldn't find a plug up here.'

Bewildered, William stared at Connie. She was coolly leaning over the side of the platform, just sufficiently to see a segment of the lower room. She held her fingers against William's thigh for him to keep silent. From below came stifled movements and the lamplight shuddered a little. Connie straightened and they sat still.

Then music began. It was the thin, cracked, cobwebbed music of a nineteen-thirties dance orchestra, scraped from the last layers of a senile record. It moaned pitifully around the lighthouse walls. William felt the short hairs of his neck turn stiff. Connie's hand covered her mouth. On the walls of the round room below them, moving around like a Victorian drum shadowgraph, were the twisted forms of two people close together, waltzing with the excruciating melody.

A remote crooner joined the band, his voice like some beggar pleading for alms. The shadows progressed like horned dragons along the white walls. Connie edged eagerly, but stealthily, to the rim of the plate again and with tense care looked over. William saw her back stiffen. Her naked arm crept back towards him and her long finger beckoned. He crawled to her.

His face went, a quarter of an inch at a time, down over the edge of the old platform. His eyes cleared the rusty rim and he was staring into the room below. Miss Tilling, wearing a blue boiler suit and a peaked cap was waltzing, eyes ecstatically closed, with one of the twelve-year-olds, a thin, string-legged child, recognizable from the rear as Theresa Thompson-Vickers.

They danced with short, hesitant steps, the music groaning bleakly from an elderly gramophone set on the stone floor near the trapdoor. Theresa was clutched uncompromisingly to Miss Tilling's boiler suit, her face buried in the blue denim, the mistress' eagle arms tightly around her.

Connie watched fascinated; William, unbelieving and horrified.

They were safe for Miss Tilling did not open her eyes, but waltzed on until the music had finally choked and expired. They pulled back their heads and heard her and the small girl applauding politely before the record was turned to its other side.

36

'You know, Bill, there are times when I can't convince myself that you're not making things up.'

'I *couldn't* make things up like that, Rufus. It was so grotesque, so horrible and perverted. It made my flesh creep to see her dancing around like that with that little girl.'

'And you say she was wearing a boiler suit and a cap.'

'I'm afraid so. People must be sick to carry on in that way. Don't you agree with me? And, of course, there was worse to come. I must be the world's greatest innocent. I mean it. Just to think that sort of thing was probably going on all the time at Southwelling and I wasn't aware of it.'

'Well you have to admit you were pretty busy one way and another.'

'That's true. I took the tennis coaching most seriously during the spring and summer terms because of this big prestige match for the Clifton Cup. Miss Smallwood told me that the school governors had set their hearts on winning back that cup after twelve years and I was the one they were confident could do it. That was a huge responsibility. The girls were coming along very well. Miss Smallwood came down to the courts every afternoon and watched, and sometimes Miss Elliott and Miss Hecht or one or two of the other mistresses would come to. I remember Miss Smallwood remarking to Miss Whitefriar that the transformation was quite phenomenal. "Mr Herbert seems to do something special to the girls," she said.'

'Many a true word, I suppose, Bill. Anyway, what about the island? This was the Easter holiday was it, and you'd gone there to observe the birds and all that sort of thing?'

'That was certainly the intention, Rufus. They had accommodation there in some converted cottages and in the disused lighthouse. Miss Smallwood thought it would be a good place for the girls, like Connie, who had nowhere special to go at Easter, or who would prefer to go bird-watching to going home to their parents; and for myself, Miss Tilling and Miss Smallwood, who had no hard and fast plans anyway. It was all intended to be good decent fun.'

'After seeing Miss Tilling do her dance in the lighthouse you saw something else, did you?'

'I'll say. It was so fantastic I don't know how to describe it. Even now I can hardly believe I saw it. I know you won't believe it, Rufus. I'm quite prepared for that.'

'Well, I'm sitting comfortably.'

'I'll begin, then.'

'Yes please, Bill.'

'It was the following evening after the business in the lighthouse. It was not quite dusk and you could see the lights on the mainland getting stronger. All day I couldn't take my eyes off Miss Tilling. She had a very strong face, that woman, and at the table I watched her munching away so calmly and chatting to the girls in her usual chirpy way. I thought, "You rotten butch."

'Frankly, I'd never heard that word for it before – "butch" – but Connie told me all the girls knew Miss Tilling was butch and I think that summed her up pretty fairly. Really carefully I watched her, especially when she was very near the girls, but she acted most cleverly. There was not a sign that she was lusting after them. I'd never come across a butch before, Rufus, and I'll make no bones about it, the whole business disgusted me. It's so bloody unnatural.'

'With young girls, too.'

'Exactly, with young girls.'

'Is your nose sore today?'

'Why, you're not thinking of ... you know?'

'It crossed my mind, I must admit. It does sometimes. Some things trigger it off. I get an almost irrepressible urge. But this time I've repressed it.'

'I'm relieved. Shall I carry on?'

'Please. Sorry, Bill; yes, you carry on.'

'After dinner, anyway, Miss Tilling announces quite brazenly that she and the twins – Mrs Ferber's twins, Tina and Claire, two lovely kids as I've said before – are going off to look for the nests of the lesser late-night godwit or some such creature. And off they went, away from the camp, which is what we called the area around the cottages and the lighthouse . . .'

'Well named.'

'Yes . . . oh, I see. Another joke, Rufus. I can spot them easily now, can't I!'

'You're getting brighter.'

'Thanks. Well, anyway, they strolled off through the dusk, naturally as you please. I made some excuse and went into the lighthouse and out of the back door. I sprinted up to the hilly part of the island and down through some heather and a series of little ravines, so that I cut back on to the path they would have to take. I made good time and eventually I'd got myself established behind some rocks and gorse and I could see them approaching in the distance. They were all holding hands and I could hear the twins laughing through the dusk. I shuddered as I lay there, hearing that happy laughter. Frankly, I didn't know what to expect. But what actually happened!

'Anyway – there was a sort of grassy depression just below me and they came along the path and stopped right there. They were only about forty yards away. Everybody seemed to know what to do. The girls stripped off to their vests and knickers but Miss Tilling stayed fully clothed.'

'Boiler suit and cap?'

'No, she was just in her normal sort of tweedy things.'

'Go on, Bill.'

'It was almost like a light-hearted ritual. The twins scampered down to the bottom of this saucer-shaped dip. They were nicely developed girls, as I've said, Rufus, and their bosoms were bouncing under their school vests as they ran down the slope.

'When they reached the bottom of the small valley they stood close to each other, both giggling, as though they were sharing a joke. They had their backs to Miss Tilling who had stayed at the top of the slope.

'I simply could *not* make out what was going on. If I hadn't felt so worried and disgusted I think I might even have been excited. I'm ashamed to admit it, but it's true. It was so secret and primitive. I felt that almost *anything* might have happened.'

'What did happen? For Christ's sake.'

'Indeed, for Christ's sake. Everthing was still, motionless, for a minute. It was like a tableau or an open-air play. Then suddenly Miss Tilling let out a sort of cackle, a terrible sound. It frightened the life out of me. And she raised herself on her toes, lifted her tweed skirt above her knees and charged down the slope at the twins like some berserk thing. My God, it was unbelievable! She came squawking down the slope at a gallop and the girls looked up and threw up their hands as though they were terrified, which they weren't, of course, because they obviously knew perfectly well what was going to happen.'

'What did?'

'Wait a minute, Rufus. You're getting all flushed, I swear.'

'Get on with it.'

'She just fell on them. She attacked them like a crazy thing. It was obviously only playing, but Jesus it looked fierce enough. She knocked both the girls off their feet and they all started rolling and wrestling together on the grass. They were squealing and panting and making out they were hurt. It was phenomenal, Rufus. As I've said, the twins were healthy girls and they could have made mincemeat of Miss Tilling if they'd wanted. But they let her pretend to savage them something appalling. They rolled over and over, bare legs in the air all mixed up with her thick woollen stockings. She jumped on them and when they pretended to try and escape she cackled again and pulled them back. It went on for minutes until, at the end of the game, Miss Tilling was sitting, all triumphant, on top of them. They were both stretched out, panting and sweating, and, I must confess, looking very eye-catching in their knickers and vests, and she was squatting on them, her woollen legs stuck out wide, one on one side and one on the other. She was making all manner of unearthly noises and the girls were giving off little imitation cries. Then, as though the spell had been broken, Miss Tilling's head dropped forward and they all started to laugh. I think that shook me more than anything.'

'Was that the lot?'

'No, that was only half-time, Rufus. Just the intermission. Miss Tilling got up and went up the slope again and brought a flask and they all had a drink of tea or coffee or something. I wondered that the girls didn't catch cold being half undressed like that.

'They were both perspiring like mad and Miss Tilling kept on pulling at her jumper and then loosening her knicks because, I suppose, she was sweating something terrible inside her clothes'.

'And there was more.'

'Yes, all right, Rufus. I'm trying to tell it as it happened. After they'd had their drinks the girls went up to the top of the bank and Miss Tilling stayed down in the hollow. It was getting quite dark now and I'm not sure what she was supposed to be doing. But it looked as though she was making out she was picking wildflowers. She walked along a bit and bent down and then went a few feet farther. Then the girls did exactly as she had done. They yelled like a couple of banshees and came dashing down the hill. It was fantastic. They hit her both at once – bang! Down she went and then the fight started all over again. How they didn't really hurt each other I'll never know. It was so brutal. Rolling and punching and getting their legs around each other. Once both the twins were on top of her at once and jumping up and down like pistons. But apparently the game was that Miss Tilling had to win in the end. She eventually overpowered them and the finale was just the same as before, with her sitting across them and them moaning in the grass.'

'What sort of birds did you see on the island, Bill?'

'Eh? Birds? Oh, all sorts, Rufus. Cormorants, puffins, guillemots, oyster catchers. Dozens of different sorts.'

'So it was worth going there. You enjoyed yourself.'

'Er . . . yes, Rufus.'

'I'm glad you did. Very easy to get bored on an island I should imagine.'

37

THE LIGHTS of Pembrokeshire lay against the sky four miles away like a low extension of the stars. William squatted like a watchman at the top of his solitary lighthouse, on the sleeping bag spread out over the iron platform, and waited for Connie. The island immediately below the pinnacle rippled away like heavy velvet in the dark and fell invisibly into the sea. No moon had arrived, but it was expected.

He heard the scrape of the metal bolt on the door at the root of the lighthouse and counted the seconds that she would take to curl around and up the steep stairs within its core. Torchlight invaded the lamp room below as the trapdoor was eased. Her shadow was wriggling tantalizingly on the wall.

'Mr Herbert.' The voice was a whisper in the white drum below.

It was not Connie. He knew who it was.

'Who is it?' he asked.

'Jackie,' she answered. He heard the metallic enthusiasm as she jumped upon the iron ladder that hung to the side of the platform. 'Jackie MacAllister.'

He squatted gloomily. She banged heavily as though staking a claim to each iron rung as she ascended before her head appeared over the edge of the round plate. She was an abysmally ugly child and this she had accentuated that night by having a great gash of lipstick applied to her mouth and environs. There was a jagged smile trapped hideously between the lips. The eyes were uncertain, but William was relieved to note immediately that there was no definite cast in them. He had never examined her closely before.

'Can I come right up, Mr Herbert?' she asked.

He nodded resignedly at her. A sturdy neck followed the hopeful face and then a broad foreshortened body, heavy breasted, and encompassed in a tight maroon sweater. A kilt of almost masculine cut and proportions came next and then the strong legs held in white woollen stockings up to the rounded knees.

She stood beside him on the platform, kilt astride, like some powerful and patriotic Scottish memorial. Shyly she looked down at him. 'Can I sit down?' she said.

'Oh, sorry Jackie,' he mumbled, moving over. 'Yes please sit down. I am just looking at the lights.'

'I would prefer to watch the stars,' she said thickly. He felt a nervous tremor go through him but she was being academic not romantic. He remembered she was a brainy girl.

'There are quite a lot,' he said inadequately.

'That constellation is Lupus,' she pointed. 'My favourite.'

'I like that one, too,' he agreed. 'It's very well . . . arranged.'

'Do you *truly*, Mr Herbert?' she turned slowly and looked into his face. To his intense discomfiture and, as though in keeping with the astronomical trend of their conversation, her right eyeball began to descend, slowly, like a small but important comet, towards the bridge of her nose. He watched it with creeping fascination until it stopped, lodged comfortably in the deepest corner of the socket.

'Over there,' she said pointing suddenly, dramatically, like some explorer opening the way, 'in Pembrokeshire, of course, they had the nineteenth-century religious rising. The Pembrokeshire Callaphumpians. Martyrs, Mr Herbert, martyrs every one.'

She swung to him again. The eyeball, he perceived, had returned to the centre of her eye, but now, as she faced him, it began to descend again as though the swift movement of her head disturbed it.

'You're very well informed for a little girl,' said William awkwardly. He forced his attention away from her eye. 'Very well indeed.'

'I'm well read, I suppose,' she shrugged. She pulled up her stout legs and let the kilt slide back towards her thighs. 'Some people do one thing, some others. I'm not much good at tennis, for instance, am I?'

'Well, if you can't get on with it, far better to stay away altogether,' he said professionally, thinking of the difficulty she would experience in keeping that eye on the ball.

'But,' she said. 'I *know* that Tenby has a population of 12,859 at the last census, and that 384 of these are engaged in the twilling industry.'

'Really? I didn't know they did that down here.'

'Twilling? Oh, yes. This used to be one of the great centres. But, of course, it's declined since the introduction of the Abbiter Separator, and all those other devices.'

'I imagine it would.'

A shy shoulder of moon came up behind distant Wales, sending threads of light across the sea to the island. 'Third quarter,' said Jackie decisively. 'According to statistics, of course this corner of Great Britain has more moonlight per year than any other part.'

'Astonishing,' he said. Then: 'Perhaps you ought to be getting back. It's pretty late to be on top of a lighthouse. You'll be too tired for nesting tomorrow.'

She glanced at him as though he had intended the innuendo. The eye had lolled only halfway to its corner, however, before she turned her head away again.

'It makes me feel very poetic up here, Mr Herbert,' she said. 'Do you know Edmund Waller? *Thoughts on the Distant Prospect of a Melancholy Death*. We've been reading it with Miss Bonner in English literature.'

'No ... No. I can't say I've read that one. I've seen it, I think, but I didn't read it. Probably didn't have time. Tennis takes up a surprising amount of time, you know.'

'I can imagine. And all the other things you do.'

'Yes, those.'

'Well, you know, the Gilbert and Sullivan and that sort of thing. Wasn't it terrible when you accidentally burst into the dressing-room like that. I was *so* sorry for you, Mr Herbert.'

'Yes, yes. It was a nasty moment.'

The land below them had become distant from the sea now that the moon was shining. The ocean breathed as though it were bored by the whole thing and a dry wind rustled the island grass.

'Would you like to hear it?'

'What?'

'I told you, silly. *Thoughts on the Distant Prospect of a Melancholy Death*, by Edmund Waller.' She turned her unappetizing face to him once more, the lipsticked mouth sagging open, the eyeball beginning its arc again. William looked away.

She continued:

'*The forward youth that would appear,*
Where the remote Bermudas ride,
What nymph should I admire or trust,
Charm me asleep, and melt me so.
Come thou who art the wine and wit,
My spotless love hovers with purest wings.
To me, fair friend, you never can be old;
Since there's no help, come let us kiss and part.
Oh thou undaunted daughter of desires
Earth has not anything to show more fair.
She stood breast-high amid the corn,
Angel, king of streaming morn.'

She halted as though on the brink of a large hole, and, to his relief, did not look at him but continued gazing out towards the vague night sea.

'Very nice,' nodded William. 'Very profound. All of it. Well, it's getting a bit chilly up here, Jackie.'

'We could go down below,' she suggested helpfully. 'It's very mysterious down in the lighthouse rooms. Let's go down.'

'You go on down,' he coaxed. 'I'll be staying up here for a while. I've got a lot on my mind, young lady, believe me. Tennis and that sort of thing.'

'Come down,' she insisted. She had climbed powerfully to her feet, so that he was looking up her legs to the great lampshade of her kilt. 'Come down and bring the sleeping bag.'

'Jackie!' he exploded. 'What are you saying, child?'

'Connie sent me,' she said looking at him squarely with no more than a tremble in her eye. 'She told me to come.' The crimson lips broke open to a badly damaged smile and she held a beefy hand to him.

He resignedly took the hand and she powerfully helped him to his feet. Determinedly she gathered the sleeping bag and stepped aside for him to walk before her down the stairs.

'Connie said,' she muttered again.

William nodded and walked.

38

'RUFUS, YOU'VE seen those ventriloquists on the television, haven't you? The ones who made a mouthy sort of doll out of their hand and the thumb is the underneath part of the mouth.'

'Saw one only last Sunday, Bill. Very clever, I thought.'

'You know how they make all the thumb and the next finger all red and the mouth opens and shuts something terrible.'

'Like a coal scuttle.'

'Just right, Rufus. Very true. Well, that's how Jackie's mouth was. God, with all that lipstick it looked just like a horrible wound. I had it all over me. Face, hands, chest, legs, back. I looked like I'd been attacked by Red Indians.'

'You had her, then?'

'This was just from the preliminaries. That red mouth! It gives me nightmares still.'

'But you *had* her?'

'Well, yes, I suppose I did really. I didn't *want* her. But that's what she came for, didn't she? Connie fixed it up. She didn't come up there to talk about the stars.'

'How old?'

'Jackie?'

'I didn't mean the stars.'

'Sorry, Rufus. Don't get annoyed. Jackie was around fifteen, I suppose.'

'You're always "supposing", Bill. It's an annoying little habit you've got. You "suppose" she was about fifteen, you "suppose" you screwed her. Don't you bloody well know?'

'Of course. It's just a . . . ufffff . . . uuuuuffff . . . uf . . . uf . . .'

'You can't breathe can you, Bill? I've got my hands right over that poor old nose and that mouth, haven't I. Say something to Rufus, Bill.'

'Uff.'

'Right, now in future no more "supposing". Let's have some straight answers.'

'. . . uf . . .'

'Okay. Now you can breathe. Ugh, you've made all this hand wet. You blew your nose in my hand, you insanitary bastard!'

'Oh, God, no! No, I didn't, Rufus. Not on purpose. Honestly. It was because I was suffocating. Don't suffocate me again, please.'

'Right, well remember what I've said.'

'Frankly I think I prefer the old nose-pulling days.'

'Just get on with the business. Did you screw the girl Jackie MacAllister?'

'Yes, I suppose . . . No! I mean I *definitely* did. I did, Rufus. Her pants were in the collection you found in my suitcase. They were the outsize ones.'

'And what about her?'

'Well, what? She wasn't exactly a substitute for Connie or Susan. That eye! Even when we were lying there in the lamp room I couldn't take my eyes off it. The way it kept drifting down like a spent firework.'

'Was she a virgin?'

'Yes, she was. The *only* one who was, I might say.'

'Wasn't that nice? Lying there with her kilt up?'

'If you think that having it away with a pipe-major in the Seaforth Highlanders would be nice, then, yes, I suppose it was. But I didn't enjoy it very much, thank you.'

'She sounds a very brainy virgin. That poem, she wrote it down for you?'

'Yes, I've kept it with me. I don't know why.'

'Who was it by? Somebody Waller. We've got a sergeant down the station called Waller.'

'He could have written this, then. The rotten little cow was having me on, just piss-taking like all the others. Why couldn't they leave me alone? *Some* poem. It's all the first lines out of about *twelve* damn poems in the *Oxford Book of English Verse*. They just picked them straight out of the index. It doesn't make bloody sense, any of it. And all this other rubbish . . .'

'Now, *I* could have told you about Lupus, Bill, When I was in the Navy I spent a long time looking at stars. Lupus can only be seen in the southern hemisphere. She was certainly taking you for a ride there.'

'And the Pembrokeshire Callaphumpians. Martyrs! Christ, she should have been a martyr. Piss-taking little bugger.'

'And the population of Tenby?'

'God knows. But they don't do any twilling in Tenby, because there's no such thing as twilling. Ignorant little so-and-so, having me on like that.'

'Who told you all this?'

'Miss Smallwood. When we were back at school in the summer term, weeks later, I said something to her about there being 12,859 people in Tenby at the last census and 384 of them being occupied in the twilling industry.'

'And she'd never heard of twilling?'

'Exactly. She thought I was having a little joke with her. She could never see anything wrong in me, Miss Smallwood. She's a nice lady, you know.'

'Yes, I know how she felt about you. She's been interviewed by other officers.'

'What did she say, Rufus?'

'Haven't I told you before! You must not pry into the Crown's case! Jesus, you'll be trying to bribe me with that motorized bicycle of yours next.'

'Goodness! Fancy you remembering that, Rufus. It's still at Southwelling. I was going to send for it later. It cost me eighty-seven pounds, you know. I thought of selling it to help pay for my defence.'

'You're getting legal aid.'

'That's right. I get Mr Decent for absolutely nothing.'

'That's too expensive for Mr Decent.'

'I wonder when I'll see my phut-phut bike again. I was very fond of it really.'

'I'll make inquiries about it. We may need it for evidence. Has it got a pump?'

'Oh yes, it's got all the fittings.'

'I'll make official inquiries. Now what was it? Oh yes, twilling. You found out it was a joke.'

'I wouldn't call it that, personally. She'd just been telling me a rotten load of lies. I checked the other things in the school library and they were all rubbish, too. Then I asked Miss Bonner – very carefully, of course – about the poem. She was a bit puzzled but she laughed like fury in the end and told me to have a look in the index of the *Oxford Book of English Verse*. She thought the poem was ingenious, she said, and asked me if I had made it up myself. Anyway when I checked with the index in the *Oxford Book of English Verse* I realized what had happened. Horrible bitch, that Jackie MacAllister. Her and her great mouth! I'm glad I didn't enjoy her sexually, I can tell you!'

'I don't want to keep harping on about these knickers, Bill. But we've still got two pairs unaccounted for.'

'Well, they sort of . . . er . . . accumulated during the summer term. Connie had recommended them of course – or recommended *me* to them, more like it. I worked very hard on the tennis that term, because of the Clifton Cup match against St Margaret's, and, quite truthfully I was more concerned about that than anything else. The whole being of the school seemed to hang about that damned cup. Miss Smallwood was on about it almost every day. She would be down at the courts whooping encouragement and giving advice every afternoon. I don't think she'd ever played in her life.'

'What about the other two girls? In case you can't remember the details, the names embroidered across the crotches of the pants were Tina and Yum Yum.'

'Tina was one of the Ferber girls, of course.'

'Indeed. I was wondering when you were going to get around to them.'

'Not *them*. Only Tina. I only visited when I was asked. And Yum Yum was Pamela Watts. I think in many ways she was the best kid in the school. So small. They called her Yum Yum because of *The Mikado*. Or did I tell you that?'

'You did. When did these two incidents happen?'

'I suppose . . .'

'You're supposing agin, Bill. You know I hate it when you start supposing.'

'July. Definitely July, Rufus. It was very hot and we had more or less fixed the team for the cup and they were practising every afternoon. Miss Hecht, the games mistress, was giving them extra physical training. Believe me, *my* mind was every bit on the tennis, but not everybody's. Connie and Susan were both in the team but, for God's sake, they only *both* came to my bed on the very night *before* the big match. They woke me up and before I knew what had happened they had both climbed in. I was really annoyed with them, Rufus. *The night before the match!* They had not an atom of loyalty those girls. I just don't know what to make of young people today.'

'Well, you made bed-partners of five of them.'

'That's a bit uncalled for, Rufus.'

'Forgive my big sigh, Bill. But get on with it, will you. We're farting about too much. You'll be in court again in two days. I want to get this straight in my mind by then. You'll be remanded again anyway but . . .'

'Again? You mean they'll shove me back in here for another week? They said it would only be a week.'

'We'll be asking for a further seven days in custody. We've got to get our case completely watertight, haven't we. Seven days – at least. Now let's get a bit of a move on. I want to take the wife out tonight.'

'That should be nice, Rufus. Anywhere special?'

'Just the pictures, I expect. But it will be a treat after being stuck indoors so long. You don't know how claustrophobic you get having to stay in all the time.'

'What a pity I can't baby-sit for you.'

'We're fixed tonight, but I'll bear it in mind. We could always bring the kid in here to you, I suppose.'

'Would you! I'd love . . . Oh Christ, you're only playing about.'

'Of course I'm playing about. Jesus, I wouldn't let you look after my bloody tom cat. Not after what you've been telling me.'

'Not even your cat, eh? I suppose it does all sound pretty damning. Do you think it will sound as bad as all that to the court?'

'Worse, much worse. I don't want to worry you unduly but, after all, I'm quite used to hearing all this stuff now, but frankly – no offence meant – it even raises my fucking hat at times. Imagine what it's going to sound like to those who've not heard it before.'

'Yes, I've thought about that point. I don't suppose there's any chance you could gloss it over, could you? I mean there's my motorized bicycle down at Southwelling and . . .'

'I *didn't* hear that, Bill. I just *didn't* hear it. Do you understand? I may speak to you about your bicycle at some other time,

209

but just now I didn't hear what you said. It was nothing short of attempted bribery.'

'Sorry, Rufus. Thanks for being so decent about it.'

'Where did it happen with the twin – Tina Ferber?'

'In my room again. But in the afternoon. I had just come in and I was stretched out reading *Tennis for Girls*, a very good book if you ever want to teach girls to play tennis, by the way . . .'

'I don't expect I will.'

'Well, she simply came in. They were a fine-looking pair. The twins, that is. But I think Tina had the edge on the other one. Claire was inclined to spots.'

'*You'll* be inclined to spots if you don't get on.'

'Yes, yes. Sorry. Well she came in bringing a tray of tea. Pot of tea, bread and butter, jam, and that sort of thing.'

'I know what tea looks like.'

'She had the blue print dress on, the summer dress of the school, and a straw hat hanging by its elastic over her shoulder. Sometimes Miss Everett, the mathematics mistress, who, for some reason, was responsible for dishing out afternoon teas, used to send one of the girls to find me with a tray, but it was always when I was on the tennis courts. On this day I'd finished a bit early and that young Tina used it as an excuse for coming to my room.'

'You pulled the blind down.'

'No. I had curtains then. The blind kept on sticking, as I told you. The curtains were pulled across anyway because the afternoon sun was pouring through the window on us. I mean on *me*. She said Miss Everett had sent her, but it was more like Connie had sent her, of course. I could see that the moment she came in. She blatantly sat on the bed and poured my tea. Then she started. I didn't even get time to drink the tea.'

'Go on. Or I'll pull your nose.'

'These things are a bit awful, sometimes. I mean, they seem to show me up in such a bad light.'

'I'll pull your nose.'

'She just took her summer dress off and the rest of her things and we lay on the bed and did it. Made love. It was very, very hot, I remember, and we sweated a good deal. She seemed to know all about it and she enjoyed what we were doing. I could tell by the way she kept biting her lip and pulling little funny faces. She had fair hair, as I may have told you, and she had it cut quite short at this time. It was wringing with sweat and sticking to her face and forehead. A strange thing happened actually, Rufus.'

'What strange thing?'

'Everything was going on . . . you know, with us on the bed, when suddenly we heard her sister Claire calling her out in the garden. Jesus, the girl stiffened like stone. One minute she had been moving, all soft and hot, and the next she was rigid. Frightened stiff.'

'Perhaps she didn't want her sister to know she was being screwed unmercifully by the tennis master.'

'But . . . well, all right . . . But remember the pair of them with Miss Tilling on the island. All that caper. They must have *known* what was going on then. And Tina knew all about what was happening between me and her. She was no novice, believe me. I don't know where these girls got hold of boys, unless they had a sort of teenage orgy every holiday, or the lads in Lewes made hay on the Sunday afternoon walks.'

'She was upset when she heard her sister calling?'

'Not upset. She merely went very still and stiff. Then she wriggled out and went to the window and pulled the curtain aside just a fraction so that she could look out. At one time it seemed that Claire was right outside the window, still calling for Tina. Then she went away and Tina came back to me. After that it was all right.'

39

HE KNEW that he would have to leave at the end of July. The long-drawn days were on Sussex, the brick school lay dry among the summer laden trees, and the river flooded with the overspill of ridiculous sunsets.

'My father would call that a *flambé* sunset,' Yum Yum had

said when they had finished on the court and she was helping him to lower the net. 'He's very extravagant with his language, my father.'

She was small and demurely pretty. Her face, arms and legs were like caramel against the tennis dress, her eyes a careful blue.

'Don't forget that forehand,' he instructed her. 'You're naturally aggressive and that's fine, but aggression is not a bit of use unless it's controlled.'

'All right,' she said simply. 'Connie said you're leaving at the end of term.'

He stopped. 'Connie *shouldn't* say,' he told her severely. 'Does she tell everything about me? For heaven's sake. I only said I *might* be going.'

'But you are, aren't you?' she persisted. 'You've had enough.'

He looked at her closely.

'I simply said I might be going,' he muttered.

'Where?'

'I don't know. Antwerp probably. I'm just going to have a look at the world, that's all.'

She smiled, turned her face deliberately to him. He took one of her rackets from her and swung it absently in its press. 'When you're out in the world,' she suggested, 'have a look out for my father. He's just run off with our German au pair girl.'

'That's a bit inconvenient,' he said lamely.

'I don't blame him, mind you,' she sniffed as they walked. 'Dagmar – that's her name. Dagmar. A terrible name, isn't it? But she was super. Only seventeen. She's a good swop for my mother any day.'

'Your mother wouldn't like to hear you say that,' remonstrated William.

'She probably will hear me say it before the end of August,' she told him when they had reached the pavilion. 'Will you wait for me out here?'

The tennis courts and the fields beside the river were fallow, idle, in the drifting evening. Pigeons were attempting muffled conversation in the eaves of the tennis pavilion. A motorcycle curled noisily away on the high road, beyond the trees, a mile away.

'All right,' said William. 'I'll wait. Don't be too long or I shall miss the staff Ovaltine in the common room.'

He did not know why he was waiting; or he tried not to know. He told himself it was a matter of courtesy not to leave a young lady at this distance from the school so late in the evening.

Uneasily he sat below a cascading oak, feeling a trifling evening breeze sniffing inside his tennis shirt. He looked at the racket in his right hand and swung it strongly first with the right, then the left, then both together. His face was tight from the sun. His forearms were burned beneath the short curving hairs. Imagine having all the achievement of your life wrapped up in a frying-pan of wood and catgut, he thought dismally. Once he threw that racket away there was nothing that the world could want with him, require of him. He remembered again his sailor friends, months ago, and how they had accepted him and liked him. Where were they now? On a dozen seas, in dangerous waters or voyaging in bland sunlight. And he was in Sussex, sitting beneath an oak, waving a tennis racket. And listening to the shower water gushing on to a pretty little girl.

The shower was stemmed. He waited on edge. After two minutes her voice came anxiously out of the tiled changing room. 'Mr Herbert. Mr Herbert, please.' He convinced himself it was urgent. Trembling he got to his feet.

'Yes?'

'Mr Herbert.'

She had hurt herself, he lied. Damn that lie. She had cut her foot on a broken lemonade bottle left lying under the wooden bench. Miss King had found some broken glass there only the previous week. The small voice, so subdued. She must be fainting because of the blood.

'Mr Herbert.'

He swung around once to make certain nobody was watching. Then, stifled within his chest, he strode in through the beckoning door. He went around the smoothly tiled corner. Yum Yum, small as a much younger child, was standing on the bench. She had dried her sunburned body and had climbed into a pair of white lace briefs.

'You called me?' he managed to say. Christ, he had never seen anything like her. The little shoulders, the dark sweet short

213

hair, the baby legs. Her miniature breasts stood out like small hubs, their flesh bashful white against the tan of the rest.

'I think there's a mouse, Mr Herbert,' she breathed.

'A mouse?'

'I saw it. It was running around.'

'It's a bit damp for mice. It's more likely to be a toad in here.' He said each word carefully and separately, so that they would not wobble as they came out. 'Anyway, I don't believe you.' He stepped decisively towards her, put his hands to her waist and lifted her from the bench. She was standing against him then, on the floor.

'I haven't got hardly anything on,' she said.

'No, you haven't.'

'Connie said . . .'

'Connie *shouldn't* say.'

'You're going away soon. To Antwerp.'

He put his dry lips against the top of her dark head which was level with his trembling chin. Her hands moved up to his arms, her palms small but firm, and her face turned up towards him.

'Sometimes the girls are very cruel to you,' she murmured. 'They're always laughing. That night in the bathroom. She wasn't really drowning, you know. They only did it because you're . . . good-looking . . . and a man . . . and nice. You're so nice, you know, that you're really a bit stupid sometimes.'

'I've worked that out,' he agreed. 'I know all about the bathroom. It was a terrible thing to do to . . . a . . . tennis . . . coach.'

He could feel the small rubbery impression her breasts were making against his stomach. 'My chubbies are small, aren't they?' she said.

'Your what?'

'My chubbies, silly. These.'

'Oh.'

'I shall get sick of my mother before a couple of weeks of the holiday are over. Can I come to Antwerp and stay with you? You can show me around?'

He groaned. 'It wouldn't suit you,' he said distantly. 'It's a terrible place. Besides which I may be away at sea by that time.'

'I've got so much I want to tell you.'

'What sort of things?'

'All sorts. Will you let me?'

'All right. You mean . . . you need a grown-up to talk to.'

'Sit on the bench and I'll sit on your lap.'

'For a few minutes, then. It's the staff Ovaltine time, remember.'

'I will. I wouldn't want you to miss your Ovaltine.'

He sat down and she climbed on to his lap, lying naked against his warm shirt.

'It's a hot evening, isn't it,' she said.

'Boiling,' agreed William.

'Oh, dear Christ,' he said to himself.

The corrugated cream skirt of Miss Smallwood's summer dress sagged sadly against her shins. The blouse had lost its enthusiasm a dozen Julys before and now sighed its summer apathy as the headmistress panted her way through the crowded afternoon. She wore a straw hat, a boater, straight and stuck out like a breadboard. Her face was pink with the sun and there were kind tears behind her spectacles.

'Oh, Mr Herbert,' she said. 'Would that you were not leaving us.'

William found himself making a short formal bow. 'If my brother in Antwerp were not in such difficulty with his shipping lines, nothing would take me away,' he said.

'It must be wonderful to have so many talents in one mortal body,' she enthused sadly. 'So wonderful. Tennis, shipping, commerce. It makes no difference to someone like you. I feel very humble.'

William choked mildly. 'Oh don't feel humble, Miss Smallwood,' he said. 'I shall miss you, too, And the girls.'

'The dear girls,' she said. 'They adore you. I hope that expression does not embarrass you. But they truly do. They *adore* you.'

William blushed. 'I adore them,' he nodded. 'And the school, of course. I have come to love Southwelling, Miss Smallwood.'

The tears slithered below her glasses. 'Oh, don't, please don't! Dear Mr Herbert,' she pleaded. 'This is such an emotional day for me, even at the best of times. One loses so many girls at the end of the summer term.'

'Yes, one does,' agreed William.

'So many. Connie, that splendid Connie, and Susan, and poor little Jackie MacAllister. I do hope they can do something about that eye. All one can hope, Mr Herbert, is that what has gone on within these old walls will help to fit them for life.'

'I'm sure it has, Miss Smallwood,' said William.

'And such friendships! We never know friendships like this again. Never. Such closeness, such camaraderie. If the school song were not in such difficult Latin I feel I would cry like a silly old woman every time it is sung. But somehow Latin and sentiment don't mix. Ah well, never mind, never mind. Now – what about today, Mr Herbert?'

They looked at the pattern of the tennis courts, red and green under the fine sky. The spectators in their summer colours were noisily filling the seats that parcelled the two main courts. Susan and Connie were knocking up in the distant court.

'A fine sight, a fine day,' breathed Miss Smallwood. 'Susan and Connie, simply *look* at them. Fine young women, Mr Herbert. I think of them like that, you know. They may just be schoolgirls to you but to me they are young women. And such friends those two, such companions. They seem to do everything together.'

'They do, I think.'

'And to think that Connie will be carrying back something of us to her homeland, across the seas. It's a considerable gratification, Mr Herbert, a considerable gratification. But enough of this sentimental headmistress talk. What of today, captain? Are we going to win? Is the cup to be ours again?'

'Let's hope so,' said William. He could see Connie and Susan moving splendidly across their court. He suddenly felt tired.

'Let's hope so, indeed,' said Miss Smallwood. She leaned towards William. 'Confidentially, I hope we give St Margaret's the trouncing of their lives. It's not just the Clifton Cup, but, quite truthfully, I cannot stand that little Frenchman they have as their coach. What's his name? Mouly. I simply abhor him. Frankly, I think he is much too familiar with those girls. I've noticed. I notice these things. Far too familiar.'

'Oh, Miss Smallwood, I don't think . . .'

'Now, now, Mr Herbert. To the pure all things are pure. I

appreciate your concern. But I'm afraid that very little surprises me in today's world.'

'No. I suppose not.'

Miss Hartley, Miss King and Miss Hecht, in print summer dresses and identical straw hats, approached and each shook his hand heartily. They ranged up about the headmistress. Miss de Berenger, from the lawn, called: '*Bonne chance!*' Miss Elliott, short blonde hair bouncing at her perspiring neck, looked at him adoringly.

'Now get your team out there, Mr Herbert,' said Miss Smallwood. 'What a pity you cannot yourself join the battle! But do your utmost. Be like St George against the French dragon. And then, the battle done, and victory ours, you can ride off to the horizon, going to conquer new and adventurous fields. Amsterdam!'

'Antwerp,' corrected William.

40

'MY GOODNESS, Rufus, that's a smart suit.'

'Oh. Oh, yes. Glad you like it. This morning I was going by the shop, right next to the motorbike showrooms down the road, and there it was in the window. And I said exactly the same thing as you, Bill. "Now there's a smart suit." So, bang! I went right in and bought it. What's more, I went back home and changed into it. After all, I thought, old Bill doesn't want to be seeing the same old scruffy detective-sergeant every morning. It's time I spruced myself up.'

'In the police force the pay can't be all that bad, then. Just to be able to go into a shop and buy a suit when you feel like it.'

'Now, Bill, don't you go prying into my private financial affairs. They're nothing to do with you.'

'Very sorry, Rufus. I didn't mean to be rude. I just thought what a nice suit, that's all.'

'Let's say we coppers get a little bonus now and again.'

'And you deserve it, doing the job you do.'

'Well, *I* think so.'

'How was the evening out?'

'What d'you mean?'

'Don't be so touchy, Rufus. You're a bit aggressive this morning, considering you've got a new suit and everything. You told me you were taking your wife out last night.'

'Oh that. Yes . . . Well, truthfully, Bill, I had to skip it. Duty, you know. You can't pick and choose your working hours with this mob.'

'That's one of the disadvantages, I suppose. Is that how you got your bonus?'

'More or less.'

'Was it a *raid*, Rufus. Did you *swoop* on somewhere?'

'Now, now, Bill, you know I can't discuss police business with a prisoner.'

'I am, aren't I. You know, that hasn't really occurred to me before. A prisoner. I've never thought of myself as one of *them*. Oh, I know I'm shut up here and they bang the door pretty loudly every time anybody goes out, just to let me know I'm locked in, but somehow I can't be convinced. Sometimes I can almost kid myself that they've put me in here as a favour – to stop the outside bloody world getting at me. Ha! It's almost as if you lot were imprisoned – all jammed up together out there – and there's me all free and safe in here.'

'They've been talking about you quite a lot, Bill. You know the old gossips, solicitors, coppers, that crowd, and I estimate you're going to be free and locked up for a long time.'

'That's why I want to get this court business over and all through, Rufus. At least when I've *got* my sentence I'll be able to start working off the days towards my release. I can't even do that at the moment.'

'You know, Bill, the strange thing is I've become very interested in you.'

'I'm interested in you, too, Rufus.'

'No, I mean I've spent far more time on this case, just talking to you, than most officers would spend on a multiple murder. The lads at the station can't understand it. For instance, now I find I'm even interested in this tennis match.'

'The Clifton Cup? That was fantastic, Rufus. I swear Connie and Susan will never play so well again in their young lives. Considering they were both in with me the night before. They were superb in the doubles, too.'

'Miss Smallwood said they worked well together.'

'She did, too. Fancy you remembering that. Actually the whole match was a very close thing. The result depended on the doubles and those two girls were dynamite. I was so choked, would you believe it? There were tears running down my cheeks when Connie put that last volley down the bye-line. Imagine how everybody went mad; all the kids. It was an absolute frenzy. Miss Smallwood tried to rush on to the court and fell over a wooden bench. Barked all her shins. But she was so excited she didn't seem to notice. I was standing there, choked up, as I say, like a fool, not just because Southwelling had won the Clifton Cup from St Margaret's after all those years, but because it would all soon be gone.

'Everybody would go off on their summer holidays; Connie would fly across the ocean, and I would be off somewhere; I didn't know where. To tell you the truth I wandered off from all the hubbub and went back to my room. I sat on the bed and drank half a bottle of sherry or perhaps a drop more. Why I did it I couldn't tell you, not even now. All I know is I felt so sick and lonely and dejected. It was like looking down a big, dark void. Just when I should have been elated, jumping for joy.

'I sat there on the bed when I heard Connie and some of the the other girls outside the window. I knew Connie's voice immediately, of course. They sounded twittery and excited, like girls do, and I heard one of them, I think it must have been that Jackie MacAllister, say: "Where's His Lordship?" I didn't realize that they meant me, but they did because just afterwards Connie came into the room.

'She asked me what I was doing and I said I was having a drink of sherry. I think she could sense I was upset over the fact that we would never see each other again because she was so loving to me. More than I'd ever known with her before, Rufus. She didn't say anything. I was sitting more or less on the end of the bed with the sherry, not even looking up at her. She came right up to me and unwound her tennis skirt – it was one of those

219

sort that wraps around – if you know what I mean, Rufus. Anyway, she unwound it and she didn't have anything on underneath. I suppose she had taken off her pants in the dressing-room. All I did was sit there just gazing at her stomach and that vicinity, and she put her hands very softly on my head and I pressed my face to her tummy. Oh, Rufus, I can hardly think about it now without wanting to weep . . . It was the last time, you see . . . I can hardly tell you . . . I know I promised to tell you everything . . . but it's so difficult.'

'Now, Bill, don't you upset yourself. I don't like to see you like this, mate. It gives me no pleasure. Let's talk about something else.'

'If you don't mind, Rufus. Just for a few minutes. Have you got that hankie? . . . Thanks. There . . . Can I have a hoot of my nose as well? I know your wife has to keep washing them.'

'Don't worry about that. She's had much worse since the baby arrived.'

'Sorry if I make a fool of myself, but it's difficult, that's all. I worry like mad about her and what will happen to our little baby.'

'Now come on, let's change the subject. Miss Smallwood is looking forward to getting the Clifton Cup returned. We're having to use it as evidence, with the knickers and the other things, of course. But I've told her that I'll take the cup down to Southwelling as soon as you're behind bars. She said to me only last night that if . . .'

'Last night, Rufus? You saw her last night? Miss Smallwood?'

'Yes, Bill, as a matter of fact I did.'

'But you told me you were on a police raid, or something. You got a bonus for it.'

'No, *You* said that. I said I was on police business. Seeing Miss Smallwood was the business. I only mentioned the bonus in the most general way, Bill. You're getting into the habit of thinking *for* me, which is bad. Nevertheless, I'm glad you brought the subject up because it reminded me of something I wanted to mention.'

'Yes, Rufus.'

'That damn silly motorized bicycle of yours.'

'What about it? It's still at Southwelling, isn't it?'

'It's still there all right. Unfortunately, it's at the bottom of the river.'

'Oh no. Oh, Christ, that's terrible. How did it get in there?'

'It was like a wild thing that bicycle of yours, Bill. You're better off without it. As I was down at the school, during the course of routine inquiries, I thought I would do you a favour and bring the machine to London to see if I could get any sort of price for it. I knew you would have liked the money.'

'That's most thoughtful of you.'

'You know how I feel about you, Bill. I sometimes get the impression that I don't *do* enough for you. So I thought I'd get the bicycle and drive up to Town on it. But I'd no sooner started the engine than it leapt away from me like a stag. You should have seen it go, Bill; it tore itself out of my hands and belted across the grass – and splash. I got myself sopping wet trying to see if I could get a rope around it and pull it up. Soaked to the skin.'

'I *am* sorry, Rufus. I suppose that's why you had to get a new suit this morning.'

'Exactly. But I'm afraid that's the last you'll see of the old phut-phut. A great pity, too, because this morning I asked the manager of the motorcycle shop, near the outfitters, how much they were fetching and he said that sort of machine kept its price very well.'

'There's the insurance, Rufus.'

'Ran out last month. I checked on your documents at the station. Just our luck.'

'Just our luck, indeed, Rufus. It's a shame because I was very fond of the old motor-bicycle. I've not had a great many possessions and I was very fond of it. Only the other night I was wondering if I could fix to have it oiled and greased, or whatever they do, and stored away until I come out of jail.'

'All I can say is I'm sorry, Bill. It just goes to show the sort of thing that can happen when you try to do somebody a favour.'

41

HIS HEAD was held, as though in supplication, against the small pillow of her stomach. He sat awkwardly on the corner of his bed and she stood sedately before him. Sadly he turned his face, allowing his cheek to stroke her skin, and put his mouth to the white drain of her groin. She rubbed the back of his neck.

'Come on, please,' he mumbled miserably. 'There won't be any more times after this – never.' He looked up at her, standing like a girl listening to her teacher. 'What are they doing out there?' he said.

'Celebrating,' she said. 'Drinking tea and soda pop. Miss Smallwood's just had Band-Aids fixed on her shins.'

'Come on, Connie,' he repeated. She obediently keeled over on to his bed, still wearing her tennis blouse, stained beneath the armpits. Its hem ran over the crown of her clean belly. Her legs and arms were red-brown, but her body was pale, untouched, almost luminous in the shadowy room. He fumbled with the buttons of her blouse.

She sighed. 'William. Let me do it, You'll just never be a Don Juan. You undress somebody like you're doing a jigsaw puzzle against time.'

He laughed a melancholy laugh. 'I don't care,' he said. 'As long as I get it off. And I don't care about the future. I'm not expecting to do this any more.'

Connie giggled. 'So tragic. So serious.' He always thought she giggled in an American way, full-flavoured, like he imagined one of their ice-creams would be. He had opened the buttons and, to save him effort and difficulty, she had unhooked her brassière. His sorry hands pushed her breasts close to each other and he buried his nose in the close cleft.

'Your nose is running, William,' she whispered. 'I can feel it all wet.' She waited a moment. 'It's not your eyes, is it?'

'It's not my nose,' he mumbled from his hiding place. 'My eyes are watering a bit, that's all.'

'You're crazy,' she said to the top of his head. 'I don't know how anybody, any man, can look so great and be so soft, so stupid. We all flipped when you first came here, you know. We thought God had smiled on Southwelling. Fifty per cent of the kids had nightmares in case you decided not to take the appointment.'

'I had doubts myself. I want to love you now.'

'Love me, then,' she said. 'Listen, they're singing the school song.'

He could hear them, through the sun-warmed curtains. The children's voices singing lustily over tea and cakes and soda pop, weaving through the trees and flattening out over the basking lawns before reaching the reddened walls of their school. He could imagine them, cake crumbs and emotion in their throats, the serious sun watching from across the river and the tennis courts, Miss Smallwood, her skinny shins bravely bandaged, conducting with gusto and an aching heart. Perhaps, probably, wondering where he was. Where Connie was.

'They'll miss us,' he said suddenly.

'Not for a few seconds,' she said. 'Do it now.'

By the last chorus of the song they were buried in it, clutching on to every second, making every movement felt to the final join; slowly because it had to last for ever, but in haste, too, like a pair of daylight robbers.

He held the tops of her slender girl's legs and then when she started to laugh, as she always did, this time he laughed as well. They rolled in their laughter and their love and finally hung on to the bed and each other, the fun and the feeling all drained from them.

'You laughed that time, too,' she said.

'I thought, this time, I would do it with you,' he answered.

'You've always been so tense and so dramatic,' she said facing him, looking into his face with her queen-bee eyes. 'Was it improved?'

'Frankly, Connie, there's not much to laugh about just now,' he said. 'Not for me, anyway. I just thought I'd give it a try that's all. As it's the last time.'

'How was it?'

'Well, I wish I hadn't,' he admitted. 'It hurts my thing – jolts it around, if you'll forgive the expression.'

'I have.'

'That's what it does anyway,' he said with finality. He reached to her youthful breasts again and ran his palms around them. 'Anyway, I think it's all right for someone very young like you to laugh. A lorry-driver once told me about a young kid laughing. I think being serious is more for people of my age.'

They heard someone crunching on the path outside, then the outer door scraped and a knock came on William's door.

'Mr Herbert, are you there?' It was Miss Everett.

'Yes, what is it, Miss Everett?'

'Are you all right?'

'Exhausted,' said William truthfully. 'Lying down for a bit.'

'Miss Smallwood wants you. Everyone is wondering where you are. I don't suppose you've seen Connie, have you?'

'No,' he called back. 'I haven't seen her.'

'Miss Smallwood wants you to play an exhibition match against the other coach. Will you come soon?'

William felt himself shake. He said wearily: 'A what?'

'An exhibition match against Monsieur Mouly. She said to tell you that it's only a demonstration – but you've got to win.'

'Yes, of course,' said William feebly. 'Tell Monsieur Mouly I'll be there in a moment.'

He heard her hurry away. Connie was laughing, turned on to her stomach with her face in his pillow. 'Go on, laugh. Have the great American bloody giggle.' He brought his flat hand down sharply on her buttocks. And then again. And again. She stopped laughing and turned viciously on him. They were kneeling on the bed, facing each other. William stared at her.

'I'm sorry,' he said. He was shaking.

'You've been damned well wanting to do that,' she said nastily. 'Don't do it again.' All the sweetness had gone from her. Her breasts stuck out angrily at his chest.

'I won't have another chance,' he said.

'No, you won't, you dirty old bastard.'

'Connie!'

'Cut it out.'

'You're just playing with me again,' he protested. 'Playing about with me.'

'And you hit my ass. Let me get out.'

'Connie, no! Don't let's quarrel now, for God's sake. I've got to go and play that man Mouly.'

She was wiping her legs with her handkerchief. 'Go and hit Monsieur Mouly's ass,' she said. He had never seen anyone dress so quickly. She was at the door before he had emerged through the neck of his tennis shirt.

'Connie,' he pleaded.

'And,' she said, returning around the door, 'I'm pregnant, Mr Herbert, I'm pregnant.'

The girls screamed and cheered ecstatically as he ran on to the court, greeting him like some rescuer of maidens, like some courtly conqueror. 'They think of their dashing Mr Herbert as something of a handsome knight,' Miss Smallwood whispered to her rival headmistress. 'I think they half expect him to turn up on a white horse.'

'He looks as though he's just fallen from one,' said the other lady nastily.

William did seem confused. He brazenly looked around for Monsieur Mouly in the manner of a killer searching out his victim. He had drunk the remainder of the bottle of sherry while he was getting into his jock strap and shorts. She was pregnant! Her accent around the door was running around in his brain. Where was that Monsieur Mouly? Ah, there he was. Very bloody dapper. Cream slacks instead of shorts. Right, I'll soon deal with that little French bugger. My God, I feel fantastic. It's marvellous what a pint of Harvey's Bristol Cream will do.

Ah, he's got the balls. Come on, Frenchie, let's have you, then. Knock up for a bit. Here, bang! Sort that one out. Don't look surprised, old man. I mean business. I know we're only knocking about, but boy, you are going to know you've played a game of tennis. Ah, here's another. Smash! What a cannonball! Don't stare, Frenchie mate, you're going to think you're playing against the artillery. Me! A father to be! She'll *have* to have me. She'll just *have* to. I shall go to America and look after her. I'll get a job in a posh country club and, once I've got a divorce from Louise, we'll get married. Just to think we'll have a ready-to-wear child even before we start! Whoa, Monsieur Mouly, steady on! That nearly hit me in the eye. The girls laughed at that. They like a good laugh, these girls. The sky looks pretty black.

Is that my eyes, or is it the sky? Where's that lovely Connie? Is she up there watching, the mother of my unborn child? Yankee-doodle came to town, Yankee-doodle dandee . . . la.la.la. la . . . la. la. la . . . and with the girls be handy.

Okay, Monsieur Mouly, you want to spin for ends. Rough or smooth? Smooth for me, Monsieur Mouly. I've had enough of the rough. Good God, isn't the sky dark.

42

'OH, RUFUS, I'm so glad you're here.'

'You *knew* I would come, Bill. Have I ever left you in the lurch. What's the matter?'

'It's the Scrabble.'

'Christ, we haven't got time for that now. You're in court tomorrow.'

'But this is important. It's to do with the case. Perhaps I didn't ought to tell you. Really I should be telling Mr Decent. It's new evidence.'

'Well tell me, and I'll promise not to mention it to our side.'

'All right. On that understanding then. Let me get the Scrabble board. There. I only worked this out last night. You remember the two girls who were arguing as to whether they could use that word in the game? You know. I told you right at the beginning.'

'Shit, you mean.'

'Yes. That's the word. Well, look, Rufus, this proves they must have *known* I was outside the door. It was all part of the plan to get at me, just like Mary Bosham in the bathroom and all the other capers.'

'How?'

'Because that child Sarah Curran was an expert at Scrabble. I told you. She played for money, even. Now I distinctly remember her saying that the word – shit – was going to be the first one on the board.'

'I remember you said that.'

'Look, I'll put the letters down. S-H-I-T. Now no Scrabble player would waste a valuable "s" by putting it on the board first. And even, so, why couldn't the word have been "THIS" or "HITS", which are decent words. Or, "HIT" and that would have saved her wasting the "s". It just *proves* that they were laying traps for me – even then. Don't you think it's valuable evidence, Rufus?'

'Frankly, Bill, I can't see it making more than, say, a month's difference to the sentence. It will just mean that you'll be out in October 1978 instead of November 1978, even with remission. In the face of evidence like we've got it's a bit pathetic; so don't pin your hopes on it.'

'Oh, I was a bit, too.'

'We'd better get on, Bill. We might as well hear the rest. We were up to the tennis match, weren't we?'

'Yes, Rufus. Of course. Well I didn't win. I won the first three games. He never saw the ball, but after that I didn't see it very well either. That's how sherry hits you. But I didn't actually lose either, because this huge thunderstorm started. You've never heard or seen anything like that storm. It got cold as soon as we started playing, and so dark. The girls were all staring at the sky. They hung on as long as possible, they were very loyal really. Then the whole heavens seemed to crack. Forked lightning and a great crump of thunder. I fell backwards and sat down on the court. I heard one of the women, Miss Whitefriar, I think, shouting for me to run. I could see old Mouly, through the net, crouching at the other end. It was like an air raid. All the kids just fled, screaming. You've never seen anywhere get so empty so quickly in your life. They just hurtled away. Then there was another lot of lightning. All over the sky. I saw Mouly pick himself up and dash off after the girls. The rain was starting to come down, thick drops like syrup. Everywhere was black and then lit up with the lightning.

'I stood for a minute, all by myself on the court. In the back of my mind I had some funny idea that I would win the match by default if I was the last one there. I suppose I was still a bit

227

whoozy from all that sherry. The rain belted down in sheets then, and there was another sizzling lot of lightning and a nasty bang of thunder. So I ran. I tried jumping the net, but I misjudged it by miles. Over I tipped. Laid myself out cold on the other side. There I was stretched out all on my own in the middle of the storm.

'I don't know how long I was lying there, Rufus. But when I came around I had some strange idea I was dead, because you remember the man who was the coach before me conked out on the tennis court and he'd been left lying there in the rain.'

'You told me.'

'The storm was still banging about all over the place and it was raining like fury. I felt oddly like a crocodile lying out there. The sherry was still working, I could tell that, and when I woke up I opened and shut my mouth a few times, just like a crocodile in a tropical storm. It's funny how you play games when you've had a few, isn't it? I had a bruise on my chin and I'd jammed my nose against the ground.'

'That's why it's been so tender.'

'Yes . . . well, it could have been. But tugging it hasn't helped, Rufus.'

'Skip it. Go back to being a crocodile.'

'It took me a couple of minutes to pull myself together and get up. Then I simply walked back to the school. There was no sense in running, even if I'd felt like it, because I couldn't have been any wetter. So I took my time. I even practised a few forehands with my racket as I walked through the thunder and lightning. I had a strange idea it would be the last practice I would have for some time. It looks as though I was right, doesn't it?'

'I have to admit, Bill, that it does. Court tomorrow. I'll be keeping my fingers crossed.'

'To win the sweepstake.'

'I'll be *interested* in that, of course, but for Pete's sake give me a bit more credit, Bill. You know how fond of you I've become.'

'Yes. You said, Rufus. You're not grinning, are you?'

'No. I've got a bit of kipper stuck in my teeth, Bill. Myra

cooked kippers again for breakfast today. Just right they were. No bones.'

'Stop. Kippers! You make me drool.'

'With a little pat of butter on each one. Very tasty.'

'Oh don't. *We're* on the fishcakes again. I can't stand them now, Rufus. Can't bear the things. They always taste so sour in here. They're not like the ones your mother-in-law made for me.'

'When you are on remand for the Sessions I'll get her to make you some more. Or if Myra's not too busy with the kiddie, I'll get her to do them.'

'Thanks. You don't suppose you could get her to send me some kippers instead, do you? Cooked. I know it would be a job to keep them warm until you got here but if you ran they might not be too bad, and I could eat them more or less right away.'

'You didn't like my mother-in-law's fishcakes, then?'

'Christ, of course I did! They were delicious. But if there's any kippers going and they could be smuggled in as it were, I wouldn't mind having them instead.'

'Bill, all you seem to do is to try and get me to contravene police regulations.'

'I don't mean to do that. I'm sorry. I've been dying to ask you something else, Rufus, but I've been scared.'

'What's that? I hope it's not another offer of a bribe.'

'There's nothing left to bribe you with, Rufus. Even my bike has sunk in the river.'

'Don't blame *me* for that.'

'Oh, I wasn't. Don't misunderstand. But what I wanted to ask is if you managed to get that photograph from the American newspaper or whatever it was. You know, the one of Connie. Did you get it, Rufus?'

'That. Ah, yes. I spent a lot of time looking for that, Bill. *Official* time and my own time. And I managed to trace it in the end.'

'You did!

'But ... stop getting worked up ... I'd made a mistake. It wasn't a picture of Connie. It was Mrs Nixon, the President's wife.'

'Mrs Nixon? You confused *her* with *Connie*?'

'Don't ask me how it happened, I just don't know. I've been very busy and this is the sort of confusion that easily arises.'

'I suppose it does. It's disappointing. I was banking on it. Well, thanks for trying, anyway.'

'Oh, I don't mind trying to help you out. You're in so much trouble that somebody's got to do it. You've been pretty unlucky with old Decent, I feel. Yesterday I heard he's already fixed your appeal.'

'But I'm not convicted yet!'

'I know, I know. That's the tragic bit of it.'

'Oh God. My *appeal*!'

'What about Connie?'

'Connie? Why, is there some news? Is she all right?'

'No, I mean what happened to her on the last evening at the school; before we picked you up?'

'Rufus – I never saw her again. Never. I went back to my room to get out of my wet things and I had another drop of sherry – I seemed to be getting quite fond of sherry one way and another – and then I flaked out on the bed. When I woke up it was about eight o'clock, in the evening that is, of course, and when I went into the school to find Connie I was told she had left for London.

'I was crushed, Rufus. Crushed. How could she go away like that, just leaving me?'

'Did you never wonder why she wasn't pregnant before?'

'Connie and Susan were taking birth pills. Susan told me. She got them from somewhere. I suppose the supply must have run out, or something.'

'One of the junior kids stole them, Bill.'

'Stole them? How do you know?'

'We have methods. We're the police, remember.'

'It's a police secret, then?'

'Apparently, Connie and Susan Belling had enough pills to keep them going until their change of life. The Belling girl got them from some source, but she won't say.

'Then this child from the juniors lifted the whole lot and distributed them to all her pals. They were taking them like

230

Smarties. God, think what a field day you could have had there.'

'Now, that's rotten, Rufus! And you know it. You make me sound like some sexual beast.'

'That's a matter of opinion, Bill my friend. Now just finish off for me. You couldn't find Connie in the school, so what did you do?'

'You know what I did, Rufus. I came to London to try and find her, but I'd had too much sherry and I got involved in all that trouble in the buffet at Victoria Station.'

'Sitting in some old-age pensioner's hamburger, egg and double chips, and trying to fight one of the staff. Actually, I think you could be done under the Race Relations Act. He was a West Indian.'

'I don't remember him. You see, Rufus, I'd had all that sherry at the school and then I had some more at Lewes station. I don't remember a thing until I was in the police cell and they were taking away my belt and shoelaces. I must have been a long way gone, I didn't even collect my wet tennis things. I just left them. One of the cases was packed and I threw some bits and pieces in the other and cleared out. I had some idea of telephoning Miss Smallwood the next day to say goodbye.

'All I wanted to do was to get away from Southwelling and to find Connie. That was all, Rufus. I'm sorry about the old soul's hamburger, egg and double chips, but I was pissed.'

'So much so you don't remember pinching the Clifton Cup and sticking it in your suitcases with your priceless collection of embroidered gym knickers.'

'I told you. I *don't!* Those girls put it there. I know they did. It's the way they *did* things to me. Don't you understand that?'

'Tell it to the court, Bill. That's where you've got to make it sound convincing. I'm going now. It's the Policemen's Ball tonight, you know.'

'Is it, Rufus. Perhaps I could come along.'

'Perhaps you could be the booby-prize, Bill. Cheers.'

'Rufus . . .

'Rufus . . .

'RUFUS! RUFUS! RUFUS!

RUFUS! RUUUFUS! RUUUUFUS!'

'. . . Christ. What do you want. I was halfway up the corridor. You're disturbing the whole prison shouting like that. What is it?'

'It's just . . . Wish me luck, Rufus . . . For tomorrow.'

'I *can't* do that, Bill. You know I can't. It's against police rules to wish a prisoner luck. Surely it stands to reason.'

'Yes, I suppose so. Anyway, thanks for listening to it all, and thanks for trying to get my motorized bicycle for me and all that. If you do hear anything of Connie will you let me know?'

'If I get any news.'

'Thanks. I can't think of a better pal than you. D'you know. Nobody ever actually called me Bill before. It was always William, which is a sort of clownish name, really just a way of taking the mickey. Always William. Even my father. Except in the Air Force where they called me Ribby Herbert on account of my falling eighteen feet off that bed and breaking my ribs.'

'All right, Bill. Cheers.'

'Cheerio, Rufus. Best of luck . . . Well, best of luck *after* tomorrow anyway.'

43

As HE walked up the corridor the warder turned the corner and walked after him.

'Trevor,' said the warder.

'Morning, Wilf. Just finished with His Lordship in there.'

'I know. I heard him carrying on. Who the hell is Rufus? He's always going on about this Rufus. It's all he talks about. Rufus is apparently like Jesus Christ. I could hear him yelling out "Rufus" just now.'

'Fantasy,' said Trevor. 'Pure fantasy, Wilf. He goes on like that all the time. Never mind, they'll sort him out soon. The head-hunters ought to have a good time with him.'

'They usually do with that sort. I like your suit, Trevor. How much did they rush you for that?'

'Fifty-five quid. Best one in the shop.'

'Looks like it, too. Did you want any more fishcakes for him before he goes to court, by the way? I know we got half a dozen stale ones out of the prisoners' store for you that day. He seems to be very partial to fishcakes, do you think the poor sod would like them tomorrow morning?'

'Don't bother. He's sweet on kippers at the moment.'

'Blimey, we can't go to luxuries. See you, Trevor.'

'See you, Wilf.'

He returned immediately to the police station. He went to the canteen for his lunch then to his office. The desk sergeant signalled to him.

'Trevor, the inspector wants to see you.'

'All right, I'll go in.'

He knocked briskly and went into the office. The inspector looked up. 'Hello, Trevor. How's your tame tennis coach?'

'Wishing me luck, the stupid bastard. I don't know whether he's a mug or a monster. He's a bit of both, I think.'

'You've spent a hell of a lot of time with him, Trevor. Most of it unwarranted, it seems to me.'

'I didn't think so, sir. I want to nail him, get him shoved away for a while.'

'Nail him, eh? Well, I should drop that hammer if I were you. And the nails.'

'Drop it? Why?'

'The charges won't stand up, Trevor.'

'*They won't stand up!* That's bloody scandalous! I knew we'd find it difficult – but, Christ, I've got what amounts to a confession. He's admitted everything.'

'The man's potty, Trevor. Absolutely potty. Surely you can see that? Besides which we can't get one trifle of corroborative evidence. Not one.'

'Not one? God, who's been fucking this up for me?'

'The girls, Trevor. One of our policewomen, in Derby, in a last-ditch effort to get the Ferber girl to talk, was chased into an ornamental pond by the family dogs last night. They swear the dogs got loose by accident. I think if another copper went to that house he'd take his life in his hands. The twins and the parents deny any knowledge of this business and the old man's threatened to sue if we bother his daughters any more. He calls us "the filthy fuzz" and alleges Tina Ferber wept and had nightmares after we'd tried to get the story from her the first time. According to her, His Lordship was a marvellous chap, kind, considerate, clean-living. She's going to miss him, terribly, she says, at her finishing school. So there.'

'What about the others? What about these embroidered knicks in his suitcase?'

'The Ferber girls said Connie Rowan put them there as a joke. She put the silver cup in there, too. You can't even nick him for pinching that.'

'Oh God. The little bitches. What about the MacAllister kid? And Yum Yum? . . .'

'Yum Yum, Trevor?'

'Watts. Pamela Watts.'

'Yum Yum still cannot be found. Her mother says her father has gone somewhere abroad with her. Apparently the parents have split up. The au pair girl's gone too.'

'And Jackie MacAllister?'

'We had her boo-ing. Her father's not contributing to the Police Orphans' Fund any more. She said she had a schoolgirl crush on Herbert and she wrote him a poem and all that rubbish. But he always behaved in the most proper manner towards her. She won't say a thing.'

'All right, what about Susan Belling?'

'I don't know whether you read your gossip columns, Trevor? Perhaps you don't.'

'I don't.'

'Well, you really should. Have a glance at William Hickey now and again. Or the one in the *Daily Mail*. It might make you a better policeman.'

'I'll start reading them.'

'Good. You might see that Susan Belling is the daughter of Sir William Belling, the industrialist who is also a Member of Parliament. She's bound for a finishing school in Switzerland this autumn. If you feel like asking her if she lost her virginity at school, you can. But I don't think her old man will be very pleased.'

'I see. This is serious.'

'No, it's very simple. All we've got on Mr William Herbert is a drunk and incapable charge.'

'What about Connie Rowan? Still nothing from her?'

'Trevor, you know as well as I do that Connie Rowan was over the age of consent – sixteen. She had an abortion in London early in August and the money was provided by the father of a young man in Derby. Connie and this chap shacked up for a week in London during the Whitsun break at South-welling.'

'Surely, the school? . . .'

'One breath of scandal and the governors will sue. We're like a stork with a broken leg, Trevor. Miss Smallwood wants to get her hands on the man who started all this. It's just as well she didn't know it was you when you went down to get Herbert's motor-bicycle the other evening. That was a strange thing to do, wasn't it?'

'I thought it might be a lead, sir. Just an idea I had.'

'Anyway you didn't give her a receipt, which is contrary to regulations, you know. See that's remedied.'

'Oh yes. Of course. What about this Major Prescod? Nothing there?'

'Chairman of the Southwelling Rural District Council, Trevor. And a magistrate. Well liked, generous, plays a big part in local life. Not a whisper against him. Apparently, he's going to marry a Miss Tilling. You try and sort a case out of that if you feel brave.'

'Shit, shit, shit.'

'Fine sentiments, Trevor, but no evidence. This thing would collapse the minute old Decent got to his feet in court. You know what a clever devil he is at the best of times.'

'Bloody hell.'

'Right, as you say, Bloody Hell. Listen, Trevor, lad, there are times when you try a bit too hard. You don't relax nearly enough. Why don't you take some leave?'

'What shall I do?'

'Do? I don't know. Go fishing. Or go to Paris and have a debauched week. After all you're not like the rest of us poor buggers, tied up to wives and families and all that sort of thing.

You could be having a high old time instead of mooning around the station every day.'

'Being a bachelor has its disadvantages.'

'Everything does, Trevor.'

'I'll go now. You say the charge is "drunk and incapable"?'

'That's all we can do him on.'

'Drunk and incapable? Drunk, yes. But incapable, that's a bloody scream that is.'

'William Herbert, you are charged with being drunk and incapable at the Victoria Station buffet. Do you plead guilty or not guilty?'

'It was the girls, sir, your honour . . .'

'HE WISHES TO PLEAD GUILTY, SIR.'

'Oh, thank you, Mr Decent. Can we hear the evidence of arrest.'

William watched for Rufus to appear. But a strange, round pedestrian policeman in uniform was in the box muttering, with a Bible held high as though he were about to throw it at the magistrate.

Then the policeman said: 'I was called to the buffet at Victoria Station at ten-thirty on the evening of the twenty-fifth of July, sir, and I saw the accused sitting on a table and leaning back against the wall, sir. He was sitting on a plate of hamburger, egg, and double chips, sir, the property of one of the customers of the buffet, an elderly lady. I touched him and he collapsed and I came to the conclusion he was drunk.'

'Good thinking, Constable,' said the chairman of the bench. 'Mr Decent?'

'All I have to say, sir, is that my client has been in custody for fourteen days because of some property in his possession which was thought to have been stolen. There was some mention of further charges, but these have now been satisfactorily disposed of. This seems to me to be an intolerable situation and, in view of it, may I suggest that the fine for the drunk and incapable charge be levied accordingly.'

'Thank you, Mr Decent,' said the magistrate. 'William Herbert, you are fined five shillings.'

'I haven't got any money,' said William.

'IT WILL BE PAID, SIR,' hooted Mr Decent, glaring at William. 'He has three months,' salary due from his last job, sir.'

The chairman nodded: 'Of course. Seven days to pay. You can go now, Mr Herbert. We are sorry the police found it necessary to detain you.'

44

TREVOR, HIS jacket collar turned up, stood with a small, crouched group of men, a traveller, a delivery man, an elderly vicar, several clerks, and a weak-eyed postman. Apparently unaware of each other's existence, they stood on the pavement, dotted about, separate from each other, observing a girls' netball match. They watched silently through spaced railings of a public park with the deep and inward appreciation of *aficianados* as the girls in blue knickers and white blouses jumped and danced laughing about the court. A small blue car drew up and a grey and red insurance agent leaned from its window motioning the delivery man to step a yard to the left to give him an improved view.

They stood, a bleak-coated tableau, their faces and eyes fixed and set. The young woman referee leaped about, caliper legs astride, stridently blowing her whistle. She did not look at the audience. Nor did the girls.

The players were all about fourteen, faces and legs red with exertion, bouncing and screeching and calling for the ball; attempting to score by leaping like salmon towards a landing net.

Their cheeks and their blouses puffed out, their plimsolled feet bounded and rebounded. One of the girls, the captain of the red armbands, had a split two inches long in the back of her pants. Each time she jumped, or stretched, or ran, it opened like a sweet white smile. The men took their attention from the general view and followed that split with their knowing eyes. Each time the girl bent for the ball the stiff congregation shuffled as though agitated. The insurance agent crept from his car and positioned himself close to the railings.

Trevor watched the smile break out and fade again on the slim blue bottom. He coughed slightly and the other experienced men glared at him as though he had interrupted an aria at the opera. Eventually, the referee shrilled the whistle decisively and the game was over. The little girls turned to the park fence and, all together, curtsied attractively. The men broke into embarrassed and desultory applause.

'Surprising, Rufus, how many people are interested in it.'

Rufus turned to him. Then he shrugged. 'It's a growing sport, I suppose.'

'Can I walk along with you a bit, Rufus. I wanted to ask you something?'

They walked. The insurance agent went by them in his car and the delivery man on his bicycle. The postman was whistling and shuffling letters. The others had dispersed to join the rest of the world.

'Rufus. I've just got my suitcases back, but the collection of knicks seems to have gone. Is it possible I can have them back?'

'I'll do my best to trace them for you. I'll let you know.'

'Did anyone get the right ticket in the sweepstake, Rufus? A five-bob fine?'

'I don't believe so.'

'Your inspector is a very helpful chap. He gave me a receipt for my motor-bicycle. Mr Decent says he thinks I've got a case for wrongful arrest. My phut-phut will be at the police station tomorrow. Strangely enough he didn't know it had been in the river. Did the police frogmen get it back, Rufus?'

'I expect so, Bill. You'll have it tomorrow.'

'The trouble with schoolgirls, you know, is that once you get really interested in the creatures and start thinking about them it's very difficult to remember what is fact and what isn't. Even some of the facts I told you in the cell may not have been absolutely right. I hope that didn't spoil things for you.'

'It helped.'

'Rufus, you know those girls playing netball at the park back there – did you notice the one with the split in her bum? Well, not actually her bum. I mean in the pants over her bum.'

'Vaguely, Bill.'

'She *knew* it was there, Rufus. She damned well *knew* it. And she kept bending and everything so that it would show more to you and all the other gentlemen. They play you along, these kids, you see.'

'You think so?'

'Definitely. Why I remember, at Southwelling, that Connie, now when she used to come into my room in her nightie she would always . . . Rufuth, thath my nothe! Rufuth! Oh for Godth thake . . . thath my nothe!'

Bestselling Fiction and Non-Fiction

☐	**The Amityville Horror**	Jay Anson	80p
☐	**Shadow of the Wolf**	James Barwick	95p
☐	**The Island**	Peter Benchley	£1.25p
☐	**Castle Raven**	Laura Black	£1.25p
☐	**Smart-Aleck Kill**	Raymond Chandler	95p
☐	**Sphinx**	Robin Cook	£1.25p
☐	**The Entity**	Frank De Felitta	£1.25p
☐	**Trial Run**	Dick Francis	95p
☐	**The Rich are Different**	Susan Howatch	£1.95p
☐	**Moviola**	Garson Kanin	£1.50p
☐	**Tinker Tailor Soldier Spy**	John le Carré	£1.50p
☐	**The Empty Copper Sea**	John D. MacDonald	90p
☐	**Where There's Smoke**	Ed McBain	80p
☐	**The Master Mariner**		
	Book 1: Running Proud	Nicholas Monsarrat	£1.50p
☐	**Bad Blood**	Richard Neville and	
		Julie Clarke	£1.50p
☐	**Victoria in the Wings**	Jean Plaidy	£1.25p
☐	**Fools Die**	Mario Puzo	£1.50p
☐	**Sunflower**	Marilyn Sharp	95p
☐	**The Throwback**	Tom Sharpe	95p
☐	**Wild Justice**	Wilbur Smith	£1.50p
☐	**That Old Gang of Mine**	Leslie Thomas	£1.25p
☐	**Caldo Largo**	Earl Thompson	£1.50p
☐	**Harvest of the Sun**	E. V. Thompson	£1.25p
☐	**Future Shock**	Alvin Toffler	£1.95p

All these books are available at your local bookshop or newsagent, or can be ordered direct from the publisher. Indicate the number of copies required and fill in the form below

Name_____
(block letters please)

Address_____

_____

Send to Pan Books (CS Department), Cavaye Place, London SW10 9PG
Please enclose remittance to the value of the cover price plus :

25p for the first book plus 10p per copy for each additional book ordered to a maximum charge of £1.05 to cover postage and packing
Applicable only in the UK

While every effort is made to keep prices low, it is sometimes necessary to increase prices at short notice. Pan Books reserve the right to show on covers and charge new retail prices which may differ from those advertised in the text or elsewhere